SPEAKERS
OF THE EARTH

Book Two: A Mountain Spruce

SPEAKERS
OF THE EARTH

Book Two: A Mountain Spruce

RICHARD JONES

SEATTLE

2020

Speakers of the Earth: Book Two: A Mountain Spruce

Copyright © Richard Jones, 2020.

Editorial & design copyright © Chatwin LLC, 2020.

Cover design by Annie Brulé.
Cover image from *Guide to the Northern Pacific Railroad* (1883).

Interior design by Vladimir Verano.

paperback ISBN 978-1-63398-110-2

Chatwin Books
www.chatwinbooks.com

CONTENTS

Author's Note

A Mountain Spruce is Book Two of a two-part work titled *Speakers of the Earth*. These two volumes are the first in a collection of closely related—though not at all chronologically ordered—tales that I think of as "The House of Windy Gap Stories." While it is possible that I may, some time in the foreseeable future, write a story unrelated to these places, people, and this way of looking at the workings of the world, I believe it is highly unlikely.

—Richard Jones,
Seattle, 2020

PART FIVE

The Home

"Nuñez! Man, am I glad to see you. I need some help, bad. I've been in this camp four days now, and I don't know anything, nobody will help me out."

"Ray boy, you lookin' a little worse for wear. Where you been this six months? Ah, never mind that. What you mean you don't know nothin'?"

"I don't know who's boss here, I don't know who to help out, who to stay away from, I don't know how to pick asparagus, I'm too slow, everybody hates me and I don't know what to do about it."

"What you need people to tell you things for? You look, you listen, you think, you get by. What wrong with that?"

"It takes too long, Nuñez, I won't make it if it takes too long."

"Looky here, Ray boy, you do your best, use that head you got, learn as fast as you know how, and leave the rest to whoever it is you talk to at night."

"Talk to at night? What do you mean? I don't talk to anybody at night." His eyebrows rose. *"Nobody? Nobody at all?"* He placed a finger on the center of my chest, tapped it lightly. *"Ray boy, you make me sad. You got to find that one to talk to. Find 'em at night, practice 'til you talk to 'em by day too."*

It's been a year since I saw him. I may be learning a little faster now, but as for finding someone to 'talk to at night', I doubt I ever will.

(California, Salinas, May 1982)

Chapter 22

I sat cross-legged on the dusty ground, looking south and slightly west to the Mountain towering over Old Desolate. The saddle between the two primary peaks of Sluiskin Mountain provided a sweeping view of Vernal Park's beauty, spreading out to the southwest eight hundred feet below me. It was a perfect place to be completely exposed to the air, the sky and sun, and yet to be completely alone. Someone on the Wonderland Trail, a mile to the west, might have spotted me with a good pair of binoculars, but that didn't seem to change the solitude at all.

After the morning's gathering—which I'd already been told was unlike any that had ever happened before—the five of us had sat in a tight little circle in our campsite meadow, my tiny camp stove in the center as if it were some kind of talisman. There had been a long period of silence, each one of us occupied with his or her thoughts. I'd looked around the circle at Hucklebark, Henry, Lyla and Lupine, and realized as I glanced their way that I loved each one, in ways I had never felt before. They had so suddenly come to mean so much to me that I didn't know what to feel about it. I'd wanted to be there with them all, and yet at the moment had felt an intense restlessness, a burning need to be moving.

"I don't know where to go next, but I have to get moving," I'd said. "I'm ready to just start wandering until the right direction presents itself. What do you all think?"

Henry had merely snorted; I could tell what he thought of "wandering." Lupine had been more specific, in a way.

"There are times when that's the right thing to do, Ray. Maybe soon you should do that. But we can't leave here until we've seen Works again."

"Any idea when he'll drop by? I can't just sit here all day, I really can't."

"First off," Lupine continued, "Works has a lot to do right now, and a great deal on his mind. It isn't just us he has to consider. Secondly, he's going to give us some time to sort things out and gather our ideas on how to move. Trust him, Ray, and wait."

"Tell you what," I'd said. "I have to have some solitude, and that won't wait. I'm going for a walk, but I promise not to disappear. Okay?"

They had all simply nodded, but then Lupine had said, "No experiments, please. We need you here."

I was reminded again why Lupine scared some people. Did she merely have a vast depth of experience to draw from, or could she see into people's hearts as if they were on display? I hadn't known exactly what it was I would try, but I'd had every intention of going off by myself to work with whatever I could find, to get some kind of feeling for what was expected of me. I could see her point, but it rankled a bit. So I had walked out of the circle and up Sluiskin to this overlook.

Vernal Park stretched itself luxuriously below, its grasses tawny in the late summer sun. Arctic-Alpine trees dotted the park around the perimeter, and the whole central meadow was alive with wild-flowers. The center and the southern end held columns of purple fireweed, splashes of red columbine, occasional furry, gray-white balls of beargrass perched atop their tall, hairy stalks, and a sprinkling of cobalt blue mountain lupine. Towards the northeastern end, where the park backed up against Sluiskin, there were great carpets of mixed green and white where the avalanche lilies were still blooming. They would have a spring lasting all of two weeks, and a summer that lasted three—very little time in which to do their work. I understood that, but I envied the lilies. They at least knew exactly what was required of them—to grow, and to reproduce—while I was still adrift in a sea of mystery, with no knowing which way to move, nor where my destination might lie.

The old man had said to me, "Get to work, child." So what work was there for me to do? How was I to set about righting what was going wrong? And what did I have to work with?

A memory bubbled up from deep inside: a time when, in my twenties, I had wandered aimlessly across all the western states, never knowing where I was going or why, always wanting desperately to know. I had been lost, so thoroughly, miserably lost that more than once I had seriously considered ending that painful life. Through whatever good fortune I hadn't, of course. And now, looking down on the great, sinuous sweep of meadow below me, I began to think about being found, and about what I had to work with.

If I looked at it correctly, it was clear that people had been giving me things from the moment I arrived at Tahoma. Everyone I'd met had given me much to think about; the trees had shown me ways of being and offered me things I hadn't known were possible; the old man and woman had somehow pulled me inside the world and through it; the others, particularly Lyla, had offered me friendship, company, safety. And it seemed, though I still hardly dared to think of it, that Works and Lupine were offering me a way of life and a place to live it in.

But it would come to nothing, as everything before had always come, if that horrid being, that *opposition* to it, could not be overcome. What was I to do with the overwhelming gifts that were given so freely?

Suddenly the beauty of Vernal Park could not hold me. I stood up and began pacing, not knowing or caring much where I was going. The saddle between the two peaks was about thirty yards across and ten yards deep, a narrow band of relatively level ground. It was bounded to the north by the slope I'd come up, to the south by a much steeper slope down to Vernal Park, and on the east and west by the near vertical, upcurving sides of Sluiskin's two peaks. I crossed it again and again, barely noticing where I was walking, as if by moving my body I could get something in my mind to move.

In the course of this aimless walking I took a step and stopped, as if I had run into a wall. My foot was tingling like I'd stepped on a live electric wire. My other foot slowly came forward, and planted itself of its own accord so that I stood balanced, and it came up through both feet.

What was happening? I felt a moment of terror, thinking that the malicious being had found a way to get to me through the very ground itself. But it only needed another second to know this wasn't the case. Through my feet I was sensing pathways through the mountain: creeks, brooks, rivers of the world's life and energy, in constant movement from one place to another. I sat down on that spot, placed my hands palms down in the dirt, and instantly the feeling increased tenfold. I closed my eyes.

The world opened beneath me, and I could go wherever I wished. Energy began to rush into me from every direction, and if I had not already experienced something like this feeling the night before with the old man, I would have panicked. But it had not killed me then, and I figured it wouldn't now. I let it flow without hindrance, passing through me. I opened my eyes and brought one hand up to hold it before them, fingers spread wide. Even in the bright summer sun, I could see light spraying out from my fingertips. I raised my hand towards the sky, and light and force, sunshine, clouds, soil and stone moved in as well as out. Feeling and energy merged, traveling, coming to me as if they had been waiting to find me, and exiting as if a task had been accomplished.

I placed my hand back on the ground and decided to have a look around the world. My eyes closed again. The feel of the ground below me was so much clearer, so much more real, than any map could ever be. The land swept away down to the southwest, and I could feel its every contour beneath the surface, over to the great mountain cirque that was the birthplace of the Carbon Glacier. I traveled the byways underneath, noting the infinite differences in the rock, the pockets and underground rills and streams of water, the spaciousness of the cirque's great bowl, filled with ice but no longer a barrier to me.

This was power, I was certain of it. But what was I to do with this power? In that moment, an obvious choice seemed to be to just ask. I placed my question before me as if it were some kind of offering, and made myself as still as I could.

Did the answer come from me, from someone else, from everywhere at once? No knowing, but answer there was.

This is not for you to be doing *with,* it said. *This is for you to* serve, *and in so serving, doing for others. Use it well, and be well. Use it wrongly, and everything will change for the worse.*

All right then, for the time being I would *do* nothing. I would feel, listen, see, and wonder. The next thing I wondered was what the core of the Mountain itself felt like. I pushed my senses to the rear wall of the cirque, where it met the Mountain, and was stopped cold. No matter how I tried to wiggle my way through the ground into the Mountain, I could not go there. Now, I thought, there was a mystery. It didn't feel threatening or dangerous; rather, it felt like a polite but firm refusal. My senses rested at the foot of the wall, and I remembered that Lupine had called this place The Home. It seemed that I would not be allowed into The Home without an invitation. The image that the old man had placed in my mind came back, of the precipitous stone wall soaring up to be lost in the clouds, and I realized he had been telling me to come here. I placed another question at the feet of my sense and spirit, facing that wall, and waited.

I felt a beckoning, as if there was in fact an invitation being offered. But clearly it wasn't an invitation to just waltz in with this newly found power that had come into me. Gradually it dawned on me that the invitation was for all of me. I was required to *show up*, in body as well as in spirit. Going to this place was one of the instructions the old man had given me, I was certain. It seemed right that I should undertake this before returning to the mountain spruce, which I had recognized immediately in the second image.

I slowly retreated from the cirque, pulling myself back through the earth until all my senses were sitting on the saddle of Sluiskin again. Leaving my hands touching the ground, still feeling the sap of the earth flowing, I chose to strike out in one more direction before returning to Lyla and the others with my news.

Down the mountainside I roamed, finding pathways of stone and water, nerves extending farther and farther into the land as I moved into Vernal Park. There had been no vegetation to speak of between where I sat and The Home, but here there was an abundance of plants. I felt the dense mats of grass roots questing down and outward in their endless search for food and water. I found the clumps of wildflower roots also so close to the surface, and followed the pathways of life through the roots and into the plants themselves. I felt the wildness of their agreement with the world, their willingness to do whatever it took to live, and their passion to go on living. I couldn't help but love and admire them, and wish them well.

Going on, I began to encounter the root systems of the alpine trees, and moving into them opened a whole new way of being with and within the trees. Their taproots pushed and clawed into the earth with a vigor that was astounding and humbling; the spread of their lateral roots and the glacial poetry of their movement filled me with joy and admiration. I found myself attracted to a single alpine fir, and after greeting it and receiving permission, I entered from below.

The tree was filled with gladness, for the sun, the air, the water underground. I shared its fierce happiness and we revelled together. But it felt like something else was happening, something of which I wasn't aware. I was afraid for a moment, wondering if I would know if I was in danger. I could feel someone else; it was a human, not part of the tree. With a start I realized it was the one who had introduced himself to me as Douglas at the gathering. In the same instant he became aware that he and the fir were not alone, and his surprise and distress were like a sudden rush of water dashing up a stream in the wrong direction. In an instant he was gone, and I was left with the fir. I did my best to apologize for the intrusion, and the fir made it clear that I had been invited, should not feel conflicted that way. I spent a few moments in wordless company with it, and then with a silent word of thanks I too retreated.

I roamed at leisure through Vernal Park this way for a while, as if I were some kind of congenial door to door salesman that generally met with willing customers, knocking politely, entering, passing the time of day, expressing my admiration for their beauty, their ruggedness and vitality, all while my body sat quietly waiting up on Sluiskin.

I felt something coming. I thought at first it might be Douglas, returning to resume his interrupted visit, but it was something or someone very different. It was still far away. I was with and in a tiny cedar, one that was no more than a foot tall despite what felt like about forty growing seasons. It had been astonishing to find a cedar in this place, at this altitude. What was coming felt like a cross between a freight train and a tsunami, and its menace grew with each passing second. It was approaching with incredible speed, from where I had no idea. From one instant to the next I went from wondering what this might be to knowing exactly who and what it was; I could feel the implacable hatred, the burning ferocity of its malice, and knew that it was coming directly to me.

I hesitated for a second, and it was nearly my final mistake. It swept up the slope from below so quickly that I had barely pulled myself out of the tiny cedar when it struck. I was moving as fast as I could from that place, so the blow that hit me was a glancing one. Nevertheless, it felt like I guessed it would feel to be hit by a train—for the tiny instant when anything could be felt. It spun me from my moorings, flung my senses into scattered disarray as it passed in a blaze of fury. There was a roaring, a tearing sound that seemed to go on and on. I had no time to be shocked or bewildered; my survival depended on pulling myself together and moving back into the mind and body that until now I had thought were all I had.

It was a bit like gathering up the contents of a basket that had been viciously knocked from my grasp as I collected feeling, thought and energy and fled back up the slope through the earth.

I reached the saddle, slammed myself back into my body and found it in the position I had left it. My eyes were still closed, hands firmly pressed into the ground, but I felt sick, and weak. I shuddered, and opened my eyes. The roaring receded; the sun was still shining, yet for some moments it seemed dark and forbidding around me. I unfolded my legs and groaned at their sore stiffness. My heart was pounding, head spinning, lungs heaving, stomach roiling, and I simply rolled over and lay on the ground.

Gradually the world stopped whirling, and stood more or less still. My breathing slowed, and I was able to determine that I was unhurt.

I decided I had come up a step since having my heart stopped under the glacier. There had been an intense, visceral fear this time when I realized that it was coming for me, but not the paralyzing terror of my first encounter with this creature, or being, or force—I still didn't know how to think of it.

I had recognized it, and known how to get away. That alone felt good. I had entered into the world in ways I hadn't suspected were there before, and stayed there for a while. But it had found me; that did not feel so good.

My mind strayed back to the beginning of this, when I had been simply pacing back and forth, and had been abruptly stopped in my tracks by a sensation that could not be ignored. I was still sitting on that exact spot, but I didn't feel that connection, the flow of energy from the heart of the world that had held me there. I wondered if I could make that connection myself, and quickly decided that as I valued my life I'd better wait a while. But were there more places like this? And could I learn how to tap into the earth this way anywhere?

So this is what power feels like, I thought. *My first notion is to play with it, to learn its boundaries—if it has any—and to see where I can go, what I can do. And my second notion is to extend it if I can.* It suddenly sounded like all the stories of magic and power I had read, where the protagonist suddenly acquires it and immediately wreaks havoc on the world and himself. It was a humbling thought, and I took some comfort in believing that Lupine knew something of this, as I was certain Works did. If I was very lucky, maybe they could help me avoid destroying myself and anything or anyone else from my own ignorance or plain stupidity.

I glanced down into Vernal Park, and my eye was caught by a patch of strange color I hadn't noticed before. After a moment I realized that was because it hadn't been there before. Well down in the great meadow was a rough circle, about twenty feet in diameter. It was an odd charcoal gray. With a chill that went to the bottom of my heart I saw that every living thing within that circle was dead, and I knew without needing proof that in the center of that circle had been a twelve-inch tall cedar tree of about forty years.

The very first exercise of the gift that had come to me had brought about the deaths of innocents. I was filled with grief and shame, and they quickly turned to rage at the thing that had done this, yet I knew at the same time that this rage was wrong. Every bit of me wanted in that moment to destroy the Destroyer. But that very morning, Works had told us, in a way that could not be ignored, that to wallow in fear and ignorance—meaning anger, too—was to throw away the solution. There was no doubt that rage was the wrong answer. What *was* the answer then?

I needed a way to think about this force, this entity, whatever it was; I needed a handle with which to grasp it. My first encounter with it had involved an apparently human form, but it was most definitely not human. Without Henry's help it would have destroyed me, as it seemed to want to destroy us all. So, then, it would be the Destroyer. I would have to be very careful not to give it human attributes and try to deal with it that way. I would have to remember this was not a human creature at all, that my own involvement with it must have shaped it that way, and to assume that what I had seen was its true form could be another fatal mistake. Nonetheless in that moment it became the Destroyer, and that was how I would place it in my mind.

Slowly, tentatively, and very much against my better judgment, I thought about opening myself to the earth again, about entering that river of life that flowed through it. And as I thought of it, it happened, and I once again felt the energy streaming into me and back out, in every direction. I was clean, and clear; the river flowed through me without resistance. I began to probe outwards slowly and carefully.

It was far away, but not far enough. I felt it turn and face in my direction, and then I could sense it rushing my way.

That was all that was needed. I pulled myself back in with a rush of movement, and concentrated my will on closing off the connection to the world I had opened. I was instantly wholly back in my body, and the river of energy and life stopped as abruptly as if I had turned a great tap. For the moment, I felt assured that the Destroyer could not reach me.

So, I thought once again, *this is what power feels like.* No wonder so many have been seduced, beguiled and bedeviled to their destruction, for it felt irresistible. But I would have to resist, and there was no doubt that I would not survive the time it took to learn to use it without the help of Lupine, Works, Lyla and perhaps others too.

The sun was well into its westward journey. I had been gone longer than I expected to be, and I began to fret that the others would be worried about me. There was much to talk about; more so, perhaps, than I could express. There was nothing for it but to try. I rose slowly, lost in thought, and headed absently back to our campsite in Meeting Meadow.

CHAPTER 23

WHEN I REACHED THE LITTLE CLEARING everyone was still there. They had moved out from the tight circle in which we'd sat that morning, but they had not moved far. I saw with pleasure that Lyla had taken my word to heart, and had felt comfortable enough to retrieve my journal; she was reading intently when I entered. Henry was puttering with supplies, and as I walked in he was eyeing my little camp stove with his customary suspicion. Hucklebark was sprawled on top of his sleeping bag, snoring gently. Lupine sat alone over on the far side of the opening, still and composed.

With the exception of Hucklebark, they all looked up as I came into the clearing. As far as I knew, there was nothing special to see in me. But Henry gave me a look that made me stop at the edge of the clearing. He took a few steps toward me, and when he spoke his voice was even and cold.

"All right, then. Who are you and what've you done with Ray?"

I thought he was joking, though his tone puzzled me. An awkward, confused laugh came out of me, but then I realized he meant it. How could I be so different as to scare my friend? Events of the past few hours flashed through me, and I felt calm; I would take care of this. I smiled encouragingly.

"Maybe some of the real Ray has finally showed up, Henry," I said. "What do you see that frightens you?"

Henry continued to hold my gaze, and he scowled. I glanced briefly around; Hucklebark had awakened and was looking at me wide-eyed. Lyla was looking with a neutral, unreadable expression, as if deciding whether or not to deal with a potentially dangerous stranger. Lupine regarded me with narrowed eyes, intensely alert for any movement.

"If I was a certain person, I would say that another garage blew up a little while ago. Can you tell me who that person might be?" Henry said.

"That would be Ev, of course," I said with a trace of irritation. "Come on, Henry, cut it out. What's going on?"

Lupine broke in. "That's what we'd like to know." She turned to Henry. "It is Ray, Henry. But something enormous has happened." She turned back to me, with an accusatory look. "I was under the impression you had promised not to do any experimenting, Ray."

"I did make that promise, and I kept it," I said. "However, I don't recall anyone extracting a promise from the planet that it wouldn't experiment with *me*. Now before we carry on with this little inquisition, or whatever it is, I want to know: is everyone here all right?"

"Of course we are, Ray," Lyla replied. "But there have been some—well, deeply troubling, at the very least—disturbances near here in the last few hours. We were worried sick about you, and Lupine went to get Works. He came for a little while, told us under no circumstances to move from here, and left. We had no idea what had happened, no idea if we'd ever see you again, and no way to do anything but sit here on the nastiest pins and needles I can remember. Now will you tell us what happened to you?"

My irritation vanished, and all I could feel was how much I loved these people.

"I'm sorry," I said softly. "I'm sorry you had to be stuck here that way, not knowing anything, wondering. I didn't have the faintest notion of what would happen; I was just going for a walk because I couldn't sit still any more. I was planning on telling it all to you anyway, but it might take as long to tell as it took to happen. Henry, am I recognizable enough to be obvious about needing a cup of coffee?"

Henry's scowl stayed frozen on his face for another moment, and then smoothed itself out into his usual deadpan. "Sounds like you, all right, and I always accept Lupine's judgment. Yeah, sure."

As I went to sit down near Henry, and looked an invitation over to Lyla to join me, Lupine interjected. "I do imagine this will take some time, Ray. I need to go find Works again, because I want him to hear it immediately, while it's still fresh in your mind."

Without waiting for a reply, she turned and darted from the clearing. Lyla came over and sat next to me; there was a tentative feel to the way she moved. She looked searchingly into my eyes, as if afraid of what she would find there. I returned her gaze, and tried to open the pathway from my eyes to my soul. She looked into me, and all I could think of was how I loved her, and I was fearful that she would not like what she found. She shivered, and broke the spell, retreating back into herself.

"Am I really that different, all of a sudden?" I asked softly.

"Yes, you are, and yet no, you aren't," was her reply. "I had to look very hard to be certain it really is you, Ray. There's not a thing about your outward appearance that's changed, but everything else—*everything*—seems different at first glance. I don't know what kind of power, or attribute, or whatever, has come into you, but it's terrifying. Terrifying and hopeful at the same time."

"Tell me what makes it terrifying."

"If you use it wrongly, it feels like it could wreck the world," she said. "If you manage to work it well and faithfully, on the other hand, it could become something wonderful beyond words."

I turned to her, gently took her face in my hands, and kissed her forehead. "You have the gift of reaching the absolute heart of the matter in an instant, and that is only one of many reasons I love you with all my heart," I said. "Whatever happens, whether or not I get to have you in my life for another minute or forever, know that that's true."

I looked again into her eyes, and saw that they were filling with tears. "Perhaps I love you too, Ray. But I'm so afraid of what may happen. And you are changing. Changing so fast I don't know if the way I feel now will mean anything tomorrow, or next week, or next year—if there is one."

"Then," I said solemnly, "As they say in all of your better tragical romances, we'd better be satisfied with today," and I put on the best over-dignified, narrator-of-heart-wrenching-love-story face I could muster.

She looked at me in astonishment, then broke into laughter, and punched me in the shoulder. "Good, you haven't changed all *that* much. You're still a brat!"

"Yes, ma'am, that's very true," I replied, struggling to keep the owlish solemnity intact. "Once a brat, always a brat."

Works must have been nearby, for just then he and Lupine emerged into the clearing. Henry and Hucklebark, who had been studiously avoiding overhearing us—as if that had been possible— busied themselves handing out coffee mugs. Works accepted his gratefully, and sat down slowly. He looked tired, worried, and wary.

We all moved to sit close to him. Henry got up immediately to start the coffee pot ritual again, as if to say in his own way, "This is going to take a while." Out loud he said, "Go ahead and get it going. I can hear just fine from here."

We sat in silence, each of us thinking that Works would be the one to start. Finally, he heaved a sigh.

"Things are moving much too quickly for my tastes," he began. "I am intensely grateful that still none of my people has died today, but I'm beginning to worry that that can't go on much longer. There has, in fact, been lamentable harm done. I already know that some have chosen to ignore my request, and have been continuing their work as if nothing was wrong." He looked significantly in my direction, and I wondered how much he already knew. How could he know, unless he was quite capable of what I had only discovered today? "Ray, I would like to hear it directly from you, with every single detail at your disposal, before I say or think anything else."

I launched into the story, starting from the moment I had become too restless to sit in our campsite any longer. As had happened before, no one interrupted. But more than once I saw Lupine and Works exchange glances laden with significance, and when they did this I almost lost the thread of the story for wondering and worrying over what they were thinking.

The sun had set behind the Mountain and twilight was filtering into the clearing when I finished. There were no questions, only a long silence punctuated by the soft hiss of the camp stove, working on yet another pot of coffee, and the softest rustle of branches as the afternoon breeze slowly died to stillness. I waited as long as I could, then broke the silence myself.

"Lupine, Works, I have watched you two communing all the while I've been talking. Is there something you need to ask me, or perhaps to tell me?"

Works shifted his position very slightly, as if not quite comfortable or settled. This was something I had not seen him do before.

"You are forcing me into a very difficult decision, Ray. I have to determine how much of what I'm thinking is supposition or merely wishfulness, and how much may be a reflection of what is to come. What I do now may have much to do with our success or failure, and many, many lives might hang in the balance."

"You make me glad I'm wearing my own shoes," I said, "And don't have to be filling yours."

"If I knew better how it was soon going to feel in your shoes," he replied, "I'd know more clearly what to say now, and what not to say." He sighed heavily again. "I'm just going to do it, I think.

"You've met a lot of people recently whose work and way of life is totally different from anything you have known before. In this circle here," as he swept an arm to include us all, "we have Change Bringers, and two different kinds of Speakers. You know that Change Bringers and Speakers come in many different forms and ways. But there are other types of work done in this way that you surely haven't learned of yet."

He paused, as if marshaling his thoughts. A question rose up in me that wouldn't be denied, and with some trepidation I spoke.

"May I ask you a question?"

"Certainly."

"What is the name for what you do, Works?"

He smiled briefly. "Rather than answer that with a word that may or may not convey meaning, I'd prefer to let our friends try to answer that." He looked over to Henry.

Henry snorted, an answer I had come to expect from him

without ever knowing if he would offer more. This time he begrudged a little more. "You're Works, and that's that. It's good enough for me." He clammed up again, and we looked to Hucklebark next.

Hucklebark looked up in surprise when he sensed our attention, as if he would never have expected his opinion to be asked. "Well, yeah, you're Works, of course. If I speak of you to someone else, it might be He Works, but," he said with a chuckle, "I suppose that's a little formal. When times were less perilous, and we were heading up here to be with everyone and have some fun, I would say 'We're going to be with He Works at Windy Gap'." He laughed briefly, then looked embarrassed, and stopped abruptly.

Works smiled. "I like that, Hucklebark, and I thank you. Lupine?"

"There aren't any words to describe what you do, and at the same time there are too many," she said. "I need no other word than your name to know who you are and what you stand for, Works."

He nodded gravely, and I looked expectantly at Lyla. She paused for a long moment, looking first undecided, then sheepish, then determined.

"When I came to this place I was an orphan in every sense of the word. You took me in, made me feel wanted and welcome, and taught me how to discover my own gifts and to find my place in the world. When I think of you as anything but Works, I think of you as… Papa." She flushed furiously, and fell silent.

Works embraced her with a loving glance. "You know you have been my daughter all this time, dear Lyla. It means more to me than I can say that my feeling is returned."

Works turned to me. "Ray, will that suffice?"

Emotions were running so strongly in me that it was hard to speak. "Yes, indeed, that suffices. And," I went on, "since I too have spent most of this life as an orphan in every way, I hope that some day I will be able to think of you as Papa." Lyla looked up at me in surprise and I let my eyes shine into hers. But we only had a moment.

"Very well, then." Works was abruptly businesslike. "Back to the matter at hand, if we may. I was saying that there are ways of work and life you cannot have learned yet. There is one way in particular that suggests itself to me, and that is the cause for my disquiet. Has anyone here besides Lupine heard of a Mender?"

Henry, Hucklebark and Lyla shook their heads and I, of course, joined them. Lupine herself looked serious and stern, and, I thought, surprised that Works was speaking thus. What was a Mender, and why would it frighten people like Works and Lupine?

"There have never been more than one or two Menders in the world at any given time," Works went on. "In fact, for generations now it's been common for there to be *no* Menders anywhere in the world. Their job is to assist in repairing the great rents and tears in the fabric of life whenever forces intrude to damage it, and it's quite safe to say—if the ancient stories are even marginally true—that their job is often a harrowing one. Menders work with the most potent, elemental forces that drive the world and all that lives in it, forces that would overwhelm almost anyone else. There are stories of Menders who destroyed themselves and much of the world around them, either by mistaking their own abilities, or from being seduced by the power they manipulated."

"How many Menders are there now?" I asked.

Works replied, "To the best of my knowledge, there has been no Mender, anywhere, in living memory."

There was a silence, broken only by the camp stove's comfortable hiss, while we considered this.

"Forgive me, Works, if this is foolish or impolite," I said. "What in this case is 'living memory'? I mean, it seems like everything I thought I knew about people and time is wrong."

Works looked down in thought, then looked back up to me. "If I tell you that I am very likely the oldest human in this part of the world, and that no tree anywhere here was alive when I was young, will that satisfy you?"

He was telling me that he was at least twelve hundred years old. It was impossible, unimaginable. And yet, when I looked into his eyes, it seemed perfectly reasonable. No eyes could have that depth, or that immeasurable, fearless compassion, without an immense body of experience to inform them.

"All right," I said quietly. "I am satisfied. But why are you telling us about these Menders? What have they to do with anything here?"

"It's so obvious—and yet so fearsome—that I'm not surprised you aren't willing to face it," Works said. "Go ahead and try it on, Ray. I could be completely wrong, which in most ways would make things much easier."

Oh. No, no—*no*. My heart nearly stopped of its own accord, without any Destroyer to menace it. No wonder he hadn't wanted to tell this. Me, useless, worthless little Ray Holdman, someone who comes along every thousand years or so and alters the course of the world, a… a *Mender*?

I couldn't *mend* my way out of a paper bag with a roll of duct tape and four staplers. And yet, and yet… This afternoon I had *played* with things that, if I took what Works said at face value, almost nobody in the world was willing or able to deal with. Power, indeed. But now it was clear that what I knew from the afternoon's events was just enough to show me how utterly ignorant I really was, and how much more dangerous it had suddenly become to be ignorant. I thought of the tiny cedar and the life that had surrounded it; I thought about how that kind of harm could spread with the mistaken or stupid use of such power, and my mind shied away from the consequences. I didn't want this! I wasn't up to something like this; who did the world think I was, anyway?

A quiet rustle at my side brought me back into the circle. Lyla was sitting next to me, looking at me gravely. With a rush of gratitude, I could tell that she still saw me, not some supernatural world changer. But there was no denial in her expression; she was struggling to see not only who I was now, but who I might become, and whether or not it would be someone she could know.

The air was electric with revelation and apprehension. I reached over to Lyla, placed a hand on hers, and squeezed it lightly. The darkness had fallen so that it was difficult to see across the circle of friends. Henry got up abruptly, went over to his pack, and returned with a candle lantern. He lit the small candle inside and set the lantern in the center of our circle. Its light was humble, unpretentious and uncertain, unlike our more modern lights. It was enough to see the faces of the people around me.

"I don't suppose there's any way to give it all back," I said quietly.

"No there isn't, Ray," Works replied, "No way at all. We have no way to know what's ahead. But we do know without the shadow of a doubt that there is no going back. The only way we can move is as it has always been—forward."

A deep sigh escaped from me. With it went all reasons to hold back, to hesitate, to wait any longer. "All right, then, forward it is. I have to go to The Home, and it has to be tomorrow morning." I turned to Lyla. "I can go alone if need be, but it would mean very much to me if you came too."

Lyla had no hesitation in her. "Of course I'll come with you, Ray."

I turned to the rest of the group. "I don't know exactly why this is, so I can't defend it. I feel strongly that no one else should go there. But I need you all to be nearby. I'm certain I'll need the help of each one of you, probably sooner rather than later. I imagine you all hate waiting as much as I do, but I have to ask, will you all wait for me?"

Lupine answered first. "You may not remember what I told you about The Home, Ray. It's not a place that people simply 'go' to."

"On the one hand, I have been commanded to go there, and on the other I have been invited," I said. "The image the old man gave me was The Home, and when I sent part of me there this afternoon, it beckoned to me very clearly. If there's anything to worry about, Lupine, worry about whether or not I can handle what's required of me once I get there."

She looked unsatisfied, but nodded. "I may not be in this exact place, but I won't be far. I could use a little time alone to think, but if you need me I'll know it."

"Thank you," I said.

"You're welcome."

Henry shifted in place, and we all turned to him. "I need to get back to the glacier. Someone has to look after what's going on down there, and get the word out if anything comes up. That's where I belong right now, but it isn't far, and you all know where to find me."

Works said, "Do you think it's wise to do that, Henry? If for no other reason, then perhaps because I have asked all the people to suspend their work for now?"

Henry looked uncomfortable. "I remembered that, Works, but I'm too worried about what's happened already. We know that this Destroyer thing is homing in on Ray, and if he's not there, I'm not likely to be in much danger, am I? Besides, I might be able to help out by being another set of eyes and ears in the earth."

Works shook his head slowly, and said with a rueful smile, "I should know better than to try and keep you in line, Henry. But—your abilities notwithstanding—I'm not comfortable with you being alone." He turned to Hucklebark. "Would you consider going with Henry?"

Henry and Hucklebark both looked as if Works had asked them to spend the night with a banshee. Hucklebark furrowed his brow in thought, and came up with an idea.

"I'm not any more of a fan of the insides of glaciers than Henry is of dry mountainsides," he began. "But how about this, Works? I'd be glad to spend a little time studying the Carbon River Canyon, and then Henry 'n me'd be close by but we wouldn't have to be in each others' faces. How's that?"

"All right," Works smiled. "That's probably the best I can hope for. Other than—in Everett's colorful jargon—garages blowing up, we are going to have to find ways to keep track of each other. Any suggestions?"

"I don't know what we'll encounter at The Home," I said, "But I would think we can arrange to meet back here in two days." I turned to Lupine. "Does that seem reasonable?"

Lupine shrugged her shoulders, a gesture that seemed entirely uncharacteristic for her. "I have no idea, Ray. But as a working hypothesis, it's as good as anything."

"Two days time it is, then," Works concluded. "I will be here too. In the meantime, I have other things to tend to."

"That's one of the words I had associated with you, Works," I suddenly said. "Tender. Funny about that word, there are at least two meanings for it. At first glance, they seem totally unrelated, but the more I think on it, the closer they seem."

Works, who had started to get up from his seat in the circle, sat back down and regarded me thoughtfully.

"I was about to say that you have many more important things to think about than what label to attach to me. But on further reflection, it might be a profitable line of thought. Promise me two things, Ray: one, you'll extend that line of thought and let it work in other directions, and two, that you won't decide you know everything about everything."

He said it with a smile, but I felt chastened, and more than a little humbled again. I was going to have to get used to being chastened and humbled, it was clear. For all I knew, it might be my key to staying alive.

I nodded my acknowledgement of his gentle rebuke, and he got up once again. He clasped hands with Henry and Hucklebark, gave Lyla a fatherly kiss on the cheek, stood eye to eye with Lupine and gently squeezed her shoulder, and then came over to me. He wordlessly took my hand, and I felt that warmth, that immense humanity that flowed out from him. I looked into his eyes, and wanted nothing more than to be able to think of him as my Papa. His eyes twinkled, and with a final, tiny shake of my hand he released it and walked slowly out of the clearing, into the night.

Chapter 24

The walk up from our campsite to Sluiskin's saddle was steep, and much of the rock was loose, but there was plenty of room for Lyla and me to walk side by side. As long as I had the breath to spare from climbing, this made talking a lot easier.

"I'm worried about Henry. In fact, I'm *really* worried. What could he have up his sleeve?"

"We're all worried about Henry," Lyla replied, and we walked upwards in silence for a while.

Henry had been long gone when we woke that morning. His gear and himself, gone as if he had never been there. Was he heading back down to his glacier, or was some other place in his plans? He knew as well as anyone that Works had intended Hucklebark to go with him. We all knew neither one of them liked the arrangement, but no one had expected Henry to ignore it entirely.

Hucklebark had sat up, looked around, uttered an expletive most unusual for him, packed his gear and left, with hardly a word other than, "See you guys soon, I hope." That had left Lupine, Lyla and I to share a muted breakfast and goodbye. Lupine had simply said she had some people she needed to talk to, but she would be close by in this area within a day and a half. We had left the Meeting Meadow of the House of Windy Gap in a somber spirit to go, at least for the time being, our separate ways.

Lyla and I stopped to rest a few minutes at the saddle between Sluiskin's peaks. She walked slowly around, looking everywhere as if to see what was different here that had led to all my experiences of the day before. She was like a bloodhound of the spirit, all of her senses seeking that difference, hunting the doorway into the world that had opened for me. I was not tempted to try my new capabilities at all; my mind was thoroughly preoccupied with the mystery Henry had presented us. Why had he felt the need to sneak away? Why did he have to be so secretive?

While Lyla investigated, touched, smelt, felt and pondered, I sat overlooking Vernal Park. The charcoal gray circle below held my eye, and would not let it go. It called, demanding and insistent. It felt all the worse not knowing what was being demanded of me. I wanted to give it a wide berth, go all the way around the extreme edge of the park if need be, but even as I thought of routes around it I knew that when we started again I would go straight to it.

Eventually Lyla came down to sit beside me.

"Will you show me where you sat yesterday, where all that happened?"

I didn't want to talk about it, or recreate anything. I wanted to get going, and yet I didn't want to go down to that circle. I thought about how I would feel if it had all happened to Lyla; I would have wanted very much to see it, try to feel it. I slowly got to my feet, and walked over to where I thought I had been when my feet had been rooted to the earth and a river of the world's energy had started roaring through me. But the spot didn't feel familiar. I looked around me, and none of it seemed like the right place. I was confused, and stood there irresolute.

"If it was me, I don't expect I'd find it again by looking," Lyla said.

Of course not. I closed my eyes, and tried to open myself up. It took all of five seconds to feel the river again; I tried to keep it to a trickle, feeling outwards in small increments. I could feel a place where it was much stronger, no more than ten feet from where we stood. I didn't bother to open my eyes as I walked that way; I could sense the contours of the ground, down to the smallest pebbles, without looking. When I was next to the place I had felt, I allowed the trickle to die away, and opened my eyes.

"Stand right there," I said. "That's where I was yesterday."

She moved onto that spot and closed her eyes, holding very still.

I waited for several minutes, feeling the urge to be moving on and resisting it.

Without opening her eyes, Lyla said, "I can't find it, Ray. How did you do it?"

"I'm sorry. I don't know. It just happened. But it seems as if someone like you should be able to find it easily if I can."

She opened her eyes and smiled at me. "No, I don't think that's right at all. Get used to it, Ray Holdman; whatever's been given to you is something very few people get." She gave a small sigh. "Maybe I'll get to experience some of it sometime, but not now. We might as well get going."

We walked back to the edge of the saddle, and I pointed to the dark circle staining the meadow below. "We have to go there first."

Lyla looked at me in surprise. "Why? What can we do there now?"

I shook my head as if to shake loose a bit of understanding that might be lodged in some hidden corner of it. "It has to be set right somehow. I wish I knew what that means. But we have to go there. I have to, that is. If you want, you can go on ahead and I'll catch up to you."

"Oh, no, you're not getting away with that anymore," she said. "If I let you out of my sight, there's no telling what will happen. If it has to be done, we'll do it together."

I squeezed her hand and said, "There's no telling what will happen anymore, regardless. But thank you."

I wanted to keep hold of her hand, but the steepness of the slope down to Vernal Park and the loose, slippery talus dispelled any hope of that. We slipped and slid to the bottom, and made our way through the lumpy grassland towards the circle. My feet were tingling again, and I had to consciously keep from opening myself up to what was in movement around and below me, though my eyes could tell me nothing about any of it. I thought I detected a murmur running across the land, far outside the realm of hearing but clear enough in my mind. The feel of it made me uneasy, and as we approached the darkened circle my trepidation rose up to constrict my throat and make it hard to breathe.

The park was crisscrossed by a myriad of tiny rivulets. The inch or two of water in their miniature courses ran merry and fast in some places, while in others it was so slow as to almost soak back into the ground rather than move forward. Several of them made their way to the edge of the blackened circle, and there they stopped. It was as if the water refused to cross the line of dead grasses and wildflowers; even looking closely it was hard to tell where the water went after deciding it would not go into the circle.

Inside that circle the plants were unnatural, darkened husks. They had not been burned; rather, it seemed as if everything that had to do with life and living had been torn from them, leaving behind shriveled, discolored corpses. They lay in disarray, as if a whirling storm of chaos had ripped away their lives. In the center I could see a shriveled stem with a few desiccated fronds still clinging; it was about twelve inches tall, and the ground around it was a black that had nothing to do with the cleansing fury of fire.

I didn't want to go into that circle. But I found my feet moving across the line between life and death, trudging towards the middle. Lyla clearly did not want to be there either, but she immediately set that aside and walked in with me. The tingling in my feet stopped abruptly, and I could feel nothing but the powdery ground under-foot. There was no sound but the crackle of dead grass as we passed.

We went slowly to the center. I sat on the ground a foot away from the remains of the tiny cedar, and extended my hand. When I carefully stroked the stem, a tiny shower of needles fell to the ground. I could feel nothing whatever; everything that had been here, in all its vigor and rightness, was gone.

I opened myself up to the earth below me, and there was nothing. The great river had been diverted from this small spot, and I wondered if it would be dead forever. The pain of that wondering was a physical presence, like a blow to the heart. I slowly stood, looking down at the dead tree.

"I'm responsible for this."

Lyla seemed to be choosing her words carefully, and when she spoke it was soft and low. "There is no one alive who really works in the world, who isn't responsible for some terrible mistake. Ray, can you simply feel the pain of it, acknowledge your part in the horror and sorrow of it, and then just try to do differently next time?"

I turned to her, anger, remorse, bitterness welling up even as I fought to push them back down. "You don't understand! It's possible that nothing will ever grow here again! That tree *welcomed* me, took me in and shared its life with me. And look how I repaid it!" I gestured around the circle. "And look at all the others who just had the misfortune of growing here when I came along. There's no *savant* in me, it's all *idiot*!"

Lyla looked searchingly into my face. It was difficult to see her, for the anger was clouding my mind, interfering with everything I needed to consider and understand. As if through a fog I returned her gaze. I must have been hoping for sympathy, for her to say, "There, there, Ray, it's not your fault," but instead her eyes seemed to harden. At first I thought she was closing herself off from me, but with a start I realized she had opened herself up further; she was showing me a place in her soul that was hard as the rock around us; it was solid, strong and purposeful.

Softly she said, "So would you allow their sacrifice to go to waste, then? Would you give up when you've barely begun?"

Abruptly I sat down again. All I could feel was despair; all the power I had felt before seemed to have drained away into a bottomless pit of fear, and pain, and futility. But Lyla spoke on in the same low, even tone.

"You don't have to decide if you're strong enough, or smart enough, or brave enough, Ray. You simply have to decide to go ahead and do what must be done anyway. It isn't a question of whether or not you'll get past this; it's a question of how you'll do it, and when."

My breathing had become ragged and shallow. I paid attention to it now, willing it to become deep and even while I tried to take in what she was saying.

"There isn't much time, Ray," she said. "How will you go forward?"

"I suppose I'll do it by getting up and walking to where we're supposed to go next." I got up awkwardly, as if I'd momentarily forgotten how to do it. "If you'd consider picking out a route away from here, I'd be grateful."

She waited until she was sure I was ready to follow, and wordlessly turned and walked out of the circle.

The moment I left that dead place and started walking through the grass, I could feel the movement beneath my feet, and the murmuring began again. Lyla's route appeared to be taking us directly across Vernal Park, towards a high ridge on Old Desolate. The murmurs were like an internal soundscape, not heard, but enough like sound that the mind might interpret it that way. It rose and fell in pitch and intensity as we walked across the park, and soon I began to sense a pattern: when we drew near to one of the sparse groves of alpine fir and spruce, it rose in volume and deepened, but when we passed by large clusters of wildflowers it grew shrill.

We came within a hundred feet or so of one of the larger groves of trees, and at once the sound made me stumble. Lyla turned around to look at me quizzically.

It was loud and strong in my mind, and getting louder. I mutely pointed towards the grove, and began walking that way. Lyla looked exasperated, then troubled, and then turned to follow. The murmuring was dominating my attention, and I couldn't explain to her. When we got to within ten feet of the grove I was forced to stop, for the sound was becoming unbearable. It was the sound of many voices. I had no idea how many voices were raised, but it felt like a whole host. Their cries were being funneled to me through the strength and skill of these trees in front of us.

There were no words, but the layers of meaning were so clear that words were unnecessary. There was accusation, and fear. There was a kind of grief that was piercing to feel. There was sorrow in an abundance that made we want to clap my hands to my ears as if I could shut it out that way. But there was no shutting this out; there was no escaping it.

I began to feel as if all of this emotion was a weight that was being placed on me. It grew as the lamentations grew, until I was forced to my knees. Pain and terror were being poured over my head like a caustic waterfall, and it got worse with each moment. I began to panic; all I could think about was being trapped, unable to move.

From some hidden recess in my mind, I heard Lupine's voice saying a single word. *Remember.* Remember what? How can a drowning man remember anything that might save him?

And yet the memories began to flow: a tiny, ineffectual trickle at first, then with greater urgency. Lupine herself, telling me in tones alternating between hope and frustration that I *did* have a place in this world; Works, and the warmth and comfort, the belonging that came with the touch of his hand. Hucklebark, a bluff, simple friend who was undoubtedly much less simple, but no less true, than he seemed. And Lyla, standing somewhere beside me, though by now I couldn't see anything for the cacophony of pain surrounding us.

The sheer weight of all that pain was flattening me to the ground. I struggled to stay kneeling. A sound reached my ears through the roaring that was running through my mind, and I realized it was Lyla gasping, being borne down too. I heard her voice, strained and far away.

"Talk to them, Ray! We can't hold this—let go of it and talk to them!"

The trees, the grasses and flowers didn't need to do anything physical to focus their feeling and thought towards us. But it helped me to do it physically, to use breath and throat to say what there was to say, even if the ones I was talking to were going to hear me in some other way.

"I'm sorry. My pain isn't as great as yours, but it's large. My fear is great, too. My sorrow is for everyone; you must know that I never meant to bring harm to any one of you. If there is anything that can be done about this, you should be certain that I'll do it. There is nothing I can do for the people who've been harmed. Please— accept my sorrow, and let us go in peace."

Nothing seemed to change; the crushing weight of all that was being aimed at us made it impossible to move, and I felt that any moment I'd be driven to the ground and squashed like a bug. But in the next moment it lightened, just a little; the pain and sorrow were still overwhelming, but the dark mist that had clouded my vision began to clear, and I could look around me again.

Lyla was on the ground, breathing heavily.

The weight had lifted enough that I could stand. I got to my feet, staggering over to where she lay. I bent down, grasped her arm and lifted. At first she didn't respond, but when I tried again she stirred, and struggled to her knees. I reached under her arms and lifted with all the strength I could find, and she rose shakily to her feet. I got us turned around, and we stumbled away from the grove, heading towards an area ahead that was as far as possible from trees, and with few wildflowers.

It felt like I was carrying two of me, and that was not counting the effort of helping Lyla to walk. We staggered and stumbled across the grassland, and the horrible weight began to diminish. We headed towards a large boulder, a glacial erratic that had been dropped there during an ice sheet's retreat and was now mostly buried in the soil, a few feet high and generally flat on top. We collapsed onto the boulder and lay silent, chests heaving, for several minutes.

When our breathing had slowed we sat up, groggy and wary at the same time, as if we expected something to attack from some unknown quarter. When nothing happened, we began to relax. Lyla looked over at me, her expression grim.

"Nothing like this has ever happened before, that I can recall. Tell me what you know of it."

"I don't expect I know anything more about it than you do," I said defensively. "As far as I can tell, every living thing within ten miles was screaming at me, and you got caught in the crossfire. If you have any other ideas, I'd love to hear them."

She looked resentful, then thoughtful. "I'm sorry, Ray. There's no reason for me to think that anything different from that happened, or that anything different could have happened. I was frightened, and I don't know that anything has ever hurt that much before."

I took her hand. "Accepted. I was scared witless, and the only thing I can think of that felt worse was being killed." I tried to chuckle, but it didn't work, and came out more like a hiccup. "What are we going to do if that happens again?"

"I need to think." She chewed her lower lip and looked towards the ground, eyes unfocused. It was still only late morning; the sun shone down from a clear sky, the air was still, and the entire meadow was overlain with a feeling of tense expectancy.

The boulder we sat on was warm from the morning sun, and it felt good and comforting. I found myself relaxing onto its rough hardness. Suddenly its solidity was an illusion, and with a jolt I understood that I had opened myself up to it without intending to. I felt all the way through it to the ground and beyond; the river of world's energy was flowing beneath and coming up to lap at me. Though I was frightened of allowing it in, terrified that if another attack came we wouldn't be able to withstand it, I couldn't resist. I let the river into me, and it moved in and out of me like a great tidal wash.

Everything connected to the ground was within reach. All of the stones, the grasses, flowers and trees, were there to touch. All of it was living, and all of it was roiled with the fear and pain of what had happened so near by. There was no sign of the Destroyer anywhere. I allowed myself to roll in the sea of being that was in constant movement around me, to let it push me here and there in its restlessness. Everything I touched communicated its fear and sorrow, and added the mass of its suffering to my own. I grew heavier by the second, until I feared I would sink into the earth and vanish without a trace. I struggled to free myself, and little by little I slowed the flow through me, until I was simply sitting on a boulder again. The debilitating sense of weight was like the echo from a cry that hangs heavy in the air, far longer than it should.

I stirred, and Lyla looked up at me in alarm. "What just happened, Ray?"

When I told her, she shook her head in wonder. "It's all happening so fast. None of us know how to deal with this. If we—if you—can't learn how to control what's happening with you, it could kill you at any moment." As she said that, her eyes grew wet with tears. An instant later she shook her head angrily. "*No!* There's no time for losing it now. I need to *think*."

I sat quietly, concentrating as hard as I could on staying exactly where I was, and being as unconnected to anything outside myself as I could manage. Some minutes later, Lyla looked up again.

"You've talked several times about the world's energy just flowing through you, like a river. And yet the pain and fear that was directed at us—at you—bore us down like a landslide. Why would that be? What is it about pain and fear that it can't just flow through, like everything else? We need to know this, Ray. You have to learn how to let it through. I mean, how could it not be a part of the world's energy?"

"It would appear that the Destroyer is a part of the world's energy, too," I said. "And if all this was directed at me, and if I failed to let it go, or something, why did it take you down too?"

"I don't know," she said simply. "I'd like to see Lupine tell us to get comfortable with *this* mystery."

"I wish she was here. Maybe it's not such a mystery to her."

Lyla sighed. "I wish she was, too. But she isn't. We'd better get going. Ray, will you think about what I've said, even though it doesn't even come close to answering everything?"

"Of course I will. I just hope we can get some help from somewhere."

"With a little luck, we're making our way towards help. At The Home," she said.

"Oh, god. I haven't even thought about what's going to happen there yet."

She managed a tired smile. "Perhaps that's as it should be. There isn't the least point in worrying over something neither one of us has a clue about." She stopped, and reconsidered. "At any rate, we have enough to be cluelessly worried over without that added in."

The next half mile across Vernal Park was uneventful. We were both feeling the effects of what had happened, and moved slowly, carefully. But the sun and the soft warm air did their work on us, and the dragging weight that had borne in so cruelly vanished, leaving only a deep weariness—something that could be tolerated easily by comparison.

As we walked I tried to think about what Lyla had said. All

the living things in this great meadow had collectively flung their agony at me in an unceasing wave; was it remotely possible that I could simply let it pass through me, and go on? Were they actually aiming it at me?

And what if it was no more than another kind of river? Why did it cling to me so ferociously? If they were two kinds of rivers, what was the difference between them?

I tried to think honestly, to face the problem squarely, and that led to what seemed like an obvious possibility I'd been avoiding. Perhaps the difference was with *me*. The question then became, how and why was I treating them differently?

Again, looking at it in another way produced a quick answer. I was afraid of the river of pain. Petrified. But why would I grasp it, stop it in its tracks, make it my own? Was it because that's what I had come to expect from life? Was pain a constant companion I'd come to believe was my rightful state, and was I terrified of a new and unknown way of living without it?

Works had told me that what I had to unlearn was as important, if not more so, than what I needed to learn. He had also said that I had been lied to, all of my life. Those were painful realizations to face, but they seemed true and important. How do you *unlearn* something that's so much a part of you that you barely know it *is* a part of you?

"How do you unlearn something?"

I didn't know I had said it out loud until Lyla, who had been walking slightly ahead of me, stopped and turned back.

"What was that, Ray?"

"How do you unlearn something?"

"Like what?"

"I don't know, maybe like something about the world, or about yourself, that's just patently wrong, and you can't move forward until you've unlearned it."

"Ah." She stood still, thinking hard. "If I consider it simplistically, I'd say that unlearning something means to replace it with something that works better. It doesn't make sense to think about just plucking some deep seated belief out of your mind and tossing it away."

"Yes," I said. "Yes, of course. That makes perfect sense. Now, how to do that?"

She smiled. "Maybe we have to find a safe way for you to swim in the right river for a while."

I stood there, looking at her in amazement. But Lyla simply turned and started walking again.

Chapter 25

We were taking an unconscionable amount of time to travel less than two miles, but there was too much to think about, and too many unknowns to work with. As well, being nearly crushed to death by the weight of Vernal Park's intense, living pain and grief had worn us out.

I walked slowly, dreamlike and clumsy. The only reason I didn't fall every few steps was that a river of energy and power was running through the world just beneath my feet, and I could feel it.

If I tried to control it like I would a machine, it veered wildly away from me or into me. Neither result was satisfying, but when it ripped into me, and flowed through like a mad tidal race, it was exhilarating and terrifying at once. Had it been less terrifying, I would have stayed with it longer. But the Destroyer was waiting and watching somewhere, and I had no wish to draw attention to myself.

On the other hand, if I let go of it, as I discovered during a moment of supreme frustration, I could sense everything that was happening over a large area, both above and below the ground. I found that it was a matter of deciding what to allow at any given moment, rather than holding onto something and shoving it one way or another. I practiced permitting no more than an awareness of a few feet in any direction. I could feel the roots of the grasses and wildflowers, brush my senses against their minute, hairy capillaries. A simple opening of my mind extended the range, and I could sense the movement of water, and the workings of the tiny but intensely hard working insect community underground. I could walk with my eyes closed if I wished, for the contours of the land were clearer in my nerves than they were to my vision.

I began to think that perhaps I could maintain this awareness and still be present in my body. Nothing was mutually exclusive; all it required was learning how to be in both places without letting one or the other monopolize my mind. The possibilities were endless, and I was filled with the excitement of discovery. I found that I could sense an acres-wide range of land, above and below, but with a light touch, as if I weighed no more than a feather. I hoped that in getting better at it, I'd be able to stay connected to all the rivers that ran through a place without attracting notice.

I could tell where there were living things, all the living beings anywhere near where we walked. Lyla, being just in front of me, was a presence so strong that I had to think and feel underneath the vibrant life she carried in order to sense anyone else. Her presence filled me with a happiness I would not have thought possible an hour before. Even though she was as tired and sore as I, she radiated love, beauty and ferocity just by being who she was. Being near her was an ongoing revelation, and coupled with swimming in the world's rivers it was nothing less than a new kind of life. I felt like someone who had spent all of their days wearing monochrome glasses and earplugs, suddenly set free to find whole new worlds of sense, color and energy.

We were heading in a southwesterly direction towards the shoulder of Old Desolate that faced away from Tahoma. We had come to the edge of Vernal Park, and were starting to head up the steep slope to the ridge. The landscape was one of loose, jumbled rock, a talus that our boots sank into as we stepped, and as it got steeper it became very hard work. We struggled up, staying on the smaller, looser stone, for even though it was slippery it was far safer than climbing on the larger stones perched on the steep hillside. I kept my attention divided between the work of moving up the slope and the rivers that ran beneath it, lightly touching whatever came my way, and extending my reach farther and farther from where we stood.

After we had climbed for a half hour or so, we reached a relatively flat place where the slope had terraced itself in some age past, and there stopped for water and a rest. Lyla seemed lost in thought, and I was busy with my discoveries, so we sat in the warm sun, letting the sweat dry from our clothes in a companionable but preoccupied silence.

I sank a little deeper into the river beneath me, and suddenly I could sense things much farther away. I could feel the entire reach of the Carbon Glacier, its immense bulk stretching three miles up and down the canyon a mile directly ahead of us and beyond the ridge. I moved into the glacier, feeling its frozen mass as I passed through it. Deep within the glacier, I came upon a living thing, and all my nerves quivered with recognition.

"Lyla, I've found Henry!"

She turned quickly to look at me. "What? Henry? Where is he? There's no one anywhere near us."

"He's inside the glacier. It feels like he's very close to where we sat together when I was attacked. I think he's exactly where we were."

"How can you know this, Ray? We're at least a mile away from there!"

"I know, but I found him, I know it's him! Wait a minute…"

In an instant, the presence that I had been so certain was Henry seemed to waver, and change. It felt like something nebulous, unformed for just a moment, and then it resolved itself into something else. It was me.

That was impossible. I was sitting here, on a talus slope with Lyla. I *was not* down in the heart of the Carbon Glacier! What was going on here?

"What is it, Ray? What's happening?" Lyla's voice was anxious.

"It was Henry—I *know* it was. But now, it's as if I'm down there myself. It's as if I'm watching myself from a mile away!"

"Bring yourself out of there. *Now*, Ray! Whatever's going on, you can't be a part of it! Get out now!"

She was right. I began to draw myself back from the glacier. But then I changed my mind; I had to know for sure if it was Henry in there. I let the boundaries of my awareness flow back out until

I found what seemed so completely to be me. I surrounded it, and pushed into the energy that was coming from that being.

It was Henry, all right; I couldn't be mistaken. But what was he doing, and how was he so convincingly pretending to be me? *Why* was he doing this?

I started to back out, and I felt it coming. It wasn't nearly as far away as it had been before, and the malice and ferocity with which it came roaring through the land was terrifying. What would it do to Henry? What could I do to keep it away?

Lyla knew something dire was happening, though she couldn't feel it directly. Her voice was sharp with urgency.

"Ray, come back now! Come all the way back!"

My words were slow and heavy; in this moment voice was a cumbersome afterthought. "It's coming. Have to save Henry."

"If you won't come back, then take me with you, Ray. Let me help!"

That would have been wonderful, but the Destroyer was getting close, and moving faster than ever. I had just enough time to devote a little piece of my mind to one more sentence.

"I can't, Lyla. Too ignorant…"

I heard a despairing wail come from somewhere. It might have been Lyla, or it might have come from another place altogether, but there was no time to consider it. With a stabbing motion in my mind that flew out to every nerve ending, I blew away the boundaries of my awareness, and the world's river of power crashed into me with a roar that felt like it might tear me apart.

The Destroyer had been heading directly for Henry. Now I suddenly sensed it changing course, and making for me. This was a game of chicken I was totally unprepared for. How close could I let it get to me before it was too late to draw myself back into this little body, to withdraw from harm's way? It was coming with incredible speed, an angry, lethal predator the likes of which I had never imagined until now.

I waited, every nerve and synapse tense, electrified and wholly present. I gauged its approach with a fineness I hadn't known was possible, but even still I miscalculated almost fatally. At what felt like the last possible instant, I collapsed myself explosively, retreating at the speed of thought back into my original boundaries. As had happened before, the force of its narrowly missed blow struck me side on, and I was pierced everywhere by the monstrous force of its hatred. I heard screaming somewhere, but I could not tell who it was, nor how many people were screaming.

An instant after being struck, I shook away the shock enough to extend myself outwards, using the little energy I had left to do it lightly, to observe without being observed. The Ray Holdman that was Henry was still emanating its strange energy within the glacier. The Destroyer had passed me by, but turned with redoubled ferocity on the glacier. The life inside there that was Henry seemed to my overwrought senses like a tiny, glowing lamp. With my mind I tried to scream a warning, and from somewhere distant there came an accompanying sound. Then the massive force of the Destroyer swept over, and into, and through the glacier, and the tiny lamp was snuffed out like a candle in a hurricane.

Chapter 26

I STILL HAD A BODY. IT SEEMED A SURPRISING thing. Another surprise was how much pain a little body like this one could feel. My heart was caught in a vise; every fiber of me was bruised, or torn, or stretched far beyond its intended use. I wondered if it was damaged beyond repair, and if I would simply die soon.

I did not die. Despite the pain, I came back into that body that some few people thought of as Ray Holdman, and opened my eyes. I was trembling uncontrollably. Lyla's arms were wrapped around my shoulders in a fierce embrace, and she was sobbing. I found to my surprise that tears were flowing down my face, and briefly wondered why. Then I remembered.

We sat, in mortal shock, for some time. Eventually, Lyla's sobs began to subside. Even though I wasn't sure my body even functioned any more, my hand found its own way to one of Lyla's, and held it awkwardly.

Lyla's face was pressed into my back, and she hadn't let go her grip on me. The back of my shirt was wet with her tears. She spoke without moving, and her voice was muffled.

"Something horrible has happened. I thought you were dead. What happened, Ray?"

Everything in me fought against saying it. There was no gentle, no kind way to say anything just then.

"Henry's dead."

Lyla stiffened against my back, and then slowly unwrapped her arms from my shoulders and drew back. I wanted to turn around to face her, but as soon as she withdrew her support I simply lay over on my side. I tried to turn over to see her, and couldn't even manage that. I heard Lyla rise, step quickly away and then back. A pack plopped to the ground near my head, and then Lyla's strong arms were turning me, gently lifting my head so it rested on the pack. I lay on my back, my breathing shallow and labored, and looked up at her.

"You just said Henry is dead, didn't you."

I closed my eyes for a moment. "Yes."

Her voice softened. When she spoke it had a hitch in it from fighting back more tears. "Ray, can you tell me?"

It was almost too much trouble to talk, but she really needed to know. I didn't have the energy to give anything but a halting, monotonic account of what had seemed to happen.

She listened intently, as she always did, and waited until I was done to comment. "It's getting stronger, isn't it?"

"Yes." It didn't seem all that important at the moment. "Lyla, I couldn't save him. Maybe if I could have waited just a second longer…"

She leaned down and kissed me, long and gently. "We may never know what Henry had in mind, or what he was trying to do," she said softly. "I thought I had lost both of you, and here I find you still alive, against all odds. I want to be extremely angry with you, Ray Holdman, for very nearly getting yourself killed again. But I can't seem to bother." She kissed me once more, and said, "Thank you for not dying just yet."

I looked up into the depths of her eyes, and there was nothing more important in the world than that I loved someone, and that she seemed to return it.

"You're welcome," I said.

THE ROCKY TERRACE on which we had rested was far from ideal as a place to spend the night. After lying still for a half hour I found I could stand and move around slowly. After a few more minutes of careful movement, we were certain that I hadn't broken anything, nor did any part of me seem to be injured beyond use. I hurt in every cell, but even though they protested loudly, each one tried, lamely, to do its job when commanded. Lyla had to get us both up the slippery talus slope to the top of the ridge. We stopped to rest every fifty feet on that slope, and I thought wryly about the day I had met her, when she had shepherded me in exactly the same way off Mother Mountain. I tried to make jokes about how much work I put her to, but they fell flat every time. All of our thoughts were focused on Henry; how could that tough, crusty old friend be dead? It was unbelievable, and yet the searing pain in our hearts told us over and over again it was so. What could he have been trying to do?

Once when we stopped I allowed myself back into the shallows of the river, skating along its surface and surveying the glacier. There was another life in the glacier now, and moving myself in closer I could tell that it was Hucklebark. He was making his way into the glacier, and was about halfway to the place where I had detected Henry. I wondered what he would find when he got there, and shuddered.

"Hucklebark is in the glacier. He's looking for Henry; I expect he has an idea of what's happened," I said.

"Ray, try and tell me again how you know these things," Lyla asked.

"Can it wait until we get where we're going today? By the way, where are we going today?"

She frowned, and said, "Honestly, I don't know how anything can wait for a minute any more. For all I know, something else horrid could happen in the next thirty seconds, and then not only would I lose you, I'd never find out how you know these things."

"Everything feels quiet right now," I answered. "With the merest luck, we have a little time to pull ourselves back together. So where are we going?"

Lyla sighed. "All right, I'll wait. We're going to a large grove of spruce that grows on the edge of the Carbon River Canyon. The canyon cliff is less than a hundred feet high there, it overlooks the glacier, and it's less than a mile from the wall that Lupine calls The Home."

"I call it that now, too," I said. "How far from here?"

"It's about a mile. It's easier than this has been, but it's still some work."

"I'll have to try to do a little more of my own work."

"Whether or not you've been making good decisions is more than I can say," she said. "But you're sure enough doing some work, Ray."

I started to laugh, and then sobered. Every time I began to laugh, I thought of Henry. I still couldn't accept what had happened. And then there was The Home itself; it was hard to simply set that aside until its turn came.

We started down the northwest side of Old Desolate's shoulder. As Lyla had predicted, the way shortly grew easier, and I could carry much more of my own weight. Soon after we began walking straight across the steep slope of Desolate, we entered the trees. The slope was protected from the fiercest of the winter's weather, so here the trees grew to be about fifty feet high, which seemed a lofty achievement after so much time with the alpine warriors higher up. I was grateful for the shade, and for cover too. Though I couldn't find any logical reason to worry about concealment, it was a comfort.

We were still moving at a bit better than a snail's pace, so it was nearly an hour before we came to and crossed the Wonderland Trail, which to our great gratitude was empty at the moment. A short, steep climb up from the trail brought us to a ridge that overlooked the Carbon Glacier.

I sat down, just out of sight of the trail, and regarded the glacier with a constricted heart. Henry was still down there. I relaxed a little more and canvassed the glacier. I found Hucklebark right where I figured Henry had to be. I wondered if I could communicate with Hucklebark, let him know that we knew what had happened, and that he wasn't alone. I tried, but I didn't know how to do it, and I had no energy left for anything but getting to a stopping place.

Lyla had remained standing. She was looking all around us, and I could tell she didn't like being exposed either, especially towards the glacier. Rather than keep her tensed and anxious, I hoisted myself to my feet and we went on.

We rounded a bend in the canyon's top, and descended rapidly into woods. It was, as Lyla had said, a large grove, at least thirty acres, mostly spruce, and mostly well protected. It felt like a forest of giants.

Another twenty minutes of walking—or hobbling—brought us to an area where the grove was very dense. Lyla led us, threading her way between trees growing close together. Without warning, we moved past two of the largest trees I'd seen in these woods, and entered a small clearing about forty feet across. It was shaded, and hushed, and the ground beneath us was level and carpeted with spruce needles and branches.

Lyla dropped her pack onto the ground. "If there's any place in the world where we can feel a little better, I think this is it."

I looked each way, taking in the beauty of the grove, feeling the protective limbs at its edge arching over us. In the quiet I could hear the deep, resonant thumps and the sharp crack of rocks tumbling down from the canyon sides onto the glacier's top, as if a couple of giant children were playing a game of marbles in the canyon. "Yes, I think you're exactly right." I walked to where she was standing, and hugged her. "What would I do without you?"

Now she laughed, and it felt and sounded like the world being reborn. "I have no idea. And for the moment, I'd prefer not to find out."

"I hope to never find out," I said.

She sobered again. "One thing, one day, at a time. Let's not burden ourselves with more than that, as long as we have this time."

"All right," I said, "I'll try not to clutter the air with my requirements of the future." I dropped down to the ground, and lay with my head propped on my pack. "As much as I dearly, deeply love your company, I believe I'm going to have to sleep until the future comes to present itself."

She looked over and observed drily, "You might want to consider at least rolling out your bag, Ray. I have to say you look as though you need a good, long sleep."

She was right as usual, so I groaned myself upright again and set things up more comfortably. Lying back down, I had only closed my eyes for a moment when I heard her gasp. I sat upright so fast every muscle I had screamed in outrage. She was facing away from me.

"Spark, forgive me. You startled me. I didn't expect anyone to be here," she said.

I looked up and saw Spark standing at the edge of the clearing, tall and composed. Although it seemed Spark must be nearly as old as Works, he walked into the clearing with the grace of a large cat, and stood a few feet in front of Lyla.

"I am sorry to disturb you. I have been looking for you two most of the day."

"You know about Henry?" Lyla asked quietly.

"I know a little, and what I know, I do not understand. Whatever has happened, I am very, very sorry. Will you tell me what you can?"

Lyla turned to me as the logical choice for speaking. I told him as briefly and succinctly as I could what had happened, but it seemed that as time went on, telling anyone about anything was getting progressively harder. Spark listened without expression, and was silent for several long minutes after I finished. Then he came over and squatted in front of me. Like Everett Longhaul, he still towered above.

"You need tending. Immediately. Lie down, please." He turned back to face Lyla. "You need tending too, daughter. Forgive me if I work with Ray first, and I promise to be with you shortly."

"I'm in pretty good shape, all things considered, Spark," she replied. "I can easily wait, and thank you."

Spark turned back to me. He eased my head off my pack so I was lying prone, and gently laid his large hand across my throat. The last time he had examined me he had only lightly held my hand, and I was momentarily startled.

"You are a complicated human, Ray Holdman," he said. His hand was warm and comfortable, like a living blanket over a place I hadn't known was sore and weary. I was looking up into his face, which maintained its air of relaxed concentration. I began to relax too, and without thinking about it my boundaries opened up and I descended gently into the world's rivers.

Spark's eyebrows shot up in surprise, but he remained motionless, and otherwise impassive. I allowed myself to navigate the clearing, lightly touching the roots of the trees that surrounded it, sending my thanks for their beauty and protection. They responded with equal gentleness, and I passed on from each one. Moving outward, I followed the land as it flowed down to the canyon, and into the glacier. I found Hucklebark, and eased into the glow of life that surrounded him. He was working, laboring at a task through an overwhelming sense of loss and grief. I brushed him lightly with my mind, told him it was me, that I knew what had happened, and that I had wept with him. I felt his start of recognition, then his wordless greeting. But it was clear he needed solitude; I withdrew, and only then did I realize what I had just done without thinking.

I focused again on Spark. "Hucklebark is burying Henry. He's almost done, and he has been crying for a while now. Nevertheless, I believe he'll be all right."

I heard Lyla draw a deep, shuddering breath, but Spark held me with his gaze. His hand moved to my forehead.

He spoke so quietly I had to concentrate to hear him. "I am glad, young man, that you have no idea of the power that's been placed in your hands. You will have to know all of it too soon as it is, and you will have to wield it to the fullest long before you're ready. I can help repair your body, but I have no good advice other than this: listen to your brothers and sisters; listen with all your heart, and remember everything they tell you. Never forget that without their help, all that is given to you will bring nothing but disaster."

His hand was the essence of comfort, and the pain I had felt everywhere was receding. "I hear you, Spark, and I hope to count you as one of those brothers."

He gently withdrew his hand with a fleeting smile. "I should think so, Ray Holdman."

I looked up into his face again. "I am grateful you are here. But why are you here? What brought you?"

"Well, then. I came here to take you to the People of The Home. They have been expecting you. But they know what has happened today, and they are willing to wait until tomorrow. You are to stay here tonight, rest, and gather what strength you can. You will need it tomorrow. I'll come back shortly after dawn."

A chill settled over my heart. How could I regain a strength I didn't have, the strength to face these powerful people, whoever they were?

Spark's hand descended again, and settled on my heart, which had started beating harder. "Be easy, if you can. They mean you no harm, as long as you are willing to listen, and act. Rest, until tomorrow."

His touch had brought my heart back into a calm and graceful rhythm. He drew his hand away and turned to Lyla. "And now, daughter, I need to see for myself how you are, *all things considered.*"

I wanted to know that she was well, that everything was all right. But Spark would care for that, and before he reached her side I was deeply asleep.

Chapter 27

I woke well before the sky had begun to lighten, and the first thought I had was that there might actually be time to make a pot of coffee. Lyla was sleeping peacefully, and I moved quietly as I could. She woke when it was almost ready, and its heady scent was stealing through the clearing.

"How are you?" she asked.

"Much better. That Spark may be a formidable person, but his healing work is incredible."

"He's almost as old as Works," Lyla said. "That alone gives him the right to be formidable."

I raised my right hand solemnly. "I promise never to quarrel with a man who is over a thousand years old."

She laughed, and tossed her head. "And what if he's only nine hundred fifty, Mr. Numbers Man?"

"Then I can be my normal, incorrigible pain in the neck self for another fifty years." I grew serious for a moment. "He is a fine person, and his advice—the little that he had to offer—is the best. I'm just not used to dealing with a dignity that huge and deep." I handed her a steaming cup.

"Many people aren't," she said. "But it's clear he thinks highly of you; all he needs is a reasonable amount of respect."

"He'd have that from me even if he hadn't offloaded a mortal ton of pain from me yesterday. I fell asleep before he tended you; did it help you as much as it did me?"

She thought for a moment. "I never know how to answer a

question like that. I think I know how much you were hurting yesterday. In fact, if we didn't have someone like Spark, I figure you might have been in serious trouble. I guess I was too, but I never seem to hurt like other people, and I don't know what that means."

"Maybe the trees have given you something more than a longer life span."

"That might be," she mused. "But I really don't know."

"Well, then, maybe it means you're already more whole than most of us, so you're just harder to break."

She made a wry face. "Nice fantasy. But look, Ray, are you awake enough to talk about how you know when people are under glaciers a mile away, and how you talk to them?"

I took a deep breath. "I can try. I need you to understand, though, that it's changing me so fast I don't know how to deal with it, let alone properly describe it to someone else."

"Try me, and if it doesn't work we can try again. And if that doesn't work, I'll have to be patient some more."

"All I know is that the energy of the world—or the life force, or the collective awareness, I don't know—moves through it all the time. To me it feels like a succession of rivers. However it happens, I can sense these rivers, and travel in them. Going into a river allows me to do things: I can explore the features under the earth, or sense life wherever it's living, and now it seems I can communicate with people other than the trees, which we knew about anyway."

"So you might be able to 'send yourself' to Windy Gap, say, to see what's happening there? And if you need to get the attention of someone there you can do that?"

"I don't have the faintest idea yet what my limits are," I replied. "I'm afraid to do much; I only found I could communicate with Hucklebark because Spark had me so completely calmed down."

Lyla furrowed her brow in thought. "That seems important. Do you know how to calm down like that yourself?"

"Not a clue. I mean, I've heard or read of all the normal things people do, like meditating, mantras, physical techniques like yoga, but I've never really tried that hard to be calm."

"You need to add that to your list of things to think about, Ray."

"If I ever get the time to think again, I promise to sit down somewhere and think myself into the thirtieth century," I said, smiling. "In the meantime, I have to think about Spark coming to take me to see some truly scary people."

"Why do you think of them as scary?"

I stopped to consider. I wanted to be honest and clear; somehow I was certain many things depended on that.

"I am afraid of powerful people. I always have been. When I was very young, everyone who had power seemed to use it to scare or control me in some way. That, or they took so little notice of people like me they didn't care if the exercise of their power harmed me or anyone else. And I am quite sure I'm expected to deal with some extraordinarily powerful people this morning."

Now Lyla took some time to think out a reply. "This is a different world from the one you grew up in, Ray. I barely recognize that world in your journal. In this one, if people are kind, and treat you with a decent amount of respect, all that's required is that you return that respect. Maybe it would be good to keep remembering what Lupine said about unnecessary fear."

"Yes. Absolutely," I said softly. "I need a few minutes to take that in, because I'll have to put it to use really soon."

We finished the pot of coffee and had a light breakfast in silence. It was lovely to just be with someone and not have to talk every moment. I was reflecting on that while we shared cleanup duties, when Spark entered the clearing.

He entered silently, and folded his long frame into a squat facing Lyla and me. Spark and I regarded each other without speaking for a moment. Something was passing between us, but I didn't understand what it actually was. It was as if Spark was talking to some part of me I wasn't fully aware of, and I was hearing a conversation in the distance, knowing it took place but not being able to discern the words.

Some silences aren't all that comfortable. It took some effort, but I waited for him to break it.

"Are you ready to see the People of The Home, Ray?"

"I have no idea if I'm ready or not, Spark. My ignorance is way too deep to have the comfort of knowing much of anything."

Again I saw Spark's fleeting smile. Though he chose not to comment, it was clear my response had pleased him. I felt encouraged, and thought maybe there was hope I wouldn't make a fool of myself or make some even worse mistake this morning.

"What do you sense in the world this morning, Ray?"

With a deep start I realized that ever since I'd awakened, some portion of my awareness had been lightly covering the area all around us. Without even knowing I did so, I had been carefully keeping track of our little place in the world, and had found everything much as it should be. This was a truly wonderful, unexpected thing, and yet it struck a strong note of fear at the same time. I wasn't even aware of what I was doing; what if I did something foolish or clumsy without thinking, and attracted the Destroyer through sheer stupidity? But Spark was waiting for my answer.

"Everything seems well. But I'm afraid, Spark. Extremely afraid."

"There is a certain amount of fear that is essential to your survival," he replied. "Can you look there to see how much of it is essential, and how much is not?"

I had done that before, when Lupine had irresistibly commanded the attention of all the people at the gathering. It could be done again now, and with a flash of insight driven by Lyla's reminder, I saw that I would have to work hard to make this winnowing of unneeded fear as deep seated and unconscious as the act of always having a hand or foot in the world's rivers.

It was becoming easier to look, and see. Naturally, most of what I found was not only unnecessary, but a serious hindrance. I looked squarely at all that fear, and named each component. As I named them, they quietly slipped away, without even waiting for me to dismiss them. What was left at the end was a fraction of what had been there, as had happened before. All this took no more time than a few heartbeats.

I looked up at Spark. "Yes, that's done now. Thank you."

"We have to be going, then." He looked over to Lyla. "Daughter, I am very sorry. Only Ray can come with me."

Lyla looked intensely unhappy. But it was clear she had known this was likely, and known as well that there was no point in arguing. I wanted her to come with us; I wanted it badly, but I never considered arguing with Spark, despite my earlier wisecracking.

To Spark I said, "Do you have any idea how long we will be?"

"That is mostly up to the People. And to a much lesser degree, it is up to you."

I turned to Lyla. "You'll wait for me, won't you?"

She hugged me briefly. "As long as necessary."

"Well, I guess we'd better be going," I said, getting to my feet.

Spark and I wound our way through the trees, heading towards Tahoma. The Carbon River Valley, filled with the glacier, was to our right. We walked fifty feet or so from the edge of the valley cliff. The way was not rough, but we were climbing rapidly.

Spark's legs were much longer than mine, but he walked at a pace that I could follow easily, apparently with no conscious adjustment. His gray felt pants and brown-checked, flannel shirt blended into the early morning light to make him seem to be floating. His pack, nearly the same color as his shirt, was unobtrusive even though it was of a substantial size.

After a half mile or so we came upon a trail that led along the cliff edge, making its way up towards what most people thought of as Willis Wall, the mountain side of the great cirque that birthed the Carbon Glacier. Lupine had effortlessly changed that name in my mind to The Home, and I grew increasingly nervous as we approached it. The land began to slope sharply downwards to our left while the cliff came closer on our right, and soon we were walking on a ridge that grew narrower as we climbed. I imagined we were at about seven thousand feet, and was astonished when I saw ahead of us a sparse stretch of a dozen or so alpine firs.

They were growing on the top of the ridge, in the most exposed place I could imagine. When we got to them I stopped and knelt next to one. Spark turned when he heard me stop, but made no comment as I regarded one of the trees.

It was less than two feet tall, and probably more than a hundred years old. I reached out to gently brush one of its branches, and discovered that I had already been sensing its roots—far deeper than its height—and that now I had completed a circuit of communication. I felt a regard for this tree, this person, so deep I couldn't express it in words, but when I touched it all my feeling went to it. The response was one of a gravity and dignity we would usually associate with an ancient tree two hundred feet tall, and thirty feet around at its base. I sent my admiration and wishes for its health and then broke the contact, for I could tell that Spark wanted us to be going.

"Thanks for allowing me to stop, Spark. There's no end to the remarkable people here, is there?"

His expression did not change, but I thought perhaps I had seen a flicker of something—maybe amused approval—in his eyes.

"No, Ray Holdman, no end at all. Come; it is not much farther."

I rose and we followed the ridge up and up as it narrowed, until we walked on a thin trail that was half its width. We came to a wall of rock on our right that formed the highest, razor sharp peak of the valley cliff, and the trail ducked around to its left. The rock wall loomed twenty feet over my head, blocking off the view of the valley and all that lay beyond it. In a hundred feet of walking we passed it, and the valley once again opened out to our right. Looking out towards The Home, it felt like I was much more than a hundred feet closer.

Now the ridge and the trail were the same. We walked along the spine of it, and it was five feet wide. We passed one more wall of rock that stood between the glacial cirque and us, and at the end of the trail was a flat space of roughly circular shape. We stopped in the center of it.

"Is this as far as we go?" I asked.

"We can go no further without their involvement," was all he said.

If I were to walk further, I would have had to scramble down a steep slope for a few hundred feet, and then climb several hundred more on the other side of the dip. At that point, I would have been climbing the wall itself. The cirque lay beside us to the right, and stretched a half mile across, a great circular bowl gouged from the Mountain over scores of millennia as the glacier ground its way down slope from the ice fields above. At this time of year the wall was free of ice and snow, but the immense gray and white fields above it seemed to defy gravity; their unimaginable masses appeared to be soaring out over nothingness.

Spark gave me several minutes to take it in. I could have stood there for weeks and not felt like I really understood or even grasped the wild, enormous beauty of it. Finally he broke the spell with a motion of his hand.

"Lay down here, your head to the north, so you are looking south, towards the Mountain. Be calm and at ease. They will come for you."

I looked up in alarm. "You're not coming too?"

He shook his head. "I am not invited, Ray. Works requested that I escort you here, and I have done so. Now do as I ask—we've kept them waiting long enough."

A surge of panic shot through me, and I fought the urge to leap to my feet and run. Lupine had told me that the People of The Home are the oldest, the most powerful people in this part of the world. The intimidation of even being in their presence, let alone the fear of their judgment, was overwhelming. I heard Lyla's voice, reminding me to think about unnecessary fear, and without considering I looked, recognized, and named it. My breathing slowed almost immediately, the terror receded, and I lay down on the dusty ground.

Spark knelt down beside me. "You won't be exposed here for long. That was well done. Close your eyes, now."

I closed them, and felt Spark's warm, strong hands cover my forehead and my heart. I noticed without concern that the darkness that came with closing my eyes began to grow darker, until it was absolute. The sounds of the wind stroking the river canyon faded away into a deep silence, unbroken even by the sounds of my breathing, or the blood pulsing through my veins.

Chapter 28

The air was warm and heavy, scented with a fragrant wood smell. I thought it must be cedar. I couldn't be sure if my eyes were still closed or if there was simply no light. I was sitting cross-legged on a surface that felt like forest floor; a firm surface underneath covered above with a soft layer of branches and leaf litter. There were others here; after a momentary stab of fear, I went through the steps of looking, seeing and naming, and I became calmer. It felt good to think I was getting better at that.

My eyes were in fact already open, for the air glowed faintly, and light from a source I couldn't identify slowly filled the place I found myself in, until I could see around me.

It looked like a room. It was not quite square, nor was it circular; there were no sharp corners, but neither were there long, broad curves. The walls of this room appeared to be made of or covered by planks of wood. If that were so, I thought that many of the planks must have been carefully and laboriously steamed to bend them into the room's shape. The effect was simple, and beautiful.

In the center of this room lay a small depression, within which burned a small fire. Next to it, on the floor, was a pile of dry branches, cut into short lengths and stacked neatly. The fire was compact and efficient, burning steadily and without smoke.

Looking up and directly ahead, I finally saw the People. There were six of them, seated on the floor in a semicircle across the fire from me. In the center were a man and a woman who looked to be as old as the Mountain itself, though their eyes shone with alertness, intelligence, and something more I was unsure of. They were different from the old man and woman of my dreams, but I gave up trying to gauge that difference almost immediately. Can a mouse make fine distinctions between thunderheads? Their hair was deep silver; the man, who sat on the right, wore a sinuous, papery robe that matched the color of his hair. The woman, to the left of him, wore a similar robe the color of a clear twilight sky.

To the left of the woman sat a man who looked to be of middle age, and to the right of the ancient man was a woman of similar middle age. Their clothing was old fashioned, with a homespun look. At the left end sat a woman, and at the right end a man, who both looked to be about my own age. They were dressed for roaming the mountains, though I couldn't tell what their clothing was made of.

The eldest man and woman in the center of the semicircle emanated power, and a depth of experience I couldn't even guess at. The middle aged ones to their sides radiated authority and intelligence, and I trembled at the thought of people such as these sitting in judgment on me. Under any other circumstances, the youngest ones on the ends would have inspired awe and intimidation in me with the intensity of their gaze; here, they were simply the youngest.

I looked all around the room, even risking a certain rudeness by turning around to see behind me. There was no entrance; there was nothing but the wood walls, and the floor like that of an old forest, soft and green. I looked up, and the walls rose into darkness.

The eldest of the men motioned me to come closer and be seated near the fire, across from them. I stepped forward and sat down. They regarded me solemnly, silently, for several minutes. It seemed appropriate to keep my own silence, and to wait for them to speak. If I had to wait all day, I would do so.

The silence stretched on. I gazed into each one of their faces in turn. Their expressions were fathomless, their eyes deep as the Mountain itself. After what seemed a very long time, I spread my hands slowly in front of me, and then dropped them into my lap. I lowered my gaze, and kept it on the fire.

"We are the People of The Home." The eldest man spoke in a

thin, husky voice.

I looked up again. It suddenly occurred to me that I was a guest of these people, and that I had brought nothing with me but trouble and questions. What else could I have possibly brought?

"I bring you my greetings, my respect and honor," I said. "I am deeply sorry that I have nothing more than that to offer."

"It was good of you to think of it," the youngest man said in a rich tenor. "Few of your people think of such things any more."

I had to smile. "Perhaps if more of them were able to meet such people as you, they might be reminded."

Now the middle aged woman spoke. Her voice was like the strong flow of a river in its cresting phase, and it carried a mild warning and rebuke. "Our Agreement requires your people to come to us. With few exceptions, that has not happened in a very long time."

I bowed my head. "Then I must offer an apology. I had no wish to offend."

The eldest man said, "You are not aware, perhaps, that we forged our Agreement with your most distant ancestors. We would work with them and teach them, so that their work might benefit the land and all of its peoples. Your ancestors knew of us, and they knew how to work with us. That was long ago; never have we dealt with many of your people, and it would seem that in this age none but the man Spark, and perhaps one or two of his acquaintance, know of us."

"I regret this very much," I replied. "I can only hope to be worthy of your time and energy, and that this lack might be remedied."

The middle aged man spoke quietly, but with the firmness of the ground on which we sat. "This is all well and good, but you are here to speak and hear of other things. How are you called?"

"My name is Ray Holdman. How would you have me address you?"

"For this time, refer to me as Riven. The eldest," as he gestured to the ancient woman and man, "are Taiga, and Fell." He pointed to the middle aged woman. "This is Rill. And these," with a gesture to the youngest man and woman, "are Tarn and Zephyr. You are a Mender, is this so?"

I took a deep breath. "Until a few days ago, I had no idea what a Mender is, and I had never heard the term. Now, though, I am told that I may be one. Yet I still know next to nothing of all this."

The woman called Taiga turned to me. "You know of the Mender's Agreements, of course."

I was forced to shake my head. "No, I'm afraid I do not."

Tarn interjected, "But you must have been taught the Components: the witnessing, the entering, and the twining?"

"I am very sorry. I have been told nothing of these."

Fell stirred, and turned to the others. "How can this be?" he husked. He turned to face me. "Young man, Ray Holdman," he said my name laboriously, "Your educated skill, strength and intelligence are essential to regaining the balance required for life to continue existing in this land. Are you prepared to tell us that you know nothing of this—nothing at all?"

I could feel the fear rising inside, getting ready to pounce, ready to paralyze me. In desperation I thought of Lyla again, and what she had told me that morning. I found the fears, and named them. It was deeply disconcerting to see that most of them remained behind; apparently there was good reason to be afraid at the moment, and I had no choice but to think and feel through it. I thought of Works, and how he seemed to believe I could learn what had to be learned, and of Spark, who would not have brought me here if he thought I could not acquit myself honorably.

To Fell I said quietly, "I can only offer you profound sorrow for my ignorance. I wish with all my heart I had better answers to give you, but I will not lie about this."

The young woman Zephyr, who had been silent until now, spoke in a voice that made me think of the wind whispering through the forest. "We are given to understand that you are very young. Nevertheless, where have you been in your life, and what part in the world have you played?"

I hesitated, thinking hard. How could I say that I have been *nothing* all my life? Was that really true? No, I decided, that wasn't exactly right.

"I've been an orphan and an outcast among my own people.

Since I was a small child, I have occasionally found someone to guide me in ordinary ways—at least long enough to keep me alive. But what little I know of what really matters I have only learned in the few days since I came to this place."

Fell turned first to Taiga, on his right, and then to the others, astonishment and consternation plain in his expression. I would never have expected to see that on a face so filled with experience and power. Again he said, "How can this be?"

Zephyr spoke, saying, "With respect, Grandfather, you may not realize the state into which the human peoples have come."

"Clearly I did not." He turned back to me. "You will have to be patient for a bit, young man, while we consider this."

I looked down at the fire in front of me, and saw that the wood had burned low. It was in danger of guttering. "Shall I tend the fire while I wait?"

"Yes, that is good," he said. "There may be hope yet." He seemed to sink into himself, looking downward to the branches and leaf litter on which we sat.

I picked up a stick from the pile and began to rearrange the brands, studying how they had been laid. The bottom layer had been laid with six sticks parallel to each other, an inch apart, covered by six more at right angles to the bottom layer. The third layer had been laid with shorter sticks in a star pattern that met at the center. It was a simple, elegant arrangement. I carefully set the remaining brands to imitate the bottom layer, and chose six new longer sticks for the second. Sorting through the pile, I chose eight short ones to place in a star pattern on top. I took my time, considering each piece and placing it with care. When I was done, the fire flared briefly, and then settled back into a steady, smokeless burning.

When I looked up again four of The People were gone, and only Tarn and Zephyr, the two youngest, remained where they had been. Tarn smiled reassuringly at me, and a spark of hope kindled that I might, in fact, make my way through whatever was to come.

"We have much to talk about. Perhaps it would be more ac- curate to say that we have much to tell, and you have a great deal of listening to do. With luck we can help you to work through some of these things without a lot of dry talking."

I bowed my head briefly and said, "I thank you for your tolerance."

"Let us begin with you. We have no doubt you have questions, and we wish to dispense with them before going further."

Where to begin? I needed time to organize my thoughts; if I asked all the questions that had arisen since I came to the Mountain, we might never get done. So to gain time I asked what I thought was a simple one.

"Where is this place?"

Zephyr spoke now, and her voice was the quiet joy of a forest breeze. "We are in a place of safety. It is removed from the places you can usually find, and trying to explain it further would serve no purpose. Its appearance is all from yourself; you have created its feeling and features, as well as our own appearance and these names you call us by. We experience them in this moment as you do." She looked around and then smiled at me. "I must say, we think you have good taste."

"Thank you. That means a great deal."

"Do you wish to ask anything else?"

"I feel like I could spend several years asking you questions. I also feel that would not be the best use of my time with you, so perhaps my instruction should begin. I hope that if I misunderstand, or fail altogether to understand, that I can ask then."

"All right, so be it," said Tarn. "Our task is to teach you the rudiments of the Agreements, and the first Component of a Mender's work. Our elders will take it in turn to instruct you in the other Components. You will have to work very hard, and listen very carefully for longer than we would ordinarily expect a human to do. Even so, when you leave here, your understanding will be thin and weak. There is no way a Mender can be taught the deeper work in so short a time. Are you willing to undergo this?"

"I'll do everything I can to make your work worthwhile," I answered.

"The first Agreement is to always—without exception—work only towards the benefit of all living things. Does this seem reasonable to you?"

Now it begins, I thought. Will I be able to sustain this? There was no point whatever in wondering about that now, so I considered the Agreement instead.

"From my place of ignorance, it seems impossible. There must be an infinite number of times when the benefit of some living things contradicts the benefit of others. But perhaps the contradiction is only my imagination. How am I to always know the difference between benefit and harm?"

"You won't," he said. "An Agreement is the best effort that can be made to hold to the condition set down. It does not require or expect perfection, particularly from one so young and untested. What it demands is clarity, humility, and the sacrifice of self-gratification. Can you hold to such an agreement within the limits of your experience and strength?"

I took a deep breath. "Yes. This Agreement is true and right, and I accept it. I will keep it as best I can."

"Good. The second Agreement concerns the fact that as a Mender, you have been given gifts of enormous power. You must agree that you will guard these gifts with the greatest of care, and pass them on only to people who are capable of using them wisely and justly. Can you do this?"

"This Agreement poses very similar difficulties," I replied. "It requires me to be a profound judge of human character, and it feels like I have to see into the future as well. It seems the best way I could honor this agreement is to not give anything away until I am much older and wiser."

Zephyr said, "That is an exceedingly dangerous way to deal with the problem, and we counsel you strongly to find another way."

I thought about what might happen if I were able to teach the wrong person how to travel the world's rivers of life at will. Then I considered teaching Lyla, and there was no question or difficulty there.

"I can think of people in whom I have absolute confidence; people who would certainly do things well if I offered them a powerful gift. There are others I would never consider, and still others I am not at all sure of. In the first two cases, my heart would tell me clearly what to do. Only in the last case is there any real difficulty, and perhaps if I think and act with care, and consult people older and wiser than me, I can hold to this Agreement properly."

Tarn nodded. "That is acceptable for now, and better than might be expected from one so inexperienced. Remember exactly what these two Agreements are, what they say, and how you must conduct yourself to abide by them."

I looked in surprise. "There are only the two?"

Zephyr smiled. "Do you wish for more?"

Oh well, I thought, I suppose I have to make at least a little bit of a fool of myself. "No, thank you, I believe these two will keep me very busy. Now that I think of it, I'd guess that everything of any importance comes from them anyway."

"That's quite correct," she said, still smiling.

Now Tarn continued. "The first Component of a Mender's work, as you have been told, is *witnessing*. What do you think that means?"

"Well, to witness is to observe. I have to be aware of what is happening around me, without missing things that should influence my actions."

"It is much more than that. To witness the world is to enter into it, to be inseparable from what is happening around you. Yet this must be done without taking from the world; you must be truly *in* it without grasping any of it, or holding it to yourself."

What did this mean? How can I be in the world without some kind of grasping or holding? This idea made me afraid, and I wondered why. I looked at the fear, and found, in the forefront, the fear of pain. In an instant I was transported back to Vernal Park, when Lyla and I had nearly been crushed to death by the pain and fear of the living things there, as they had reacted to the coming of the Destroyer.

"Not knowing how to do this almost killed us, only yesterday," I said. "Here you find maybe my deepest, most dangerous ignorance. Is there any way you can help me learn how to witness the world without being destroyed by it?"

Zephyr said, "Witnessing—whether it be pain and fear, or joy and love—without being consumed, is a simple endeavor, but mastering it takes time for someone who has never known that it can and must be done."

"You will begin this work now," Tarn continued. "You will start with your own pain, as it is clear you carry a great deal of it with you."

I looked up in alarm. "What shall I do?"

"You will look all the way into your own heart and mind. You will *witness* the pain that has been there since before your memory began, up until this moment. And you will neglect to grasp it as you have always done before, as if the pain itself were a thing of value. You will understand all of that pain, and recognize it, and remember it with complete clarity even as the weight and substance of it is shed from you. What remains will be knowledge, understanding, and compassion. This is subtle work, and we will grant you as much time as you need. But be aware that you will not be done with it today, or tomorrow, or for some time to come. Begin now." They sat calmly, and waited.

Just be quiet, I thought. Be quiet, and allow things to happen. But what things? My mind showed no inclination to be quiet; I let it run, and like a border collie it darted this way and that, sometimes in tight circles and sometimes randomly here to there and back. Very soon I noticed that every direction it ran, every corner it sniffed into, it found pain, or sorrow, or fear, or uncertainty. No wonder it refused to stand still!

It darted suddenly to Tarn and Zephyr. They were nearby, exactly as they had been, and yet I began to feel their presence more strongly. It was as if a strong and gentle hand was laid on my mind, and the frantic back and forth running slowed itself. I retreated inward, and spiraled down into places I had thought I would never go again. Memories, images and stored feelings were bubbling up from depths I had been certain were closed off forever. They were massive, clumsy and powerful, and simply rediscovering them was pain itself. A series of scenes from long ago: flashing red lights, angry, shouting adults, and the roughness of the tree bark I was pressed against so tightly. Hands grasping me, irresistibly strong, dragging me into a waiting car. Sterile, fluorescent lights that never went out pulsing down on hard, gritty cots; hulking bodies whispering hideous threats into my ear while I pretended to be asleep. Jails, drunk tanks, dirty, despairing field worker barracks, people weeping, disappearing, reappearing only to be lost again the next day. Running headlong through trash-strewn alleys, fleeing into the darkness, running…

The weight of all this was going to crush me, and I began to panic. The fear rose in me, a corrosive flow that ate away at my reason and my strength. In the midst of this chaos a name echoed faintly in the distance: *Lyla*. She had told me something important; she had reminded me of something vital someone else had told me. The cacophony of pain and fear nearly drowned it out, but with a desperate stretch of will I heard it. I clutched her name like a talisman, and looked squarely at the rising bedlam of memory. I chose an image as it lurched by, and stopped its movement. I stayed with it; I gave it a name.

Javier. My little brother from what I now thought of as The Other Home. His disappearance had been a devastation. There had been the long time of uncertainty, the worry over whether or not he was safe with someone else, or lying dead in a ditch somewhere, or—worse still—in the thrall of someone's twisted power, as had happened to other young boys I had known of later. There was the feeling of betrayal, of a trust and comradeship summarily thrown away. And then there had been the certain knowledge that after he was gone, I was truly alone. The averted eyes when I asked people about him, the blank refusal to give me at least the solace of knowing what had happened to him. I'd been shut out of human places as long as I could remember, but nothing had hurt more than this.

In my mind I stood before this agony of spirit, still and waiting. It seemed to be holding my heart in an iron grip that was unbreakable. Another type of river, altogether different from the living force of the world, flowed through me with a scorching toxicity that made me want to scream. I struggled within its grip, and was unable to move.

I became still again. Quietly, stealthily, my perception seemed to turn inside out. Now it looked and felt like I was holding this pain in my own personal death grip, instead of its holding me. It was not as simple as closing my hand around a rock or a branch, but it was similar. Instead of struggling or holding, I tried to relax, to let go of something so deep inside I couldn't see it. Something, the deepest part of my spirit perhaps, searched for the way to release what it was holding so fiercely. There was a beginning of that letting go, and immediately I felt a trickle of that mortal pain fall away from me. I had no idea where it was actually going, but it was leaving.

The pressure in my heart eased a little, and I sat there in wonder. A little more, perhaps; if I could let go of a little more, maybe I could breathe and think again. Another rivulet of pain flowed away, a bit more than the first time, and the intense, exhausting grip I maintained loosened further.

Javier slipped away, to become a place in my memory that would always be there, but without the crushing weight of loss and grief. I stopped another piece of the maelstrom, and allowed my understanding to see how I was gripping it. I started to relax that grip, and more pain fell away.

There was no question of losing anything that I truly needed to keep. It did not appear that I needed to worry in the least about for-getting the things that had brought so much pain; as Tarn had tried to tell me, it was possible to possess all of this memory without the lethal freight that had controlled my thinking, feeling and actions for most of my life.

I practiced. There was no need to go looking for the sorrow, grief and fear. They came to me, insistent, demanding to be looked at, requiring my agony; instead I regarded them carefully, saw the way I was holding on to them, and practiced releasing my grip. The detritus flowed away, leaving the essence, the lessons, the love and sorrow. I began to believe it was possible after all to be truly *in* the world without being borne down by it. Then something presented itself to me that made the whole work feel like an instant train wreck.

Henry.

It slammed into me like an ocean wave I was utterly unprepared for, as if I'd been standing in the shallows thinking I knew everything about the sea.

Henry was dead. He had been murdered by a force whose manifestation was due at least in part to my presence here. Henry had saved my own life: once for sure, in the glacier, and very likely once before by the simple act of convincing me to come here. But I had not been able to return the favor; I had tried to help him, certainly, but in the end it had meant nothing.

I felt the full impact of Henry's death for the first time. Until now, there hadn't been time to feel it. There had been too much to deal with, to think about, too much worry and uncertainty over events past and coming. Now the pain of losing him, atop a lifetime of losses—only a few of which I had just now managed to let go of—threw me down like an angry child flinging a doll to the ground.

I struggled against the wave pressing down on me, violently at first, but then more feebly as it went on. I couldn't tell if this was something I was holding on to, or if it was in fact gripping me. I was suffocating in it, and growing weaker by the moment. How was it possible to hurt so much? How does a person get past feelings that blow so far beyond intolerable?

Fighting with all of this guilt, remorse and grief exhausted me very quickly. There was no longer any point in trying to resist it, because there was no more energy to resist with. I became still, both inside and out, and discovered that I was flat on the ground and had been shaking and thrashing. There were hands resting on me. One was on the shoulder that faced up, and another was lightly wrapped around an ankle. They pressed gently down so that I felt the ground beneath me.

Stay where you are.

The words cut through the confusion and fear, firm and convincing. Even though I was desperate to escape from all I was feeling, it seemed natural to obey.

My heart still felt like it was being squeezed beyond the limits of its endurance, but I stayed. The grief and remorse continued to wash over me in waves that made me want to run, run anywhere to get away, but I did what I was told, and stayed. Gradually, over and through the haze of pain, I began to think.

I could still feel the ground beneath me. It was solid, reassuring and comforting. I began to wonder about how my understanding had been turned around, and I had seen myself holding on to the pain of all those memories in a fierce, unbreakable grip. Henry's death must have been the same for me, but it was so much harder to see it that way. Perhaps it was too new. I wondered suddenly if the ground below me would accept all of this dangerous and poisoned pain if I offered it.

Could the earth take it in without becoming polluted? Could all the energy it had taken me to create, experience and hang on to all that pain be broken apart, recycled as it were, and put to better use elsewhere? I began to consider how highly I valued all I endured. From the standpoint of the planet, though, my pain was one small thing out of billions of small things. Perhaps it was just another tiny tributary of one of the great rivers that flowed around the world, and if I released it, it would simply merge with a great flow of life that was quite prepared to take it in and transform it into something more useful.

I tried with all my will to let go of the grief from Henry's death. For several long moments nothing at all happened, and it all stayed exactly as it was, squeezing the life out of me. Then, a little trickle of that grief began to slip away, and leak into the ground below me. It wasn't much, but soon it was enough to make me feel that I would get past it, in time. The hands that had been resting on my shoulder and ankle were gone. I sat up laboriously.

Chapter 29

Tarn and Zephyr had disappeared. In the places they had sat before I saw Riven and Rill. My head was pounding, and it was hard to focus on them. The rest of me felt as if I had fallen off a roof. Riven's voice was firm and commanding, though it held a large measure of kindness in it too.

"Breathe."

I drew in the air, and I could taste the cedar, and the lightest tang of wood smoke. They blended with the rich fragrance of the leaves and needles on the floor, and it felt like medicine. I sat quietly for several minutes and breathed.

Riven and Rill waited patiently. When my breathing was back to a normal depth, Rill spoke.

"You have worked hard so far, Ray Holdman. There is promise in you, and it seems well to continue. Are you ready to go on?"

The pounding in my head had lessened, but I still felt battered and dazed. "I doubt it, but I don't think that should stop anything. If this is my only chance to learn from you, I wish to do whatever can be done now, ready or not."

Riven's faced eased into a faint smile. "That is how we would expect a Mender to answer."

Rill said, "The man Spark has told us that you have already begun the work of *entering*, though you do so with no knowledge or understanding. Are you aware of the dangers in this?"

The answer to that seemed obvious enough, but I decided to stop and think anyway. Attracting the Destroyer came to mind instantly, but I figured that Rill was trying to get me to consider other things. I remembered the first time, up on the ridge overlooking Vernal Park, when I had almost lost myself in play while happily exploring a new world. The things I had thought about then—*so this is what power feels like*—came back forcefully. How seductive, how gratifying it could be! Suddenly I saw in my mind's eye the old woman's opened palm, and all the rivers that ran through the world. Some of them were not just uninviting, but now in my memory I saw them as places of mortal peril.

I answered slowly, "I have been lucky beyond reckoning to have not made a fatal mistake so far. It's happening so fast! I have no idea of limits, or boundaries, I haven't any notion of my own capabilities, or where they should be taking me. And on top of all that, I have to constantly be careful to not attract the Destroyer."

Rill nodded. "Your intelligence is quick, and you appear to be capable of learning from first mistakes. For one with no time to learn, this is vital. For a time now, you will accompany us. We will attempt to show you some of the answers to your ignorance."

My stomach tightened at the thought of what they might have in mind, but at the same time a charge of excitement and anticipation ran through me. "How will this be done?"

Riven replied, "You have some notion of how to enter these rivers, as you think of them. Use that knowledge. You will be joined with us. Begin when you are ready."

I took a deep breath, let it out slowly, and opened my mind towards the flowing life beneath and around me. Until this moment, I had felt nothing of the world outside this room, but now the ground came alive beneath where I sat, and the rivers were there, running as I had sensed them before Spark had brought me here.

The boundaries of my body melted away. I was surrounded by two presences; though I was certain they were Riven and Rill, in a way that I could not understand they were other than that, too. I was not exactly a part of them, but we were somehow a single awareness all the same. We expanded, growing and moving out into the world, moving through the heart of the Mountain. I had come here before, alone, and been firmly refused entrance. Now, I passed into and through the heart of Tahoma with two of its residents.

I could feel the different layers of rock as we passed through them, the incredible stew of mineral, chemical, heat and cold, the unimaginable pressure of the weight of the world. Though my body was far behind waiting quietly for my return, I felt as if my arms were spread wide, and the power that roiled a scant few miles below the surface rippled through me. I could sense the movement below, and the never ending contest between the forces pushing upwards from the center, and those pressing down from above. My senses were spread farther than I could have imagined, connected to all of it at once.

We moved faster, extending our sense and awareness out and downwards, following the rivers of energy that flowed everywhere. In each direction I explored, there was life of some kind; deep within the earth all of it was microscopic, but life it was. Whole communities, civilizations of tiny creatures lay in places I would never have imagined, living out billions of lives where the pressure, the heat, the lack of space and air made life seem impossible. It was clear that where life was concerned, nothing was ever truly impossible.

Faster still, until we seemed to be ranging through the world at the speed of thought. Something beyond us attracted my attention, but by the time I had started to wonder about it we had abruptly stopped. We faced what felt to all intents and purposes like empty earth, but in effect was a wall, high, wide and forbidding. Passing through it was out of the question. It was a place in the world where we simply could not go. The rivers we had been riding veered away from it, and I cautiously probed it with my senses. The wall seemed to lash out at me, sending a wave of energy that felt fatally poisonous, and I recoiled in shock.

We moved back from the place that had stopped us. I tried to learn its dimensions by feeling carefully near it without touching in any way, and found that it extended great roots down towards the center of the world. I posed a wordless question, and as one we moved downwards farther into the earth, following beside the wall where it descended.

It was huge, an upside-down mountain of—what? Something

Works had tried to teach me came to mind. I thought perhaps it was a mountain of *opposition*. As we traveled slowly down, we came to places where it extended outwards in great streamers, exploiting some weakness or opportunity in the earth that I couldn't understand. We moved carefully around them. A feeling of foreboding stole into me, and the farther down we went the stronger it grew. I began to want to leave that place, but Riven and Rill continued down, and I had no choice but to go with them.

We were moving along the contour of this vast, mysterious place of no life along the small tributaries of energy I had come to recognize as a part of life itself. I remembered times, such as in Vernal Park, where the rivers I'd joined had felt wide and strong. Here, we followed a trickle; unlike far above, closer to the surface of the world I knew, I could now feel no connection to any of the far places where life existed. The energy of this little tributary was weak, and I wondered how it existed at all so close to its apparent opposite.

My distress kept increasing as we descended, and I began to understand that it was tied to the waning strength of the little rivulet of life we were following. The fear that had been building in me began to assert itself, and I was again on the verge of panic. The life path we followed grew weaker still, and with one last gentle push downwards, we came to a place where as far as I could tell it was gone altogether, and there we stopped.

To be in this place was to be in the absence of all life. It was as if the whole world was a charcoal gray dead circle. The feeling of panic grew until I didn't think I could control it, and I began to struggle, trying to move away from this horrible place, back to where there was at least some hint of life. A soundless voice said something I had heard before.

Stay where you are.

I didn't seem to have a choice in this. With all the will I could muster, I stopped fighting and stayed still. The moment I did this I heard the voices of Lyla, and Spark, and Lupine, all telling me in their own way to examine the terror, and deal with it.

The hardest part was to simply be still and look at it. In my imagination, I would have to look at something awful beyond reckoning, something so huge and impersonal it would either crush me or swallow me whole.

What I did see was different. I saw that the terror I was feeling was the fear of being alone. Not just by myself for a while; this was another matter altogether. Something in my heart and mind was convinced it was possible to be utterly, truly *alone* in the world—disconnected from every living thing, adrift forever—and the prospect of that was fearful beyond expression.

Here was a place where logic and the heart might work well together. Logic told me in no uncertain terms that the world was filled with life, and that being totally isolated from all of that life wasn't *ever* possible. The next step should be to integrate that knowledge so that it was embedded in my heart and mind. Perhaps that would allow me to deal with a place such as I was in now, so that I could exist here for a while without falling apart, even though I'd much rather be somewhere else.

Riven and Rill were a comforting presence I could feel, and then logic reminded me of the others. I thought about all of the people that had come into my life since arriving on the Mountain, and my heart reached out to them. Whether or not they felt my reaching in that moment didn't matter, for I knew they would always respond when they could.

The panic receded, dying back into normal fear, which itself shrank down to a feeling of deep unease—something I thought might make sense in a place such as this, but would not cripple my ability to think and act. Finally, I could start to pay some attention to my surroundings and consider the meaning of this place.

I wasn't actually "seeing" the things around me, of course. Understanding where I was and what was here came from different ways of awareness that had nothing to do with my physical senses. Nonetheless, as I remained quiet and attentive, I could make out the great mountain-shaped mass of not-life that permeated the earth here. Since the awareness I could make use of depended on the rivers of life energy that flow through the world, it was difficult to perceive it clearly, but I knew we were still very close to it, and that it extended a great ways above and below us.

Why had Riven and Rill brought me to this place? They were to teach me how to *enter*, and we had certainly done that, I guessed. I thought about looking into the rivers of life that flowed in the old woman's hand, and how some of them had come to seem uninviting, even forbidding. Riven and Rill had carried me to such a place, to what purpose?

I cast about again, trying to make sense of this place. The lifelessness of it was so oppressive my original fear and panic seemed quite justified. Yes, this would be an appropriate place for the Destroyer to have come from.

At last, the thought arrived. If the Destroyer came from here, or a place like this one, perhaps it would have to be returned here. This would be where it belonged, locked inside this mountain of opposition-to-life, not roaming the world bringing death and horror to whatever it touched.

That, I thought wryly, will happen around the same time I learn how to stuff a thunderstorm into a bottle.

Abruptly I started feeling edgy and restless again, and for a moment I didn't know why. But it began to seem that Riven and Rill themselves were becoming impatient to move on; being here, in a place where the river of life dwindled away, was a lot like trying to breathe in a place that had no air.

My teachers apparently decided I had learned what they brought me here to learn—or perhaps simply that I had learned all I was capable of. We began to move away from that mass of lethal, contrary energy, and back up the tiny rivulet of life whose end we had reached.

As the rivulet became a creek, and the creek a stream, so we increased the speed of our movement through the earth, until we were going so fast my perception couldn't keep up, and I became disoriented and afraid.

Relax and pay attention—both at once.

Did I trust Riven and Rill to not make some fatal mistake while I was dependent upon them? Of course. Once I remembered that, it was much less difficult to relax *and* pay attention, "both at once."

Then I was able to clearly sense the way we were moving, and how following an energy river at this rate of speed required less reactionary skill than it did elemental trust. I decided I believed that the rivers themselves were right and proper, and our traveling within them was also right. Once I could truly get that belief into my deepest being, I was certain there would be few limits to what was possible within this web of life and energy. In the meantime, there was already more possible than I knew. A fierce exultation swept through me.

A few more moments and awareness leapt back into my body, which was still sitting quietly in a mysterious room redolent of cedar and wood smoke. When I opened my eyes, Riven and Rill were gone, to be replaced by the ancient visages of Taiga and Fell.

They sat still as statues, gazing at me intently. I had no idea what they wanted or intended at that moment. Knowing it was absurd with such people, I still tried to cover my confusion by looking around me, hoping that by delaying whatever was supposed to happen I might get my bearings and composure back. Glancing down at the fire before me I saw that it was almost out, and had started to smoke. I looked inquiringly at Fell, who nodded; with relief I again spent several minutes tending it carefully and minutely.

But I could only spend so much time on a tiny fire. Eventually I was forced to look up at the two of them. Not knowing what else to do, I waited. I found that I wanted them to tell me how I had done, whether or not I had acceptably met their requirements. I even considered asking them outright, but common sense prevailed. If they had thought I was a complete failure, I would certainly not have been there any longer. As it always did, it came down to a level of trust; I would have to trust them to either direct me or throw me out. So I waited some more, and tried to breathe and think calmly.

Presently, Taiga spoke.

"Ray Holdman, you have entered into the Agreements. You have taken the first steps towards witnessing the world, and you have begun to enter into it. The work will become more difficult now."

More difficult? How could it get any harder?

Now Fell said, "The last of your first steps requires you to pick up all you have been taught and make use of it. The work of a Mender is the work of restoration, which means you must employ forces enormously more powerful than yourself to repair parts and places of the world that encompass vast ranges of life and energy. To accomplish this, you must do what is thought of as *twining*. Tell us what you think this twining might mean."

The words "tell us" were like a blow to the head, even though nothing like that had happened. It surely wasn't intended that way. But as nerve wracking as it had been to try and answer first Tarn and Zephyr, then Riven and Rill, these two ancients were far more intimidating. Fell radiated power in a way that made me feel he could reduce me to a pile of dust without making a motion. Taiga's power was less overt, but the wisdom and authority that circled her were overwhelming.

I tried desperately to think; what did they want me to understand? What was *twining*? My mind circled uselessly around the word, but all I could think of was that I had already taken in more than I could hold, and there was no room left in me for new knowledge. I looked down at the ground before me and said, "I'm sorry. I don't understand."

Taiga's voice rescued me. "It's all right, young one. Listen, then, to what we tell you. Hold it carefully until you do understand it. You think of the world's life and energy as being rivers. Go to some of these rivers, then. Enter into them, and wrap yourself around them. You must do this gently, respectfully. Carefully, and with much thought, bend them together and help them to move in the direction that is needed to do the work that wants doing. If you do this properly, you will be able to change the world in accordance with the Agreements you have made."

I looked up at them. They were focused on me more intensely than ever, willing me to understand and know. Their eyes were bright and fierce, but they held no threat, only the sharp and urgent need to teach.

Now Fell told me, "The way to approach this is simple: ask, offer, and join. Each of these must take place in turn, and the way that you ask, and what you offer, is as important as how you join with them. Never forget that without the truest humility, the forces you attempt to work with will kill you very quickly."

Ask, offer, and join. I was completely spent, and I fervently hoped that I could at least remember those words until I could learn how to use them. But at that moment two things totally dominated my thought: sleep, and the fear that I would forget what I had been taught. What I said then surprised me.

"I am spent, and very afraid."

Taiga answered. "You are quite right to be afraid, young one. But remember what your brothers and sisters have taught you, and act anyway. For now, rest a bit. Then you must return to your people and your land, and get to work."

Just like the ancient man had said to me: *Get to work, child.* I briefly wondered if this work would ever get truly underway, let alone accomplished. I looked up at them again, with the intention of thanking them for everything they had done. But Taiga had raised her hand, palm outwards, towards me, and then gently drawn it downwards. My eyes followed it, and immediately I slept.

Chapter 30

I woke to cool air and spaciousness. I was lying flat; a slight movement yielded the crunch of dust and gravel beneath me. When I opened my eyes I was looking at a pale blue sky studded with stars. I sat up slowly and saw that the sky to the east was lightening. A glance around showed me to be in the exact place where Spark had laid me down on the ground—when? Dawn would be coming soon. Since he had set me here somewhat after dawn, at least a day had passed while I had been within the Mountain with the People of The Home. But had it been one day, two, or more?

I went to rise rapidly to my feet, and found that despite Taiga's admonition to rest, I had not managed to do so. I was so stiff and sore that my legs buckled under me, and I had to drop to my knees to keep from falling. I impatiently checked myself; there was nothing wrong whatever except the ache and fatigue. Had I lain out here, utterly inert, for whatever time had passed within the Mountain?

The only way to learn how long I had been gone would be to get back to Lyla and ask her. Ignoring my body's protests, I rose again—a little slower this time—and began the downhill walk to our campsite.

I walked lost in thought, barely taking in the magnificence of the land and the coming day. I went over all that had taken place with The People, rehearsing how I would tell it all to Lyla, eager to hear what she thought of it, and the suggestions she would have for what to do now.

After a quarter mile of walking my joints began to loosen again, and I could move in a more natural fashion. I quickened my pace, and without conscious thought opened the boundaries of my awareness, lightly touching upon the rivers below me to learn what was ahead.

I expected to feel her presence immediately, and was convinced at the moment that I could sense Lyla wherever she might be on the face of the planet. But I could not find her.

I opened further, expanding the area that I touched, thinking at each moment I would feel her and so know exactly where to go. Everywhere I searched there were no human people. A small herd of mountain goats were grazing beyond the nearest ridge, and I noticed with surprise that their sentry started when it felt my questing touch. But I was not interested in anything or anyone but Lyla; where was she?

I went faster, until I was moving at a jog, sliding down gravelly slopes and panting back up. Most of the way was downhill, and as I got closer to our camp I ran harder, until my breath came out in ragged gasps. Still it was as if the landscape had been cleared of all human presence.

I entered the woods and zigzagged through the trees, nearly tripping over outstretched roots, catching myself and plunging on. I burst into the beautiful little meadow where we had made our camp and came to a clattering halt.

My pack with the sleeping bag strapped to it was still lying in the grass, exactly as I had left it. The early morning light showed a sheen of dew over everything in the meadow. Nearby, all of Lyla's gear was there too. But search as I might, I could not find her. Unless I was completely wrong about it all, she was simply not there.

I walked over to my things, then over to Lyla's. They were undisturbed. I began walking aimlessly around the meadow, trying to think what to do. After several useless circuits I left the meadow by the other side, with no purpose in mind other than looking until I found her.

A few steps beyond our camp I came into the heavy smell of charred wood. I turned in the direction it was the strongest. Moving around a small grove of young fir, I faced the blasted, blackened stump of what had been one of the great trees of the wood.

There was nothing left but the stump, rising to a jagged point about six feet from the ground. There were no torn branches, no debris of any kind; it was as if the rest of the tree had simply been vaporized. The stump lay in a circle about twenty feet across, and everything within that circle was a dead, charcoal gray.

A glint on the ground on the other side of the circle drew me. When I approached, I saw a water bottle nestled in the dead grass. Next to it was a small canvas bag that would be for storing trail food, and I knew at once they were hers.

For several long moments I refused absolutely to believe what my eyes were telling me. Then I felt something break inside me, as if a beam that held up the entire edifice of my being had snapped, and I was falling while everything around me collapsed.

Reason began to drain out me, hemorrhaging from my mind and heart as if a dam had burst. When it was almost gone, I picked up the last of it and flung it away from me. I would find this Destroyer and obliterate it, or die in the attempt. Nothing else mattered.

I flung my senses into the earth, feverishly searching for wide and strong streams of life and energy. I found them, and joined them abruptly. When I was running through several of them at once, I broadcast a bellow of defiance and anger that I hoped would reverberate across the planet, to attract the Destroyer's attention. I was satisfied to feel its approach almost instantly.

My reason was utterly gone, but my senses were sharper than they had ever been, tuned to a pitch that was nearly unbearable. I could feel the Destroyer racing towards me, and a moment later I could see it again. It was much the same—lank hair framing the skeletal face with its red-rimmed, hate filled eyes. Unlike the first time I had seen this foul visage—when he had approached me slowly—he was moving faster than ever, and his image wavered before me.

My own rage was so far beyond my control that I welcomed him, taunting and beckoning. He plunged on towards me, growing larger and more powerful by the instant. I cared nothing for that; there was room in me for nothing but vengeance.

I reached out to all of the streams of energy I had joined, and brusquely wrapped my intention around them, pulling them together. Each one bucked and thrashed, and I tightened my grip on them until they seemed to be, all unwilling, melded into a single, huge flow. I held them together with the strength of maddened passion, my whole purpose in life the destruction of the Destroyer, and faced the evil thing racing towards me. Its hand was raised to strike me down.

Just before it reached me, the streams I was holding so fiercely began to rear and plunge every which way, as if I was holding for dear life to a great fire hose that whipped me around like a weightless piece of fluff. The Destroyer struck us a glancing blow, and the collision of hostile energies screaming through me tried to tear me apart. That only served to inflame my rage further, and I wrestled with the streams with all my might, trying to wield them to strike at it.

I was engulfed in a chaos of swirling energies. It became hard to tell which was trying to kill me and which I was trying to wield. The streams writhed and bucked, and the Destroyer struck and feinted along with them. I brought the streams around and tried to strike with them; they refused my commands, and careened off in the wrong direction each time.

I was mad with hatred and anger. I could see the contorted, inflamed face of the Destroyer each time it came around to strike. Each time I dodged enough to avoid being directly in its path. But I could never completely elude it, nor could I compel the streams I was riding to strike back.

The Destroyer turned, faster than I could sense, and struck from behind. If the streams had been obedient to me, it would have hit me directly. Instead we bucked sideways, and I felt another intense, glancing blow. The streams wrested themselves from my grip and streaked away. There was nowhere to fall, and yet I was falling. I couldn't tell if I was falling up, or down, or in any coherent direction at all, and there was nothing I could do but wait for the final strike that would finish me. From somewhere came a long, despairing cry; it dwindled, drew farther away, fell to a whisper, and the darkness closed over me.

Part Six

Lyla

*I have been lost many times before, but never like this.
There is no moon, no stars; clouds blanket the sky, and from
horizon to horizon there is no one else. There is nothing
but a cold, lifeless ribbon of pitted asphalt and the endless,
hollow land.*

*I don't have the heart to describe how this came about.
What difference does that make now? To be utterly empty,
standing in an empty land, turning ineffectually every way
in the cold darkness and seeing nothing: now I know what
it really means to be lost.*

(Eastern Nevada, November 1998)

Chapter 31

Something was wrapped around my neck. It was squeezing, and fear and anger welled up in me. Something else was pressing down on my chest, hard. I had no idea where I was, and I could see nothing. There seemed to be no alternative but to struggle, so I began to thrash and writhe.

From somewhere above, a voice sounded. "For heaven's sake, Holdman, stop fighting me."

That voice belonged to Spark. Was it possible that I was still alive? I quieted immediately, and the warm, firm pressures on my throat and chest returned, but now that I knew them, they were a comfort. My eyes popped open to see the stern face of Spark directly above me. Looking past it, I saw Everett Longhaul hovering beyond Spark. Ev's face was stricken with fear and worry.

Without cracking the merest hint of a smile, Spark continued, "Young man, if you absolutely insist on being killed once a week, you're going to have to submit to my treatment until we can rid you of this obnoxious habit."

I blinked and sought vainly for a suitable reply. Unsurprisingly, none came to mind. Instead I croaked, "Where am I?"

"With the combination of an iron constitution and an astounding amount of luck, I believe you are already sufficiently recovered to sit up and learn that for yourself."

Spark and Ev both slipped an arm under my back and helped raise me to a sitting position. The moment I sat up and glanced around, it all came crashing back in: the stupid, reckless battle with the Destroyer, my fight to control the rivers that had so obligingly carried me before, how the Destroyer had struck and struck again, never quite hitting home, and—

I was sitting near the edge of a circle blackened into charcoal gray. Everything around us was dead. Spark and Everett Longhaul squatted on the barren ground beside me.

Up to now, Ev hadn't said a word. Now he looked into my eyes and said, "Ray, where's Lyla?"

Lyla. My throat constricted so tightly it was hard to breathe, and speech was impossible. I turned and mutely looked at the charred tree stump. From my position on the ground it seemed to tower over me, a testimony to heartbreak and an accusation all at once. I closed my eyes to try and shut it out. I heard Ev let out a long, low moan. Spark remained silent.

We sat that way for what seemed a long time. I could not talk, and I didn't want to see. Spark and Ev remained still and quiet, absorbing the facts as they presented themselves pitilessly to us.

I heard Ev stir and draw a breath that caught before it completed. "Ray, we need to get you away from here."

I turned to look at him. His face was streaked with tears. I turned to Spark, and his face was set in stone that even in its impassive stillness revealed a breaking heart. So, I thought, there should be no surprise that these two loved Lyla in their way as deeply as I did in mine.

Spark turned to Ev slowly. "Do you have a suggestion for how to move him? He is alive and mostly unharmed, but he cannot walk far today."

Ev seemed to shake himself, and returned at least part way to his own immense competence. "I've carried him before, I can do it again. I need to get my pack apart, and then we can get started."

I felt helpless and useless, and the thought of walking anywhere made me realize how weak I was. "Where are you taking me?"

"Back to Mender's Camp," Ev said.

"Mender's… Where is that?"

"Where you all stayed at Windy Gap." Ev looked over to Spark. "I can't think of a better place for now, can you?"

Spark shook his head slightly. "That's the right place. I can repair Ray's body, and perhaps a little of his spirit, but for the rest we'll need Works."

Ev and Spark began discussing the technicalities of lashing me to Ev's pack frame again. Even though they were still next to me, they seemed to be receding into the distance. I fell into an uneasy sleep, and dreamed.

I was in a forest. It was utterly dead; each tree was a blackened hulk, and the ground as far as I could see an ashen, dark gray. The low and menacing sky was the same color where it showed beyond the corpses of the trees.

I needed to find Lyla, and it was extremely important. She held the key to some terrible problem I absolutely had to solve, but I had no idea where she was. As I walked through the forest, I began to notice people. They were shadowy and indistinct, and seemed to be coming from the direction I was heading. I stopped everyone that passed, and asked if they knew where Lyla was. Each one answered me in exactly the same way by saying, "Do me a favor—don't decide you know everything about everything."

Each time they said this I began to argue with them, but without another word they glided past me and disappeared into a deep veil of mist that had crept up behind me. There was no way to go back, and nothing to look forward to. It was an endless journey, a pointless journey, and it made me feel heartsick and sore. The light grew dimmer, and I became weary. Finally I sat down and leaned against one of the charred tree trunks. I would stay there forever, and nothing would ever matter again. I opened my shirt and reached deep into my chest. I pulled out my own heart, and flung it away from me. The last of the light in the dead forest faded away, and I was done.

Chapter 32

When I woke I was lying on my back, looking up into a canopy of green. It might as well have been brown, or black or gray, for the dream was still with me, and everything was dead. The soft, late summer mountain air, that should have been so clear and sweet, tasted like ashes.

I thought about sitting up, and wondered why I should bother. Lyla was gone; what point to continue? I had thought I knew about pain before I ever came to this place. Then I—we—had been nearly crushed by the pain of a meadow that had been visited with obscene death. On the heels of that, Henry had been lost to us. But neither of those traumas remotely resembled how it felt to know that Lyla would never again walk beside me, or cajole me into reaching the right decision, or ask me one of her penetrating questions, or delight me with her brightness and life.

I lay on my back inert, staring upwards, and my mind was dull and quiet. Nothing mattered now, so there was nothing to do or to think. My body was made of stone, and covered with a nondescript blanket of haze. I watched disinterestedly as feeling drained out of me.

Abruptly, I saw Tarn standing before my mind's eye. I did not want to see him, but he was directly in front of me, and his face bore a fearful anger.

"This is what you do with our teachings? *This* is how you repay us for reaching out to you? We excused much because of your un-fathomable ignorance, but this cannot be excused."

I stared dully back at him. What did he want from me? Didn't he know my life was over?

"A Mender does not behave this way. A Mender goes on, moves forward, because that is the only Way that can be taken without forsaking all that has been offered and accepted. And you—perhaps you do not want to be a Mender. Do you suppose that humans simply choose to say yes or no to such a thing? You are what you *are*, Ray Holdman, and many, many lives depend upon you remembering that, and acting accordingly."

He seemed on the verge of turning away, but stopped himself.

"To have to speak this way is disappointing and distasteful. We have never in all the ages turned away from an Agreement with any people. But you make this Agreement meaningless, and it appears that our work is wasted."

Tarn vanished as rapidly as he had appeared. I hadn't thought I could feel worse than I had upon awakening. It was far from pleasant to realize that it was possible.

All right, fine, I thought. Even if my life is in fact over, and moving or doing is entirely pointless, I would rather engage in pointlessness forever than to know that what Tarn said was true, and that I had been the one to poison a relationship of unimaginable antiquity and importance. I hated the thought that it took searing shame to motivate me now. But it was so; and when one is lying at the bottom of a deep well with no apparent hope of release, why bother any more with denying reality? I slowly hoisted myself to a sitting position, inwardly cursing the intense weakness I felt in doing so.

At that moment I discovered just how self-absorbed I had been upon waking. Not three feet to my left side sat Works. He sat cross-legged, calm and still, regarding me with what felt like a stern sort of compassion. Turning slightly I saw Everett Longhaul directly in front of me. He seemed to be asleep sitting up, though I had begun to wonder if Ev ever slept. And a little farther away to my right was Hucklebark, looking down at the ground before him, apparently lost in thought.

What could I say to these beloved, stalwart friends? What

should I say? I sat mute and bewildered, torn between shame and grief and fear.

The deep, measured tone of Spark's voice rescued me from behind, issuing with its immense authority and dignity.

"Before you get too involved with things, friends, he needs food and water. Hold yourselves in patience while we build him up just a little."

Ev shook himself into action. Up from the ground with lithe and lanky grace, he was at my side almost instantly. He placed a water bottle and a steaming bowl of soup next to me. I took a dainty, disinterested sip of the water and looked without enthusiasm at the soup. "I don't want to eat now."

Spark, in the meantime, had moved around to seat himself between Works and Ev, facing me. He said, "When are you going to learn that what *you* want is unimportant?"

It was like a heavy slap to the face, or perhaps an intense electric shock. A jolt of anger shot through me. It was instantly extinguished by the shame and grief that held me like a fossil creature encased in solid rock. I looked down at the ground. A wave of anguish drew itself up inside and engulfed me. It would not be denied; my efforts to contain it were swept away as if they didn't exist. The sobs wracked me from places in my heart and body I usually forgot were there. They slammed from one side of me to the other, so far beyond my control that I felt a new and piercing kind of terror.

It seemed to go on and on. A distant part of me wondered if it would go forever, or until I really did die. I sat in shame and humiliation, gasping, choking and sobbing.

Nothing lasts forever, and in this case that was a particular blessing. Eventually the waves began to recede; my breathing slowed into a long series of hiccuping sighs, and I began to be aware of my surroundings again.

No one had come over to comfort me or put an arm around me, and for that I was profoundly grateful. It was bad enough to behave this way before witnesses, let alone to arouse more compassion. I wiped my face with a shirt sleeve, drank two thirds of the water bottle, and reached for the rapidly cooling soup bowl. When it was half empty I set it down.

"I'm sorry. Sorry for many things, including my ignorance, my attitude, and my self centeredness." I was speaking to no one and everyone at the same time. "All I can say is that I see what I have done, and how I have acted around it. I'll do whatever it takes to do better in the future."

Works stirred, and softly said, "That's good, Ray. It's all that can be asked."

I looked to Ev and Spark. "How did you find me? I really don't understand how it is I'm still alive."

Spark took in turn to say, "You may not be aware it was yesterday that I left you with the People. This morning, I encountered Everett on my way back to where I had left Lyla. We were both coming to see how you two were doing, in our respective ways. About a mile away, we detected a disturbance deep in the earth that was far worse than anything we had yet felt. We began to run, and the disturbance lasted so long it ended only shortly before we found you. Naturally," and here he graced me with a faint smile, "Mr. Longhaul arrived first."

Ev picked up from there. "As far as I could tell, Ray, you were dead as a doornail. It was puzzling, since there wasn't a mark on you. Fortunately, Spark is a great deal faster than he looks, and got there soon after I did. He saw that you were still just barely alive, and started working on you. After a couple of minutes you started struggling, and then you woke up."

"There's no way for me to properly thank you for saving my life—again," I said. "And I may never get the hang of not getting killed once a week, but I promise to keep trying." I turned back to the soup. Now that I had begun to wake from despair—perhaps only from its paralysis—my body started to reassert its imperatives.

They were all silent while I finished the soup, and set the bowl down again.

Works, who had been sitting with a stillness that made it hard to tell if he was breathing said, "Now Ray, are you ready to tell us what happened?"

A chill went through me at the prospect of talking about it. I didn't know if I could say Lyla's name without breaking down; it was hard enough to hear it. I took a deep breath.

"No, I'm not ready. But what Spark said was true: what I want or think doesn't matter. If I'm going to pick this life up again and move, and not waste what's been given to me, I'll need the help of all of you."

Spark nodded. "We have as much time as you need. There is nothing to be done that I know of, until we have heard what you have to say."

I began at the moment when Lyla and I had left this very place. Ev had called it Mender's Camp; I wondered if it would become a place to be remembered, or one to shun. I told every detail I could recall, from Vernal Park to Henry's death, to our camp in the woods by the Carbon River Canyon. It was very difficult to describe leaving Lyla to go with Spark to the entrance of The Home.

It was also difficult to describe what had happened there, with the People. But it had not been so long ago; all the things I had been bursting to tell Lyla came out now, in a very different tone. The final part of the story, when I had returned to our camp to find Lyla gone and the destruction of the tree—with all that that meant—was hardest of all.

Works now did something he had never done before. He broke into the story.

"Ray, are you saying that you never saw Lyla after you were returned from The Home?"

I nodded my assent.

"And then what happened when you made this awful discovery?"

"I—I went crazy, I guess. I didn't care about anything but killing the Destroyer." Describing the battle, and my misuse of the power that seemed to be entrusted to me, was like telling the story of a despicable character, one unworthy of anything but scorn.

Works was silent for a moment, and then said, "Is there anything else that you can add, Ray?"

I shook my head, but reconsidered. "When Ev and Spark were bringing me here, I had a dream. And when I woke up here, and decided to give up and never move again, one of the People came and told me some very hard things." I had briefly thought about not mentioning these, but I wanted these friends to know what kind of person so much had been entrusted to.

When I got to the part of the dream where each of the people I stopped replied, "Do me a favor—don't decide you know everything about everything," Works' eyebrows lifted.

"Do you happen to recall hearing that message anywhere else recently?"

I stopped, thought, and flushed to the roots of my hair. "Yes, of course, Works. It came from you."

Works, who had been leaning forward very slightly, eased back into his customary, straight upright sitting position. "Very good. Are there any implications you can draw from this?"

I groaned inwardly. I was sick to death of being tested. I felt rebellious, as if a deep part of me had decided that it was all just too hard, and I wasn't going to cooperate any more.

Another deep part of me—the part that still maintained a shred or two of common sense—crushed the rebellion with ruthless efficiency. I had been given an opportunity I'd never dared to dream of: the chance to enter into a life of meaning, a life with work that actually gave something useful to the world. How much doubt, self-examination and humility was that worth? Easy answer—whatever it required.

The task, then, was to understand why it was important to reconsider having decided 'I knew everything about everything.' Or at least to understand why Works thought it was important.

On the other hand, I must think it important too. Otherwise, I would not have dreamed a whole crew of shadowy people telling me that.

What would there be that I'd decided I knew, that was likely not so? Or to put it another way, what assumption was I laboring under that might need to be jettisoned? Before I could stop myself and avoid the incredible pain it would bring, I thought, what will Lyla have to say about this?

Lyla. Was Works telling me to deal with the lethal thoughts and feelings that swirled around her loss? What had *happened* to her?

I looked up sharply at Hucklebark. I had essentially forgotten he was there, and now I saw why. He sat immobile, staring at the ground. I had always considered the size of his heart to be commensurate with the rest of him, and now it was clear that his heart was broken. It was wrenching to realize that, absorbed in my own sorrow and guilt I had not even noticed how Hucklebark was suffering. Now I spoke to him, as gently as I could.

"Hucklebark."

He raised his eyes slowly, coming reluctantly back from some place very far away. Holding his gaze took all the strength and courage I could summon, for his grief flowed through him like a great tidal bore of pain. But it was *flowing*—not lodged motionless in his heart and crushing him. I could see that at some time he would go on living, go back to his work, and spend the rest of his life doing what life asked of him. I saw how much he could teach me, and I knew why Lupine seemed to cherish him.

"Hucklebark, I have to ask a hard favor of you. If I didn't need your help right now, I wouldn't do it."

He sat still, nodding his head so slightly I almost didn't see it.

"I need you to tell me what you found when you went under the glacier to look for Henry. Everything. It's important."

Hucklebark grunted softly, drew in a breath and let it out in a long, slow whoosh. "Not much to tell, Ray. I knew somethin' bad had happened already. I went in slow, and moved slow the whole way. The light wasn't good, since the only light I got is real small. When I found him, he was kind of slumped over. I made a pit, laid him in it, and covered him with rocks just like I'd do for someone up on the mountain. You came into my head while I was doing that, so I reckon you already knew that."

"Did it look like he'd been hurt in some way? Were there burns, or injury of any kind you could see?"

Hucklebark shook his head slowly. "No, funny about that. Henry looked for all the world like he'd just gone to sleep. Nothin' out of the ordinary, 'cept he was gone."

"Thanks. That's all I need for now." Hucklebark looked down again and receded back into his grief, letting it run through him with a sorrowful patience that I hoped someday I'd find for myself.

My own grief was still mixed with too much rage and fear, and I didn't yet know how to let it move. The only thing I could do now was to think.

When the Destroyer had killed me—truly killed me, as it had Henry—the first time, I had suffered no lasting damage once Henry had convinced my heart to start beating again. And this time, when it had been Spark who had saved me, the same: nothing shattered, burned, broken, nothing actually destroyed. Only a heart struck still. And with Henry, it must have been the same. *Then where was Lyla?*

Something different had happened to Lyla, but what?

Think, I told myself fiercely. What do I know; more importantly, what do I believe I know that's wrong?

I took the deepest breath I could, held it for ten seconds, and let it out slowly. It didn't seem to help that much, so I did it four more times. I assumed that Works, Spark, Ev and Hucklebark were all still sitting quietly nearby, but I didn't look around me; there was too much work to do.

I knew that Lyla had deserted all of her gear. I knew that she had left a water bottle and some food very near the destroyed tree. Had she sat there? Maybe, maybe not. But I could be pretty sure she wouldn't casually walk off from the equipment that helped her to live here. The first question to answer was—where was she? Or, if it came to that, where was her body? Answering that would solve the real question—was Lyla dead or alive?

Working through this was like cleaning a deep cut with iodine and then stitching it closed myself, only a great deal worse. When you're halfway in, though, it hurts just as much to pull out as to go through, so I kept going.

What did I know of Lyla that would help me to find her? I began to catalog everything I knew, which was surprisingly little. I began to carefully add what I believed of her, examining each one to see if it needed discarding.

Lyla was very strong—physically and emotionally. Her integrity was impeccable, meaning she would not have been doing something stupid or self serving. I knew that I loved her more than I had ever loved anyone in my life, and to lose her would...

Time to shake my head and move on. I knew that she was a highly respected and skilled Tree Speaker. *And that she had taken me to store my memory in a tree not thirty yards from here.*

I stood up suddenly; as it happened, a little too suddenly, for I plopped back down in a thoroughly undignified fashion. Ev was startled, but Works and Spark simply looked at me expectantly. Hucklebark seemed not to have noticed.

"I'll be back in a few moments. There is someone I have to talk to." I got up more mindfully, and walked to the corner of the camp where we had been the night of my conversations with Lupine and Works. I'd been so exhausted and filled with ideas that I remembered little of how she took me to that tree. I headed slowly out of the clearing in what felt like the most likely direction, filled with worry that I wouldn't find it. The trees drew closer together outside of the clearing, and the undergrowth made walking difficult.

What had the tree said? *Get yourself near, and you'll find.*

I moved clumsily through the thicket of alpine trees for twenty steps or so. Then I stopped; which way would it be? I closed my eyes, tried to still my racing mind, and asked, *Where are you?*

No words returned. But it suddenly seemed obvious that I needed to move a little to the left and forward another ten paces. Now I was in a hurry, and I crashed through, letting the branches whip my arms and face as I passed. A few more steps and I faced a tree with one branch about eye level that was the right size to wrap my hand around.

I raised my arm and noticed it was trembling. What would I find in this tree? How much more pain could I stand without losing my mind? What if this wasn't even the right tree?

I heard Tarn's voice in my mind: "You are what you *are*, Ray Holdman." Why did that return in this moment? Perhaps I was made to feel and endure pain. Perhaps there was more to my life, too, but I'd never find out with a tremulous arm half raised to a branch. I reached up and gently took hold where the branch met the trunk.

Calm. A settling, a resting, whose roots ran deep into the ground. A capacity for acceptance that transformed me into a great and spacious forest. I lived in the world, and it lived in me.

I said, *Thank you for showing me how to return.*

There was no corresponding answer. Instead, I was suddenly standing in a great clearing, surrounded by each of the memories that had flowed from me into this tree. They stood distinct, as if I was with a great company of people, each of whom I could see clearly. Each was willing to give themselves back to me for the asking.

My attention was drawn to one of them, and in an instant I was sitting on the slope of Sluiskin, drenched in moonlight and facing the immensity of Tahoma. Lupine sat beside me. She said, 'If you're going to get through this next part of your life, Ray, you're going to have to get pretty comfortable with mystery.'

I turned to another nearby and heard myself say, 'It seems hopeless, Lupine,' to which she replied, 'Why would it ever be hopeless unless you've misplaced your hope?'

Another, and then another, and then Works was sitting on a flat rock, holding me with his gaze. 'Have you considered the possibility that what you need to learn is no more important than what you need to *unlearn?*'

There were more. So many more; I stood in awe of the feeling that I was surrounded by a company of immensely powerful friends and allies who would be with me, whatever happened. I felt a rush of gratitude for this tree, and let it flow out from me. The wordless response was one of perfect calm, perfect acceptance.

I said, *Can you help me to find Lyla?*

She is hidden. Where, I cannot know.

A flame leaped inside of me, so fierce its heat seemed to scorch my heart. *Are you telling me she's alive?*

I do not understand your 'alive' and 'not alive.' She is hidden.

But can you help me to find her?

Use what you've been given. You have all that's needed.

Can you tell me what I must do?

It is all yours. Grow it, tend it, use it.

My hand released the branch of its own accord, as it had done before. I stood next to the tree, shaking and wondering. Tears started into my eyes, and without thinking I turned downwards, let them flow into a tiny puddle in my hand, and then placed my palm against the rough bark. *I will honor your people as long as I live*, I said. The tree stood, calm in late afternoon's gentle breeze, and was silent.

I stayed there for several minutes, lost in thought. The serene, unshakeable acceptance of everything in the world that the tree had shown me lingered, helping me to consider how to respond. One thing I was learning about the trees—in fact, realized with surprise I had always known—was that they mince neither words nor ideas. What they expressed to me in a handful of words or concepts embodied whole realms of understanding.

The tree had tried to make me understand that I had already been given everything I needed to find Lyla, whatever state of life (or not) she might be in. So what had been given to me? The list had recently grown almost too long to manage. Between what Lupine, Works, and the People of The Home had offered and given, I didn't know where to start. I began to walk slowly back to the clearing, thinking hard.

When I returned the others were all still there, though they had spread out into a more comfortable configuration. I was surprised to see Ev still there, since I'd never seen him in one place for more than ten minutes, except at the gathering. I stopped more or less in the center of a circle formed by everyone's resting places.

"I need to talk to you all for a bit, about what to do next."

We all seemed to silently agree to move ourselves over to where Works was sitting. I was surprised at first, but a moment's reflection made it seem natural; everyone here, including me more and more, revolved around Works.

When we were situated I went on. "Before I do anything else, I need to make some amends."

Spark broke in. "Forgive me, but explain please—what has changed in you in the few minutes you've been gone?"

I looked over at Spark in surprise. "Have I changed so much in that time?"

"At the risk of repeating myself to tedium, you are a mysterious young man, Ray Holdman. When I return you from the moment of death, you are filled with a despair that might kill you despite all my efforts. A mild rebuke from me releases an incredible torrent of emotion, which turns that despair into excruciating remorse. And after a disappearance of a few minutes, you return invigorated and ready to move on. I am tempted to ask, 'How many of you are there?'"

I turned his question over, and treated it seriously. "It would be easy to think that there are several of me. But they are different sides of the same human. A rather ignorant human who is changing—being *changed*—much too fast for it to be graceful."

Spark nodded, at least provisionally satisfied. I explained how Lyla had taken me to that tree and asked it to store my memories, and what had happened just now when I returned to it. "So you see, I am surrounded by a multitude who wish to help me. Not at all the least of which," I said, looking at Works, Spark, Ev and Hucklebark in turn, "is this group of cherished friends here. I have some ideas, and I hope you'll help me sort them out."

All four nodded agreement.

"As I was saying: before I go any further, I need to make some amends. In particular, I need the forgiveness of the world's rivers I tried so clumsily to control, and also forgiveness from the People of The Home. Once those are accomplished—assuming it's possible to make those amends—I can think about next steps."

"Let's begin with these rivers," Works said. "Consider, if you will, that humans are pretty much the only beings in the world that indulge in judgment. The rest of the world, and especially the oldest and deepest parts, simply respond, and we are the ones who perceive that as valuation and consequences. The rivers you manhandled are not capable of anger, Ray. They're far too ancient and powerful for such a middling emotion. I'm inclined to think that if you do no more than approach them the right way next time, things will go much better."

After a short pause, Works continued, "As for the matter of the People of The Home, I would suspect that Spark will have the most useful opinion."

I turned to Spark. "Do you have thoughts on this?"

"I believe I'd prefer to have you work it out on your own," he replied. "At this point it's safe to say that the People know you a great deal better than I do. However, if you should choose to discuss your ideas with me, I might be able to provide something useful."

"Thank you, Spark. Your opinion is important to me. As well as your willingness to drag me back from the brink over and over."

Spark rewarded me with a faint smile and a nod. From him, it felt like much more.

"I have to re-establish my relations before I can go further," I said. "But when that's done, I'll need to return immediately to our camp by the canyon. If we're to find Lyla, it has to be quickly."

I turned to Hucklebark, who had been silent so far, still enduring the grief that washed through him.

"Hucklebark, would you consider coming back with me?"

In answer he rose to his feet, strode to his pack and in one motion scooped it up and onto his back. He stood there, looking at me expectantly.

I couldn't help but smile. "I never imagined I could have such friends. Can you hold off for just a little while, so I can get this other work done first?"

Hucklebark managed a grin that somehow muscled its way through everything else he was feeling.

"Ready when you are, Ray." He slipped back out of the pack, and sat down to wait.

Works now said, "It makes sense for you to return there. It also makes sense—to me, at least—that Spark and I accompany you. Do you agree to this?"

"Yes, yes of course," I replied. "I—I guess I figured that the two of you would have other things that needed doing, so it didn't occur to me to ask."

"At the moment," Works said calmly, "and for many reasons, I don't believe there is anything more important for us to be doing.

Do you know how you're going to, as you say it, re-establish relations?"

I hadn't actually thought that out, but a few seconds were all I needed to decide what to do. "I'm going to walk up to the saddle that overlooks Vernal Park, and start over from the beginning."

Spark lifted an eyebrow. "Do you imagine this might take a while?"

"The way I figure it, it will either take a short time or it won't happen at all," I said. "I'll be back soon—I think."

The last time I had walked up to that saddle, Lyla had been beside me. She had tried hard to sense the things I had told her and the others about, with no success. At first I had been afire to get going, to go around the dead circle in the Park, and then instead I had marched straight down to it.

Nothing had changed in the landscape of Vernal Park in the short time since I had sat here. The dead circle below looked exactly the same. I stood looking down into the Park for several moments, and then shook myself. There was no time to waste if I had any hope of finding her. My heart lurched in my chest as I struggled to keep hope under control.

I walked near to the spot that had stopped me in my tracks. I opened a tiny fraction of myself to the ground, very slowly. Nothing happened until I realized I was trying too hard, squeezing my awareness through the smallest possible pinhole in my being. With a conscious effort to relax, I opened more, and instantly felt the place I needed to be, about two feet to my right.

I moved there and sat on the dusty ground. I moved into the earth gingerly, expecting at any moment to encounter resistance or rejection, or worse, the Destroyer.

Instead I felt the rivers running near enough to touch with my mind. I reached out and carefully, gently touched one. I felt like someone trying to handle a traumatized animal that could turn dangerous at any instant. Then I remembered what Works had said to me, and tried to concentrate on just doing things well. I entered the river, and traveled slowly, staying close to where my body rested. So far so good, I thought.

How would I be able to 'twine' rivers, as Fell had said I must do? I rummaged through memory: "You must ask, offer, and join." Taiga had said it with more words, some of which I remembered: 'enter,' 'gently,' 'respectfully,' 'wrap' and 'bend.' Very well, I would ask, first.

The more I thought about what words to use for asking, the more I came to realize that words in this situation were encumbrances to avoid. How to ask without words? What did I want from these primal energies?

I wanted to join with these rivers of life. I wanted to work with them, to have them help me repair things—I wanted them to help me mend. When I thought about it that way, the mending seemed to be both an inward and outward moving thing. I wanted them to be my partners, and I wanted to be theirs.

The more I thought about this, the more I felt a kind of yearning emerge, a desire for strength without need, without ambition. I let go of trying to describe it, and instead simply placed that yearning before me, as if making an offering of some kind. I offered them my desire, and I wrapped it in the Agreements I'd made with the People of The Home. I left it sitting there before my awareness like a bowl of food lovingly placed on the steps of a temple.

Suddenly I felt myself sinking into the river I'd been slowly drifting along in. This was not like any other time before; I was dissolving, and yet there was no fear, for I was still perfectly aware of who and what I was, and where I had come to. The river took me into itself, and though there was still me and the river, there was no barrier, no important distinction.

We moved this way. I felt the power of the life river in ways I hadn't imagined before. I knew what a two hundred mile long tidal race feels like; I knew with my own nerve endings and my own mind how the thunderhead feels, rolling across the sky. The mountains undulated in waves whose periods would be measured in millennia, and I understood.

There was another great river moving nearby, almost in parallel with this one. I reached out to it, touched it lightly, firmly with my mind, and laid my offering before it. I sank, and I was integrated into the two of them. I traveled with them. Perhaps we moved around the planet; I wasn't watching for distance, I was taking in the feeling of being a welcome visitor to the work of the world.

I could sense everything around me, and discovered that the rivers were everywhere. They crisscrossed, ran parallel for a time before branching apart, looped in and around each other; always in motion, graceful even when in conflict.

I could stay here, moving through the planet this way, forever, I thought. But merely thinking that brought me back to what lay ahead, the work that must not be put off or ignored. There was Lyla, and I realized that if I were to find her, it would be by searching this way. And the need to reach the People of The Home, and find a way to make amends. Then there was the Destroyer. I was still quite uncertain whether or not these great rivers of the working planet would allow me to wield their power to bring some semblance of balance back to Tahoma and its peoples.

Not having the least idea of where I'd traveled or for how long, it was still a simple matter to backtrack to where I was still sitting on a dusty ridge overlooking Vernal Park. It was not at all like trying to walk upstream in a creek; I simply sought myself, and returned.

My eyes opened. The sun did not look like it had moved very far in its westward journey; I hoped wryly that it was still the same day. My stomach felt like an empty cave, but I had not eaten much lately, and could not take that to mean any great passage of time. I stood, stretched hugely. It was time to be in a hurry again. I needed to get back to our camp at Carbon River Canyon, and I needed to find Lyla. What would I encounter if—and when—I found her? This was something to put away until the time came; I tried to place the thought with all its terror and hope in a place where it wouldn't get in the way, but it refused to move, and I stood irresolute. Finally, the best I could manage was to just barely shoulder it aside with the next thought: there was much to do.

It was late afternoon when I strode back into Mender's Camp. I noticed with some surprise that the name had moved through my thought without a ripple; perhaps I was ready to accept it, with all of its implications, regardless of what happened next.

The sun was behind Tahoma, and the clearing was already in deepening shade. Works, Spark, Ev and Hucklebark were all still there in various attitudes of rest or readiness. I went to retrieve my pack, looked around and realized it wasn't anywhere to be seen. Of course, Ev had been thoroughly occupied carrying me back to this place—there hadn't been any knowing if my pack would ever matter again at that point. Fortunately, I thought, the pressing business at hand required that I return and rejoin it as soon as possible.

I stood in the center of the clearing. "I need to go back to the Carbon River Canyon right away; is everyone ready?"

Hucklebark, who had been sprawled in the tufted grass next to his own pack, picked it up and stood waiting. Ev—whose pack wasn't here either, I suddenly noticed—rose too. Works and Spark got to their feet much more slowly. They both looked tired and worried.

I had expected someone to question whether we should wait for the morning to move, but no one raised it. To have such friends and allies—how lucky could a person be? I wanted to say something that would reflect my gratitude for them, and how they honored and humbled me. But the few things that came to mind all sounded pretentious or overly formal, and I let them lie without voicing them. Instead, I simply turned and walked out of the clearing.

Chapter 33

Ev caught up with me first. "Ray, I need to go back quickly, get my pack and retrieve some supplies for us. Can you do without me until I can get back?"

I turned to him. "How long do you figure you need?"

He looked thoughtful. For about three seconds. "I can be back by morning."

"Honestly, Ev, I don't even know what I'm asking of anyone. So let's hope that by morning will work, because I think I could eat you out of house and home otherwise. And…and thank you, Ev. Thanks for everything."

He looked astonished for an instant, and then recovered just that fast. Putting on his best W.C. Fields voice, he said, "Why sure, my boy, it's all in a day's work, ya know. All in a day's work." He walked ahead of me with his immense stride, still in character, muttering something that sounded like "There's a Mender born every day, you know that? Never met a Mender I didn't like, but you don't wanna trust 'em…"

I was still smiling when Hucklebark came up. I realized that I hadn't been able to speak to everyone in the clearing because I needed to say what I wanted to say to them individually. Hucklebark matched my pace, and fell in beside me.

"Hucklebark, I don't know how to say this gracefully. But you've been as true and as strong a friend as I've ever had in my life. I'm grateful to have met you; in fact, I can't think of anyone else I'd have preferred to find me trying to talk to a willow by the side of the Carbon."

Hucklebark looked at me blankly, with the look he always got when he was trying furiously to process something totally unexpected. Slowly a grin cracked through the grief he was immersed in.

"Well, Ray, I reckon that's graceful enough. Almost too graceful. But I thank you kindly. It's been a pleasure." He suddenly looked anxious. "You know something you haven't told yet? End of the world, or something like that?"

I couldn't help but laugh. "If you haven't figured out yet how clueless I really am, I bet I can buffalo you for a long time to come." Sobering a bit, I said, "No, I don't know anything. But some things need to be said whenever the chance arises, maybe precisely because I don't know anything. But look, Hucklebark, can I ask you a question?"

"Sure, that part's easy," he replied. "The chancy part is whether or not I can answer."

"All right, I'll take my chances. What did it feel like when I came into your mind, when you were under the glacier?"

Hucklebark rubbed his chin while we walked. "I don't know if I can answer that well. But I knew it was you, right away—no doubt about that. If it had been someone I didn't get along with as well, it might have been more of a problem."

"So was it like I was trespassing, or being somewhere I shouldn't, or anything like that?"

"I confess I was a tad shaken up for a moment. And now that I think about it, it's kind of strange, and maybe worrisome. But you know, at the time it seemed natural."

We walked along in that companionable silence I had come to cherish, both with Hucklebark and with Lyla. The thought of her came rushing back in, with the wave of grief I had been holding back all afternoon. I slammed my hope against it, fought it to a standstill. *Not yet,* I told it—*not until I say so. Not until anything and everything that can be done has been.* I took a deep, shuddering breath and kept walking.

Hucklebark, who apparently hadn't noticed anything, suddenly said, "Why d'you ask, Ray?"

"Hm? Ask what?"

"If it bothered me when you came into my mind."

"Oh. Well, two reasons, I guess. One, like I said, you're a friend who means a great deal to me, and if I did something wrong I'd want to know about it. Two, I expect I'm going to need to do it again. Maybe with you, maybe with everyone who's with me. And I want to know if it's going to cause resentment, or anything like that."

"Can't speak for anyone but myself," Hucklebark said. "Or shouldn't, anyway. But I'm willin' to bet if it's got something to do with settin' things right around here, none of us'll kick too hard."

We walked another quarter mile, and I found that I couldn't see Works or Spark when I turned around to look. I asked Hucklebark if he knew whether or not they were coming.

"Oh yeah, they're bringing up the rear. Works has to take his time, you know."

"Why's that?"

Hucklebark looked uncomfortable. "I'm not supposed to talk about it. But I guess you'll have to know sometime, Ray."

"Know what? Out with it, Hucklebark."

He sighed. "Works has been kind of, well, sick I guess. He's mighty old."

"Tell me more."

"Not much to tell. I don't know what's ailing him, and I don't reckon anyone does unless he's told 'em. Seems unlikely, unless it's Spark. But he's moving a whole lot slower than he was just a few years ago, and a lot of us have been worried for some time."

I had not had very much time with Works, and I thought then about each of those times. I remembered what it felt like when he grasped my arm, the incredible warmth and strength that flowed from him, and what it would be like to have that taken away too soon. I thought about the effort it would take to be weak and unwell, and to still give something like that away, and I decided if I ever became a thousandth of the person Works was, I'd have done better than I could have dreamt.

"I think we should wait for Works and Spark, Hucklebark."

He walked in silence for a bit. "I don't guess he'd care much for that, Ray. If you're dead set on it, I won't argue. But he's got Spark with him, and if anyone can get him to your camp, it'll be Spark."

"All right, I'll go with what you say. You're right, I need to get there." I picked up the pace even though I was getting tired, and Hucklebark moved along with me.

RATHER THAN TAKE the precipitous route Lyla and I had taken, down from the saddle overlooking Vernal Park, I had decided to go around the west and north side of Sluiskin. We were retracing the steps Lyla, Henry, Ev and I had made when we first went to the House of Windy Gap for a gathering. Though it had only been a few days ago, it seemed like so much deep history; memories were all I had now of Henry, and my mind shied away again from the fear that I would have no more than that of Lyla. I was filled to bursting with fear and hope for her. The only way I could bear the war between hope and despair was to walk harder, and I grimly brushed aside the complaints of my legs and lungs, and moved faster. Hucklebark, whose stride was at least a foot longer than mine, was visibly working to match my pace, and there wasn't breath between us to spare for further talk.

It was fully dark when we crossed the Wonderland Trail as it skirted Old Desolate to the southeast. The moon had not yet risen; glancing upward for the first time in an hour I saw that it wouldn't matter when it did, for a thick blanket of cloud lay over us. On Tahoma, the weather can turn not only inclement, but dangerous, any day of the year. I began filling with anxiety, worrying that if it turned bad I might not be able to find her. Lupine came to mind, then: "After that, work on eliminating every scrap of unnecessary fear that keeps you in the *idiot* state and out of the *savant*." No better advice would I find, for I would need every bit of 'savant' I could produce. No point in obsessing over the weather, yet. It would do what it would do, and I would simply have to remain aware and ready to respond.

I was glad that the terrain between the Wonderland Trail and our camp was relatively easy. I didn't want to use a light if I didn't absolutely have to, though if you had asked me why, I probably couldn't have answered. Hucklebark was so accustomed to not using one that his feet seemed to know where to place themselves without any help from his eyes. I tried to emulate him, and made a shambling, stumbling mess of it until I remembered to relax. Still, I moved much more slowly. By the time we reached the woods that overlooked the Carbon River Canyon, I was quivering with impatience.

Once under the trees, the darkness was complete. I turned to Hucklebark. "I recall you saying you used a small lamp under the glacier. You happen to have it handy?"

He fished through several pockets and produced a tiny flashlight whose beam was barely bright enough to illuminate the path at our feet. "Does Ev bring you batteries now and then?"

"Doesn't use batteries. I have to remember to leave it out in the sun once in a while, which is why it's just about dead now."

I held the little thing in front of me, but it didn't shed enough light to make a difference. I grew frustrated, tried to move faster, and nearly brained myself running into a tree that loomed out of the shadows. *What am I afraid of?* I'm afraid I won't find her. *And how will smacking my head on a tree help this?* Don't suppose it will, will it? *And if I drop this fear, what is revealed underneath it?*

Oh. What's *underneath* is an unending series of rivers, who have so far taken me where I needed to go (whether I knew so or not) every time I've entered them, and who took me there without the need of eyesight or light.

I opened up, and they were there as I knew they would be. I descended just enough to spread my awareness in a circle of a few paces. The ground was revealed, and I knew exactly where to step. Just a little more opening and I could sense the clearing ahead of us. I let the hand holding Hucklebark's tiny lamp fall to my side, allowing it to point to the ground, and moved forward confidently. I heard a short intake of breath from Hucklebark as he started to ask me what was going on, and then felt rather than heard him reconsider, and remain silent.

I threaded us through the dense thicket of trees that surrounded the clearing where Lyla and I had camped. The darkness in the clearing was a shade lighter than it had been under the trees, but it was still almost complete. Hucklebark set his pack down, sat down beside it, and looked up at me expectantly. I handed him the little flashlight, and he immediately switched it off. Though he was only four feet away from where I stood, I could barely make out an outline of different darkness. I sat on the ground to be more or less level with him.

He spoke softly. "What's next, Ray?"

"I need to find her," I replied. "But… I need something else, too, and I don't know what it is, and I don't know how to find out. You ever have that feeling?"

"Sure," he said. "Any chance it's something from me?"

I hadn't gotten there yet, but he was right. "You know, I think it must be. I need to ask you about something, and I can't get to it."

In the darkness I couldn't see Hucklebark rub his chin in thought, but the soft, sandpapery scratching sound of his beard was unmistakable. "If I was to guess at what you might need from me right now, I'd have to start with whatever there is I got that others don't. There isn't much of that, so it ain't a long search, Ray. I knew Henry a lot better than anyone, so I'm figurin' maybe you need me to talk about him. Maybe somethin' more you're after than just what happened in the glacier."

I looked over towards him in growing wonder. How could Hucklebark know that, when I didn't know it myself? But now that it had been said, it was clearly so. "I think you're right. Would you be willing?"

He shifted to get more comfortable, and his pack creaked as he leaned back against it. It was an oddly comforting sound, a gentle but definite difference from the night's silence. It made me all the more grateful for Hucklebark's company, whether I needed anything else or not.

"I don't actually figure *willin'* enters into it so much, but that's all right. Any place in particular you want to start from?"

"Not really, I guess. Wait a second. There's no point in pretending, Hucklebark; what was it between the two of you that went so hard?"

"Hm. Might as well get right to it, huh?" he said. "Okay, then. I brought Henry up here the first time."

I sat up straight. "You? So it was you prowling around Pioneer Square, all those, I don't know, how many years ago?"

"Yup, it was me, and I don't know how many years ago it was. Don't rightly care much, neither. I can bet it was a lot different down there than it is now. I used to go once in a while when I needed to see some different faces. I don't get that way any more, and that's fine with me, but back then I'd run into lots of interestin' folks there. And Henry was one of 'em."

Hucklebark paused for a moment, taking himself back to those times. I waited quietly for him to get there.

"Soon as we got back here I figured I'd made a big mistake. Henry wouldn't hardly just *talk* to anybody, even though everybody was nice as could be. It wasn't like he was mean or anything, he just didn't seem to get on with people. He'd ask a lot of questions, get a lot of answers, and then go off by himself for weeks on end. Then he'd show up somewhere and start asking more questions. People got to feeling like he was a one way kind of guy, never giving much back for everything they gave him."

I asked, "What did Works think about all this?"

"Works didn't meet Henry 'til he'd been up here a year or so. That made a difference all right, and Works got him settled down a bit. But Henry always wanted to move too fast, go places he wasn't ready for, do stuff that would have been hard and scary for someone with ten times his experience. He got in a lot of arguments, and people kind of decided to just let him be. I worked pretty hard at staying friends, but it wasn't never easy, and it got harder as time went on."

"I didn't know him as well as I would want, but I'd say he was pretty complicated. Henry saved my life, most likely twice," I mused. "Now there's no way to repay him."

With a rueful smile in his voice, Hucklebark answered, "I'd never've called Henry simple either, Ray. And as far as repayin' him goes, I'd say if whatever he did helps show you how to do somethin' important, he's paid in full."

"No, there was nothing simple about Henry." I shook my head

slowly in the darkness. "Nothing anywhere seems to be simple in any way."

"Wouldn't be much of a world if it was all simple, now, would it?" Hucklebark said.

"No. No, I don't suppose so."

"Anything else you want to know, Ray? I don't reckon I have much more, but if it'll help, I'll scrape the bottom of this old brain pan."

I thought for a minute. "Hucklebark, *why* do you all live for so long?"

He paused, just as I had. I could almost feel him roaming through his mind, searching for an answer.

"Haven't thought about it in a real long time. But there was a time when I did, and when I reached an idea I liked, I let go of the whole thing. It's like this, I think: you told us that with the People of The Home, you made two Agreements. All of us here have made Agreements with the world, one kind or another. I think the world wants us to keep those Agreements. But humans are slow learners, Ray. I figure the world—whatever face you want to put on it, whatever voice you got to hear it in—is helping out by giving us more time to get it."

Most people would have found a more elegant, a more mystical way of putting it. But Hucklebark's bare-bones assessment appealed to me strongly. I found, a little to my surprise, that I was satisfied with it, though I wanted to know why he was satisfied.

"How did you just let go of it once you got that idea?"

"Had to—otherwise, it felt like lookin' a gift horse in the mouth," he said. "A horse that was already takin' me on a longer, better ride than I ever imagined. Maybe it's a mystery, but I don't have time for 'em all, even if they were all meant for me anyway. Make sense?"

"Yeah, that makes sense, Hucklebark. Very good sense."

"That it, or you need any more mealy chestnuts from this old squirrel's stash?"

That should have been enough, but I couldn't leave things alone.

"Did you ever bring anyone else up here besides Henry?"

"A couple of folks before Henry's time, and one after. That one didn't work out so well, and after that I pretty much gave up on it."

He shook his head and muttered, more to himself than to me. "Poor old Bill. Wonder what ever became of 'em."

Everything inside me went still. There was no reason for it; the world was full of men named Bill, and more than one of them had to be Tree Speakers, successful or otherwise. But the stillness would not move. I thought furiously; when would Hucklebark have encountered Henry—1920? 1885? 1940? I had no way of knowing, and it was clear Hucklebark hadn't counted years in a great many of them. The idea had lodged itself in me, and nothing I could do would make it go away.

After a long pause, I said, very quietly, "Did he walk with a limp on his right side? Was he about my height, kind of thin, his voice kind of high and strained?"

"Huh? Who?" Hucklebark replied. He had clearly moved on to thinking about something else.

"Bill."

I heard Hucklebark's vertebrae crackle under the rustle of his shirt as his head snapped up to gaze at me, though I could see nothing of this in the darkness. The tone of his voice was baffled, almost frightened.

"Now how could you know that, Ray?"

"He failed, didn't he, Hucklebark? I mean, failed totally. Tell me what happened with him, would you?"

"Not 'till you tell me how you could know about someone who was up here before you was born, Ray. I know you're on your way to bein' a Mender 'n all, but you don't need to scare me over it."

I spoke with a low, unsteady voice. "His name was Bill Holdman, and he was my father. He died twenty years ago in a mental institution, because he couldn't live with trees and he couldn't live with humans either. Will you tell me what happened?"

I waited long enough for him to answer that I began to think I didn't want to hear one. I was about to get up when he let out a long, slow sigh.

"Don't know quite how to talk about it—can't hardly believe it. I found him wandering around the Square, kind of in a daze, and I figured it was about the trees, and not knowin' how to live with 'em. After we got up here I started to figure out that Bill was in some kind of pain, not the leg, I mean, something else inside him, and it wouldn't let him rest. Seemed at first like he'd get it worked out and things'd be okay, but he couldn't calm down enough to just work, and it seemed like nobody could help him neither. After a while, the trees wouldn't let him in anymore, and the human folk here gave up tryin' to get him to quiet down. He was up here for a year or so, then one day he just up and disappeared. We never heard hide nor hair of him again."

He was silent for a moment, then said, "I'm sorry, Ray."

My father had been here. No, that was just the beginning. *My father had been brought here by Hucklebark.* And he had made the same mess of this spectacular chance that he had made of the rest of his life. What would my life have been like if he'd been successful here? I told myself angrily, *What a useless, idiotic question!* I said, "There's nothing to be sorry about, Hucklebark."

"I'm just sorry there ain't nothin' I can say to help it be less hard."

"Oh. Well, for that, I thank you. For that, and a lot of other things too."

"Nothin' to it," he replied. After another short silence he said, "But look, Ray. This is a right kick in the head for both of us, 'n I wish there was a couple years we could both take to work it out. But we came up here in a tearing hurry, didn't we?"

What am I doing? Get to work, Holdman! I had to stuff this into a box and put it away, instantly. If Lyla was still alive, how long could I expect her to wait while I gnawed on ancient history? What box inside me could contain this?

"You're absolutely right, as usual, Hucklebark. I need to start my searching for real, and right now. I'm not sure where I'm going first; I'll have to let the rivers lead me, and hope our purposes are the same."

"Anything I can do besides sit around and be useless?"

"I can't imagine you ever being useless. Hang on a second."

I found a river that ran more or less in the direction of Windy Gap and followed it, feeling carefully. It was a lot like trying to move quietly in a forest where it was vital to not attract the panther's attention, though in this case the panther was becoming capable of destroying an entire region. About halfway between our camp and Windy Gap I found Works and Spark. They were moving slowly, and I could feel that Works was in pain, and not bothering to conceal it. I resisted the urge to touch them, to encourage Works, and I was filled with dread at the thought of losing him.

I returned to the campsite and Hucklebark. "There is something important you're needed for. Works and Spark are about halfway here, and moving slowly. It would be a good thing if someone was ready for them when they get here; I figure they'll both be pretty worn out."

"So, like have a little fire going, something warm to drink, beddin' down places picked out, all that?"

"You have it thoroughly worked out already," I said.

"No problem," Hucklebark said. "So, you're off, then?"

"My pack is around here somewhere. After I find it and eat everything in it that doesn't run away, I have to look for the place I can begin to search from."

"You need a special place to start from?"

"I can't tell you exactly why, but I think I do," I said. It was too dark to find my pack by just looking around the clearing, so I started quartering it, keeping my awareness open a few feet in front so I didn't run into anything. I found it pretty quickly.

It was exactly as I'd left it; nothing had been disturbed, including what food I had in there. I devoted a few minutes to wolfing several large chunks of stale bread with the eternal peanut butter, and then returned to where Hucklebark was working. His dim flashlight lay flat on the ground as he cleared a small space for a fire.

I said, "I don't know when I'll be back, or where I'm off to, or what I expect to do. If there's something useful I *can* tell you, just ask."

Hucklebark looked up. "Come back and tell me you found her," he said softly. "Til then I don't need nothin' else."

Chapter 34

I walked across the clearing, letting my mind lightly brush the rivers below. They led me unerringly out of the clearing, towards the charred dead circle, in whose center stood the great tree that was now a blackened snag. I walked around the circle, heading down slope in a direction just east of north, having no idea why I went that way or how far I would continue.

I let my awareness of the surrounding landscape expand, slowly and carefully. My greatest worry was that in seeking Lyla I would attract the Destroyer's attention. Avoiding it was a lesser concern; what I really cared about was not being distracted from the search.

I was tending towards the cliff that marked the eastern wall of the Carbon River Canyon, walking slowly, steadily over the increasingly uneven ground. With the moon not yet up to offer even a dim glow through the cloud cover, and the woods overhead, the darkness was a heavy, final presence that arched over me. I settled lightly into the river below my feet, gave it my senses, and allowed it to show me where to move. I stepped lightly, softly around rocks and trees, and my feet knew where the earth would be when they descended.

I traveled this way for about a half mile. Off a quarter mile to my right and upwards a hundred feet I sensed the Wonderland Trail, abandoned by humans for the night. A few dozen yards to my left I felt the yawning space of the canyon, and the great, massive presence of the glacier below. My feet turned decisively towards the cliff, and I let them move without question.

I came to a moderately deep depression in the ground. Here a boulder the size of a small shed had lain for years, perhaps centuries or millennia. Some time in the relatively recent past, gravity and the glacier had called it down. What a sound that must have made! What remained of that huge sound was a bowl about twenty feet across and ten feet deep, with sides just far enough from the vertical for my feet to pick their way downwards.

The bottom of the bowl was layered with forest duff. Years of erosion and litter had left a level space more than ample for sitting comfortably, and I sat. Without conscious thought, I composed myself on the ground facing Tahoma.

To my right now, where the great boulder had crashed to the glacier below, the side of the bowl opened out onto empty space, an airy darkness. It felt like coming to sit in a room that had long been lived in by someone very powerful, whose departure left behind a lingering residue, the echoes of a great and strong spirit. The room's one window was wide open to the night.

I was certain this was the right place to be. At last, there was nothing to think about but the search for Lyla. As best as I could, I shouldered aside the thoughts that were clamoring for attention, and opened myself into the ground below. There were several rivers running very closely together here. Without any great preparation I lightly touched all of them at once, and entered each one. It was possible to enter them without moving and without exerting the effort to stay still, something I had not known before. I remained where I was, and considered again what Fell had told me: *ask, offer, join*. I still had no real idea how I would search; perhaps if I just did as I'd been told, something would present itself.

A request for help; a strong current of gratitude; the Agreements a Mender must make; the notion of a partnership that repairs the world. These I set before my mind, held them up and waited silently.

Almost as if I had been sitting over a trapdoor, something opened abruptly below me, and I sank. The sensation of *joining* with those rivers was overwhelming. It was as if until that moment I had been skating over them like a water strider, so light I couldn't penetrate the river's surface tension. Now I was in them—deep inside them.

There were three rivers of the world's energy flowing in parallel under this place, very close together. On either side of where I sat they diverged again. I was simultaneously inside of each one, and without going anywhere I was aware of everything around, above and below me for a long way. Nearby I could sense a family of tiny pikas nestled in their burrow, already asleep against tomorrow's search for food. The roots of each and every one of the trees in a great swath around me lay open, ready to be asked for an invitation. I flicked a tendril of awareness, and instantly found Hucklebark in the clearing. He had collected a night's supply of firewood, and the little campfire he'd built was efficient and cheerful. A minutely stronger flick, and I found Works and Spark laboring up the slope that led to the Wonderland Trail crossing. What were the limits to seeing the world this way? I had no idea.

I roamed slowly, aimlessly, over an ever increasing area, probing, feeling, and thinking. Was I wasting time? Maybe, but what else was I to do?

I allowed myself to wander into the Carbon Glacier, and immediately thought of Henry. What had he been trying to do when the Destroyer had found him? How had he been able to mimic me so perfectly, and to what possible purpose?

I felt it coming. It required only an instant to know where it was, how fast it was moving, and how much time I had to elude it. Not much time at all; I retreated at the speed of thought, left the rivers and slapped back into my body with a jolt that toppled me over on to the ground.

Frustration threatened to derail my whole train of thought and effort. How could I search for Lyla if I couldn't do what I had been taught?

How should I work through this?

What is going on in you right now?

Well, I'm extremely angry.

Why?

Because I can't search for Lyla!

Not good enough, bub. Now why?

What—are you Henry or something?

No, I'm you pretending to be Henry pretending to be you. Now answer the question! Why *are you angry?*

I am afraid. If I don't find her, I won't want to live in this world because of the pain.

Good. Now you know it's about fear. What have you been taught about that?

Lupine taught me the only way to survive is to eliminate all the unnecessary fear. What's left can be considered and dealt with.

Nice work, bub. Now—do you really have to be terrified that you won't find her?

It's a self-fulfilling prophecy, isn't it? I'm afraid of not finding her, which makes it hard to think, which means I can't find her.

Perhaps there's hope for you yet.

Henry, may the Creators, whoever they are, bless your pointed head and blunt tongue—even in death you pester me into intelligence. Now what were you doing in that glacier? Why broadcasting an engraved invitation to the Destroyer?

Silence.

All right, let's try again. I'll let go of the fact that I don't have a clue how you could mimic me so well as to fool it. To what end?

Silence.

Frustration rose up again; this was becoming a distraction. Wait—

A distraction. A chill settled in that shocked me to stillness. Had Henry been that powerful, that devious? Had he been practicing to lure the Destroyer away from me so I could learn what I needed to learn? It was impossible. *Henry?*

And yet there was no other explanation that would cover it.

However he had done it, it *had* worked. The Destroyer only came towards me because my 'invitation' had outshouted Henry's, and it veered away the instant I escaped back into my body, screaming back to him instead. I had to think Henry had not planned on it actually reaching him. What then? Was he going to feint, to wave it aside? The sudden memory arose of a tree in the Elysian Fields that had tried to show Lyla and me that very thing. We had told Henry that story in all its detail; there was no scrap of doubt left concerning Henry's intention.

Elation. Grief. A stabbing, savage sorrow. Henry had been working out a defense that could make Mending possible, and he had lost his life in the practice of it. I mourned. I wept.

What the hell are you doing now?

What do you think? I'm mourning the loss of a friend, a brother. *Time for that later, if you insist. Get to work!*

He was right. No, I was right. No—well, whatever. Henry had given me what I needed to get back to work, if I could only figure out how to use it. I took several deep, shuddering breaths, and settled into the ground. I made my request and my offering quickly, and was almost instantly deep into the three rivers again.

A short time before, I had sent my awareness here and there, with a simple mental flick. Was it possible to send something less, and to send it farther? I thought about what an insubstantial echo of my awareness might be like, tried to send it out without any of me following it. Nothing happened.

Maybe what I needed was a better way to think about this, a metaphor. I concentrated, mentally squeezed, trying to force one to arise. Naturally, more of nothing followed. I tried to relax my thoughts, stop pressing. Maybe if I thought about something totally benign, like sitting on the bank of a slow, quiet stream…

Fishing. Not just any fishing, but fly fishing. I'd never done it in my life, knew practically nothing about it, and yet it seemed exactly like what I wanted to do right now. If I could fashion a lure out of some wispy echo of myself, cast it far out into the world, and then break the line at the last moment, would that do?

I tried. The first several times produced nothing. But I liked the idea; it made sense to me, so I kept it up. I pretended to do it the way I'd seen on film, whipping the line back and forth over the water, and finally sending it out far over the stream, always ready to let go of it at the right instant. This time, though, I was aping a technique I knew next to nothing about, and my purpose was not only quite different, but failure was certain to be fatal. I tried some more.

It was coming. There would not be time to try this more

than once; if I was wrong about it all, maybe not even that much time. I sent my lure soaring through the world, and with a mental snap I released it. The lure—nothing more than the memory of a thought—went streaming on away from me. The Destroyer veered sharply to follow it, screaming through the ground. At the furthest edge of my awareness, it struck the ephemeral lure, and veered yet again, moving farther and farther away.

I rested, silent and stunned. It had worked. Would it work again? I would find out when it was needed, and not before.

I floated lightly, quiet and alert, far within the three streams. Slowly, tentatively, I began to explore the world around me, finding life in every place I looked. The trees, plants, insects, mammals, bacteria and viruses, all the myriad, uncountable forms life takes: even this somewhat sparsely populated part of the world was bursting with life. Was Lyla still in this world somewhere?

Finding and tracking Hucklebark, Works and Spark had been almost effortless. If Lyla was alive, and if she was anywhere in this region, I would find her.

Joining three streams had a consequence I had not anticipated: it was as if I had three distinct minds that I could marshal and order as needed. I let my senses expand outward from where I was, slowly, carefully probing and examining everything I found. I worked hard at keeping my touch light, so light that the lives I observed were unaware of the observer. Time was an uninteresting side issue; this work would take whatever time it required, and as long as I didn't fail to maintain the body that made it all possible, I would burn time like kindling to find her.

I became intimate with each place I examined. I knew every single life form that was there. Gradually, the places and lives accumulated, until I was part and parcel of a wide swath of Tahoma's flank. Still I had found not even the tiniest trace of Lyla.

I reached a point where there was resistance to expanding further. I considered that, and realized the resistance came from myself. I didn't want to move out any more. Why not? Was it hopeless, and was I going to have to return to the unthinkable assumption I had begun with—that Lyla was gone forever?

You're not done yet, bub.
If I'm not done, what next?
Perhaps you figure you've done all that can be done.
The thought had crossed my mind, yes.
What have you been taught about assumptions?
That they often lead me away from the truth.
Then what's next should be obvious.

What was I trying to tell myself? All I could come up with was that some deep, unknown part of me held the conviction that if I were to find her, it would be here, and not farther away. That seemed better than an assumption, so I mentally turned myself around.

There didn't seem to be any point to just moving back and doing the same thing over again. But what should I be doing differently?

Ask around, bub. There's a lot of people in the neighborhood.

Who *are* you? Is it Holdman pretending to be Henry, or Henry pretending to be Holdman?

Yes.

I never knew I was such an exasperating person. Nevertheless, the point was made: the next step, which was, after all, obvious, was to ask for help. But how, and from whom?

A sense of urgency had been building, almost unnoticed. If it became much stronger, it would be intolerable. Whatever I was going to do, it had to be *now*.

I stopped thinking. I picked through my heart, choosing the strongest feelings I had for Lyla, and the things I loved about her the most. The beauty and vigor of her life, her clarity, her fearlessness, and the fierce devotion she felt towards the trees and the people she loved. I wore them around me like a robe, and decorated it with my fear and worry for her. Then, I moved back inward towards the center where I had begun my search, moving slowly along the three rivers, keeping my heart and mind quiet as I could.

I came to a place where the root system of a great tree spread itself into the earth. The roots twisted, gnarled and serpentine, through a vast area beneath the surface. They were inviting, somehow. I hesitated, thinking at first that I had no time to go visiting. Another moment made it clear that I was being invited in, and there might be a reason to accept. I approached, lightly brushed my awareness over the nearest stretch of root, and entered.

You come from the other one. That one was here, but no longer.

I paused, baffled. What other one? Hucklebark's revelation cut through me like a knife. I placed before me the only memories of my father that I had.

You knew *him?*

We knew him. We wanted to help, but he would not allow it. Now we see that he gave himself to you. You will allow, and we wish to help.

How could he have 'given himself' to me before I was born? There was no time for this mystery.

Yes, I accept your help with all my heart.

You seek the Lyla.

Yes, yes! Can you help me find her?

She is hidden, and I do not know where.

Yes, I've been told she is hidden. Is there nothing you can tell me that will help?

She was with the elder when it happened.

Who is the elder? What happened?

The elder is gone now. It was destroyed.

Gone… The elder is dead? Please—who was this elder?

The oldest, the strongest. I do not understand dead. *The elder has gone on.*

Is there anything else? Anything at all?

Search in stillness. Only then can you find. We cherish the Lyla too, though we cannot help her now. You must be the one; be still, and find.

The tree had nothing more to say. I placed my gratitude before me, and moved on. Outside the confines of the old tree's life, I rested quietly, the energy of the rivers rippling through me. My senses were becoming confused, and it was difficult to concentrate.

How should I 'search in stillness'? I had read accounts of the power of being still, and how remarkable things could happen in that state. But I had never understood how it was done. Yet I was absolutely certain that time was rapidly running out, and I would have to do it now.

Be still, and find. Did I trust this advice? What choice did I have? For that matter, why would I ever distrust a tree that loved Lyla too?

I floated, stationary within the rivers. It seemed likely that I would not 'do' anything in becoming still. Rather, I would neglect to 'do'. The best I could manage was to focus my attention on the rivers themselves, and try as I had never tried before to let go of everything else.

Thoughts crowded in, clamoring for attention. I resolutely did nothing to discourage them. In time, they simply wandered off, to be replaced by new ones. Whenever my attention drifted away from the rivers I gently brushed it back into place, carefully neglecting to scold or remonstrate.

Eventually the thoughts barged in less often, and I found small, isolated moments of deep quiet and clarity. Without any fuss or change in effort, I kept doing what I was doing, which was less and less. The moments of quiet grew longer, and the disruptions more sparse.

In a long moment of no thinking, my senses suddenly blossomed outward; they spread away from me in the purest silence, moving deliberately, efficiently out into the world. I was aware of more than I had known possible. The details of the life surrounding me would have been overpowering if I had not already been so still that it all simply washed over and past me. I wasn't merely aware of the pika family sleeping in their burrow; I felt what they felt, dreamt their dreams, slept with them, all in the space of a heartbeat. There were others, innumerable others, and I knew each of them: trees, plants, grasses, the squirrels, the marmots, the cougars, ravens, grey jays, the stones, the dirt, gravel, and sand. I moved through the rivers without moving, embedded in a stillness that brought all the world into me. Hucklebark was an immense presence, not far away. The strong but laboring glow of Works, and the stronger one of Spark, near him. I allowed my sense of them to pass, glad to know they were there, but in need of another.

Something reached me and did not pass. It was incredibly faint, even to one who could hear the thinking of the lichens, and I wondered what it might be. I lingered with it; a life that should not be so faint, for my senses told me it was not far away. I began to move gently, carefully, following and feeling. I did not dare to hope.

I had no idea where I was going, for maintaining contact with that ebbing life required everything I could offer. I did not have to go far.

It was Lyla, and she was alive—for the time being. In this moment, where she was did not matter. Her stamina was at its final extremity, and if I could not find a way to sustain her she would be gone in a matter of minutes.

Ask, offer, join. I was enmeshed in the three rivers, and if ever I needed to *twine* them, it was now. I asked, with all the respect I could summon, in all the desperation I felt. I offered the chance to save a life of worth and importance, and I thought back on how much Lyla meant to so many of the trees, and to many other good and useful people. I asked once more: *let me join, help me to help mend.*

My mind reached out to surround the rivers, almost of its own accord. I brought them together with a softening touch, a touch with an integrity and a firmness I never imagined I possessed. They came together willingly, snaking around each other and me. Together we went to her, and I wound them around Lyla's life. They flowed, pulsed, washed over and through her.

I could tell that she still lived, but by such a slender thread it was a wonder it didn't break at any instant. I thanked the rivers, encouraged them, twined them together and untwined them, wrapping each separately and in concert around her, and I began to hope.

I played the rivers, worked them, kneaded them into different shapes and plied Lyla with them, all as if I were making a song that, played properly, would bring her back to life. The rivers allowed me to play them, and I suddenly understood they were playing me too, and that the changes we brought about would have had no meaning without the deep agreement of both of us.

I felt a quickening of the life we sang silently to, and my hope blossomed. We played on, entwined in a song of energy, flowing to and through her. A small corner of my mind considered the likelihood that she would need physical help as soon as she was safely brought back to the living. I could not imagine leaving her now to return to my body, learn where in the world she actually was, and go there. Instead, while the rivers and I played each other, I sent to my body, followed the faint trail back to the shallow bowl by the canyon's edge, and summoned it. I dimly perceived it rising from the ground and scrabbling to scale the side of the bowl. Then I had no more time for it; I would trust that body to do its job, for the rest of me was consumed with doing its job here.

Lyla—alive! The thought raced through my mind and my heart of hearts, leaping from place to place, cavorting through the landscape and the rivers I was immersed in. My joy flew through the world with the same mad vigor that my pain and despair had used to nearly drag me down to my end. But there was still work to do, this instant, and be done correctly. The rivers and I washed into her again and again, but she was perilously frail. So close had she been to death that only someone with her own native strength and ferocious love of life could have held to it. I worked; the rivers wrapped themselves around me, and we wrapped ourselves around her, and we worked.

From far away the corrosive, discordant note of blind hatred sounded. It was coming. The Destroyer had heard the song, and was tearing through the earth, directly towards us.

There was no decision to make. I would not leave her, not even to escape the Destroyer. I would either deflect it, or we would both be taken together. Most of me stayed working with the rivers and her; another, smaller part of my mind collected a scrap of memory that looked very much like me, held it in a grip of iron, and with every ounce of energy I could spare, flung it from us.

I pushed against it as it streaked away from us, screaming through the land in a northeasterly direction. I was astounded by the speed at which it roared across the landscape, and amazed at the reverberating thunder that followed close behind, as if it pulled all the sound in the land along with it. After all, it was nothing more than a scrap—an echo—of me, and yet it made the same kind of bellowing fuss I had made when in my madness I had sought to kill the Destroyer.

It was with only a little surprise that I felt the Destroyer change its direction in a broad, sweeping arc that turned away from us and followed my roaring decoy. I turned back to Lyla, for there wasn't time yet to do or to think of anything else.

The rivers and I had worked in and through her without pause during the moments the rest of me had been distracted. They had bound me to themselves, and while I had sent my decoy shouting across the world, I had kept on playing and being played, singing and being sung.

She was stronger now, and I felt that with a little more work, she would be able to sustain her life, and so be safe and whole again. It occurred to me to wonder where the rest of me had gotten to; where, in fact, were we? I searched for the body that until very recently had been all of me that I knew of. It was not far from wherever we were, but it didn't seem to be moving. I roamed over it, wondering absently what the problem might be. One of the rivers unwound itself from around Lyla, moved with me to where my body seemed to be lying, and the two of us worked into and through it.

It was not damaged beyond repair, but something had happened to prevent it from finding us. We worked it, running energy, poking and prodding. I sensed it slowly rising from the ground, and beginning to make its halting, clumsy way towards the place where Lyla was almost revived. I would figure it all out later, when the rivers and I had finished our song of life and living.

That song was nearly done. Wherever her body was, I could feel her heart beating properly again. Her lungs were reaching for air, and her blood pulsed through her. A finger twitched somewhere, and suddenly her hand clutched spasmodically.

It was time to complete the finding of Lyla. The rivers and I washed through her once more, and then I gently unwrapped them from her, and from me. The song had been played and sung, and it had done what was needed. I was too filled with feeling, and I didn't know what to do with it. I wanted to hug the rivers to me, to cry out my gladness and gratitude, to give them something, grace them with something spectacular as if I were a grateful monarch or a loving nation.

None of these were relevant, and I knew it. I was overflowing, but all I did was to hold myself open to them, my spirit holding its arms wide, allowing it all to spill out of me. Works was right, of course: the rivers of the world's work simply did what they did, and emotion was something for humans, a few other equally ephemeral, living communities, and perhaps for no one else in the world. I relaxed my hold, and they simply moved away, returning to the courses they had been following when I had found them.

Where was *I*, then? Lyla was safe, for now. I turned my awareness aside from her to hunt for myself. The trail was short; I found my body almost immediately, and gently entered. There was pain—a lot of it. I shouldered the pain aside, and tried to get my eyes to work again.

There was light that looked to be the aftermath of a grey dawn. It was difficult to see, and I could not tell why. Impatiently I wiped at my eyes, and found that I was facing the great, charred snag that stood in the center of the dead circle near our campsite. She was inside it; it was patently obvious now. I reached into the ground, found a river that was moving slowly around the perimeter of the circle. I asked it, begged it, offered all my spirit, and after a moment's hesitation it entered the dreaded circle. I twined it around me, and we burrowed down deep into the taproot. We worked our way upwards, pushing against the dead tissue of the tree, separating, cracking the blackened wood as we went. I could hear it rending as we moved upwards, and with a final, deep throated crack the trunk split wide.

The tree was hollow, and Lyla was in its center. She was slumped to one side, held up by a knob about three feet from the ground. With a shuddering groan a great slab of charred wood fell away from the tree, and I clumsily stepped over it to reach her.

She was alive, but not conscious. I stood directly before her for a minute, thunderstruck. I moved to her, took her face between my hands. My tears fell softly on her face, streaking the soot that had settled on her skin. My lips brushed her closed eyelids, and my hands moved wonderingly over her shoulders, down her arms to her hands, hardly daring to believe that she had been returned to me.

There was blood dotting her face, and more of it on the front of her shirt, which was tattered and scorched. I looked anxiously for the gash or cut, needing to find it so I could staunch the flow. I heard a voice behind me.

"Don't worry about it, Ray—it's yours."

All right, good—it was my own blood. In my confusion, all I could understand was that it was not Lyla's, and that was all that mattered. My hands dropped softly to my sides. I watched her intently, and saw her chest rise as she breathed. With that, I knew I could pay attention to whatever else was happening in the world.

I turned slowly around. It was Hucklebark who had spoken. He stood just off to one side, his face radiating joy as he gazed at Lyla alive. I saw his glance move to me, and it changed abruptly to a concern that bordered on panic. I wondered vaguely what could be bothering him. Lyla was alive! What else mattered?

There was someone else standing nearby. No, there were two someones. I squeezed my uncooperative eyes, forced them to open wide and saw that Spark and Works stood there only a few feet away. Works was smiling broadly, and made to move towards me. Spark abruptly put up a hand and stopped him.

"Not yet, my friend," Spark said softly to Works. Then he turned to me. "Look at me, Ray."

I could find no reason to disobey. I looked into Spark's face, impatiently wiped my eyes again. Now I could see him. Yes, it was the Spark I knew. His face seemed hard and stern, and yet I was sure I detected beneath its steeled exterior the softness of deep concern. I had nothing to hide from him. I opened myself up, far behind my own eyes, and allowed him in. I let him see everything that had happened, all that I had done, all that had been done for me and with me, and for Lyla. Whatever he could see and understand was his to take, as far as I was concerned.

Spark was someone who never seemed to need much time to reach a decision. He nodded briefly to Works, and without a word moved swiftly to Lyla. I moved clumsily out of his way while he lightly placed a hand over her heart, listening and feeling with every cell in his body. His hand moved to her forehead. After a moment he straightened slowly, and turned to face me.

"Very well, then, she is safe and whole. There is, as usual, much we need to discuss, Ray Holdman. Not now, certainly. In the course of your most remarkable work, you have once again managed to very nearly kill yourself. I suspect you will keep me far too busy for some time to come."

Nothing—*nothing*—mattered right now. No one in the world, with all the power in the world, could make the merest scratch on the surface of my joy. I drew myself up to the most dignified pose I could imagine, and in the process felt a stabbing pain that raced from my left foot to my shoulder. It yanked out an involuntary gasp, and I gulped for another breath.

"My dear—Spark," I finally said, "You of all people should know two things: one, that I am not accountable for the fact that the world has seen fit to bestow such gifts upon an *idiot*. The second, and hardly less important, is that becoming a *savant* requires a great deal of time, something we do not have at present."

I felt it was a grand speech, an unanswerable speech, delivered with all the dramatic verve that it required. Unfortunately, whatever effect it might have had was ruined as I toppled over to the ground, and fainted.

Chapter 35

I floated, warm, drowsy, comfortable. I was happy; whatever reason there was for that didn't seem very important right then. Some small part of my mind was holding me within a world river, where I lay cozy and still as the river's energy gently flowed through and around me. It felt like a slow, mellow electric current running past, radiating comfort.

It would be easy to lie here forever, pretending, perhaps, to lie in the shade of a maple or an oak by the side of a murmuring stream, on a blessedly sunny summer's day. It would be so simple to just stay here, dreaming and loafing, with nothing to do and nowhere to go. I was in no mood to think seriously about anything, so I let the idea float beside me, and the two of us loafed together.

A sound intruded, softly at first, and then gaining in strength. It was a light, almost airy pattering. I wanted to remain lazy and incurious, but the mood began to slip away, and in spite of myself I wondered what it was. It seemed to be coming from above me somewhere—but since I had no idea where 'here' was, 'above' didn't mean much either.

Why was I happy? And why did I suddenly feel that, happy as I was, something important was waiting to be done? I didn't want to leave my little paradise. But it began to desert me instead, and as I slipped upwards into my body, my eyes opened.

I was gazing upwards, but there was no sky. Instead, only a flat, featureless expanse of something colored like the fir trees. The pattering was happening on the other side of that surface.

Slowly, something of the world I had known came back to me, in bits and pieces. Of course—this was a *tent*. What was I doing in a tent? The pattering sound was *rain*; a gentle, motherly rain that soaked the ground gradually, forestalling the floods and erosion that came with the vigorous, driving rains. And then I remembered why I was happy: I had seen Lyla again. I had missed her so terribly, and then she had been there again. How had that all come about?

A sigh escaped from me. There was a rustle off to my right. Someone else must be in this tent, I thought. A face came into my view, and it was Lyla's.

Everything that had happened slammed itself back into me then, with a force that seemed like it might lift me from the ground. The horror and desolation, the mad battle with the Destroyer, the shame and reconciliation, the search, and the finding… Lyla gazed down at me, and softly said, "Ray."

I looked up at her, still afraid to believe it. I reached out and rested my hand on her arm. It was her, and to fear it for another instant would be to deny the miracle. I said, "It really *did* happen."

"Yes, it really did." She smiled. Lyla bent down and kissed me, and I reached up to wrap my arms around her. There was the memory of a stabbing, intolerable pain. But now all I felt on my left side was a stiffness that could barely hold my attention. I drew her down to me, and held her tightly. I could not keep the tears from starting from my eyes, and they wet her cheek as they wet mine. I stroked her hair with both hands, and silently did something I had never before done in my life: I cried for joy.

Some time later she pushed herself up from me and sat upright. I could not stop looking at her. "I thought I had lost you forever," I said.

"I would have thought the same, had I been able to think anything at all," Lyla replied. "I think you might be as happy as I am we were both wrong."

"Lyla. I love you with all my heart. I hope you don't get tired of hearing me say that."

Her eyes twinkled. "I doubt I'll get tired of it for some time to come." She sobered suddenly. "But I'm afraid, Ray. Afraid of what's been done so far, and even more afraid of what remains to be done."

"Then we're both afraid, and with the best possible reasons. Help me sit up, would you? I think I've rusted, or something."

She took my hands and gently pulled me up to a sitting position. I didn't hurt anywhere, but I was amazed at my weakness. "How long have I been sleeping?"

"Since yesterday morning. Works told me that right after you found me, you fainted. You were so broken up that it took Spark an hour just to get to the point that they could move you. And all the while he was fussing over me too."

"I've been working him much too hard," I said. "I seem to recall saying something about that and being absurdly proud of the way I said it. But for the life of me I can't remember it now."

She laughed. "I heard Spark repeat it, but I'm not going to tell you now. I'm going to make him say it to you like he said it to me."

"Hm. I imagine I can wait for that. But what about you? Are you all right?"

"Fine as could ever be expected. I came around a couple of hours after you found me—or so I'm told. Spark was fit to be tied; he said he found seven broken bones that had set themselves and knitted of their own accord, and three or four internal injuries that were almost completely healed when he examined me."

"Ah. I wonder if that's what happens when we wrap ourselves up in world rivers. But Lyla, what *happened?* How did you come to be in that tree?"

She sobered again. "As Hucklebark would say it, 'Not much to tell.' You'd been gone all day and into the night, and I was worried sick. The tree you found me in is—was—one of my most valued people, and I knew it intimately. That was why I chose this place to camp. I actually just went to sit with it sometime in the middle of the night, because I needed company and someone to share my worry with. But it invited me in, and I accepted. I'd only been with it for a few minutes when the Destroyer hit. It happened so fast I had no time at all to get out of the way, and the next thing I knew the tree had drawn me inside of it."

"Inside? How did it do that?"

"I don't know, Ray. I never knew there was any tree that carried that kind of power. It knew that if I stayed outside, I'd be killed instantly, and that if it took me in, I might survive even though it certainly would not. I did survive, but there wasn't time to do anything gracefully, and for the few minutes I was conscious I hurt in ways I didn't know were possible. It didn't last long, but while I was awake the Destroyer struck several times. It was awful; the tree deflected what it could of that horrible force, but each strike weakened it, and finally the Destroyer killed it, with me hidden inside. After that, I don't remember anything until Spark woke me yesterday."

I placed a hand over hers. "You've lost someone important. I'm sorry."

She looked down at our hands, and sighed. Looking back up to me, she said, "Ray, you already know that the trees have a radically different way of thinking about life and death. The elders of them are more different still; they have taught me more than I can tell you about now. But the fact remains, I am still a human, and we have our way of fearing and grieving. It hurts as much to have lost this tree as it did to be pulled inside it. But it had no fear, and it knew that it would be going on to some other way of being. I'll miss it terribly, but it would be impatient with me if I grieved for very long."

I looked down, shaking my head. "Another valued friend, gone because of this foul thing. What can be done to get rid of it?"

Lyla looked at me squarely. "There may be ways I can help, Ray, but we all know it will have to be you that figures that out."

"Yes, it will have to be me," I said glumly. "Why would the world pick someone like me to be a Mender?"

She reached out, gently grasped my shirtfront, and drew my face to within an inch of hers. Lupine's way of doing this might have been subtler, but Lyla's was no less powerful. Softly, she said, "Because, buster, the world knows a lot more about things than you or I do. It's time to stop questioning it."

She released me and I sat back, stunned. The look on my face must have been one to remember; she gazed at me for a moment, and burst into laughter. "Ray Holdman, you are the dearest buffoon I've ever met!"

I loved it when she laughed, and I didn't care how it was managed. I laughed, too. "Madam, I will gladly be buffoon, baboon, or balloon if it comes with you laughing and happy."

She stopped for breath, still smiling. "So be it, then."

I looked down and finally noticed something. "Huh. I seem to have different clothes on." Looking back up at Lyla, I said, "As do you. How did that happen?"

"You and I were both very pretty messes when it was all said and done," she said. "Ev was kind enough to bring us a couple of changes of clothing, along with the tents and supplies."

Of course, Everett Longhaul would not bring just one tent, or one of anything. "How many trips did it take him to get all this stuff up here?"

"One, of course," she laughed. "He said something along the lines of, 'This stuff is so much easier than carrying humans it was like a holiday'."

I winced, hoping fervently that Ev would never again have to strap me onto his back and climb several miles and several thousand feet that way.

Every time I looked up at Lyla, it was like a new gift had been granted me. I was filled with gratitude, joy and yearning, and I leaned forward, took her face in my hands, and kissed her. At first she allowed, then she joined; she placed a hand on my shoulder, stroked it gently.

A stentorian throat clearing just outside the tent flap made us both jump. A moment later the flap opened, and the thin, bright-eyed face of Ev Longhaul peeked in.

"Begging your pardon, my dears, but the Powers That Be have requested I enquire as to the well being of one Ray Holdman, and one Lyla-known-only-as-Lyla. Would either of you happen to know anything about this?"

Lyla and I both answered at once, saying "Nothing whatever!" and looked at each other in amazement before breaking into another laughing fit.

Ev, who would follow a joke as long as anyone I'd met, replied solemnly. "Then I suppose I shall have to pick up my lantern, toddle off into the darkness and continue my world-weary search for honest miscreants."

I said, "On second thought, perhaps we can spare you such a tiresome journey, good fellow. What would the Powers That Be want with such a pair?"

"Why, to roast them on the spit of merciless interrogation, of course," Ev said, smiling wickedly. "I understand they taste best when they're tired, and slightly giddy."

"Oh, well, that's all right then. We'll be right along. How are you Ev?" I asked.

"Never better, occasionally worse, and sometimes quite different," he said with a flourish.

"Hmph. I'd be inclined to say, 'Always *very* different,' myself. But listen, Ev—thank you for bringing everything all the way up here, I really mean it."

He favored me with a broad wink. "Not at all, dear boy. The trail to this place is broad, flat, and lined with eiderdown. Especially when our beloved Lyla is brought back to us, and waiting to be honored." Ev reached into the tent, took Lyla's hand, and gave it a chivalrous, theatrical kiss. "Madam, I believe our superiors are waiting."

Despite the years she had known Everett Longhaul, and her own formidable self-possession, Lyla flushed deeply, and then shook it off with a laugh. "Come on, Ray, we're keeping them waiting."

I rose unsteadily to my feet outside the tent, and found the little clearing transformed. Besides the tent I had been resting in, three others had appeared. Two smaller tents, which I thought must be for Lyla and Hucklebark, and one that was significantly larger, likely housing Works and Spark. They were all of colors to blend in with the landscape, looking more like neat, modest hillocks than modern outdoor equipment. I wondered where Ev had acquired them, and then wondered further at knowing that he had brought them all, along with food, clothing, and who knows what else, in a single trip up from the lowlands. I turned to Ev, who was standing nearby, waiting for us. "I doubt I will ever stop being amazed by you, Everett Longhaul."

He bowed, with a courtly fluttering of his long, thin arms. "My goal and satisfaction, sir." Gesturing towards the largest tent, he said, "This way, if you please."

The rain had diminished to a light drizzle. In the few steps to the tent, I saw that its peak had an opening, set opposite the prevailing wind's direction. A thin, almost invisible stream of smoke issued from the opening, vanishing altogether by the time the light breeze had carried it to the edge of the clearing. Ev opened the tent flap, and I followed Lyla inside.

The tent's interior was spacious and airy. The floor, which appeared to be in sections, was rolled back to the walls. In its place was a thick layer of dry fir needles and boughs, which made a soft, sweet smelling carpet on which to sit. The misty, gray daylight from outside was softened even further as it passed through the dun colored walls. In the center was a small cleared area that enclosed a modest campfire, beautifully and efficiently laid, and tended with loving care by Hucklebark, who sat next to a small, neat pile of wood. Works and Spark sat near each other around the fire; all three of them looked up expectantly as we entered.

I was happy to see them, and my happiness had surged when, entering through the flap, my arm lightly brushed against Lyla's back. I recognized a further source of pleasure as the smell of freshly made coffee reached me. Ev, Lyla and I sat down, completing the circle around the fire. Hucklebark reached over to the coffee pot placed near the fire, and made a comradely ritual of pouring and passing.

He passed the last mug around, and looked to me saying, "All present and accounted for, hey Ray?"

"Present company is very close to being more than I could ever have hoped for," I replied. "The only one missing is Lupine. What word do you all have from her?"

Works looked gray and worn, and now his expression took on a note of worry. "We haven't heard from Lupine for several days, Ray. While I don't know anyone who is more capable than she, I confess to some small concern."

I considered all that this might mean. Had Lupine gone off to try some daring idea, as Henry had? I had not thought until that moment about the part she might play in what went forward. Now I suddenly felt that without her, everything would be much less likely to work out. "I understand that concern. When we're done here, I'll look for her. She's the only piece in my puzzle that isn't here." What did I mean by 'my puzzle'? Had a way to move forward been forming itself in my mind, quietly, stealthily? It would seem so; parts of it whispered themselves to my inner ear, but it was not yet whole.

"So," Ev spoke up, "Is this a council of war we're at?"

I thought a moment before answering. "I think I'd prefer to consider it a council of *response*, Ev. I really don't know who might have started this whole thing, but whatever happens next will go better if we think of it that way, instead of like some kind of fighting."

Spark gave me a look of appraisal, underlain with a hint of satisfaction. Works simply nodded his head, as if this was something he'd always expected me to figure out, and I had finally gotten around to it. I was worried about Works, more so than about Lupine. I started to ask him what was wrong, and then bit the question back. Perhaps he would tell me, perhaps not. But I would wait for a chance to ask him alone.

I glanced towards Lyla. She was watching me carefully, waiting. Perhaps she was still waiting to learn who and what I actually was, and if that person would be someone she recognized. I was swept with a feeling of love for her that made me catch my breath. I wanted to talk with her—alone—reassure her that I should be hers, we should be us. But now she spoke.

"What do you have in mind, Ray? Are you ready to move forward?"

I spoke to the group while I looked towards Lyla. "It hasn't all come together yet, no. Maybe it won't come together at all, and I'll just have to make do with what little I understand. I know I need the help of all of you, and I also need Lupine's help. It's pretty clear what I need to do—I just don't know how to do it."

Spark leaned forward slightly. "You are a Mender, Ray. Do you acknowledge this?"

I thought carefully before speaking. Everyone allowed the moment to rest quietly, and waited for me. "Yes, that's what I am, Spark. But," I went on smiling, "Even you have to agree that I'm one seriously green Mender. If there was someone to be apprenticed to, I'd think of myself as an apprentice."

"You are apprenticed to the world and some of its most potent people. We can be of some assistance, but your teachers have already taken you out of our hands."

What did he mean by that? "Lyla told me you said when I fainted I was so 'broken up' you had to work on me for an hour just so I could be moved. What does that mean specifically?"

Spark grimaced. "Essentially, every bone on the left side of your body was broken. How you managed it, I don't know. Perhaps you fell fifteen or twenty feet while you were returning here, and your mind was elsewhere. How you completed the work of locating Lyla and freeing her is even more mysterious."

"I hurt spectacularly just before I passed out, but it doesn't seem like it was nearly bad enough. What happened then?"

"After I got you situated, which as Lyla said took some time, I was, shall I say, politely pushed aside. You were healed by forces I have only heard stories of. They did not reveal themselves to me. I have never seen such damage repaired at all, let alone in the space of a few hours."

Spark, *pushed aside?* Who would have done that? What kind of people had taken me out of the loving hands of Works, Spark, and the others? I asked, "Do you suppose they were the People of The Home?"

Spark's expression was as serious as I had ever seen it. "As I said, I have only heard stories; I may not have met the People of The Home on the same terms as you, but I have some acquaintance with them. It is likely not even appropriate to think of those who are helping you as 'they'. I will remind you once more: No living being in this part of the world—perhaps anywhere in the world—has ever known a Mender. You are enmeshed deeply within forces that no human we are aware of has had relations with in well over a thousand years."

Lyla's hand rested on the floor of fir boughs near me. I placed my hand on hers, and grasped it firmly. She did not look up, but I felt the pressure of her response.

I said quietly, "There is nothing I can do but keep on working, and hope that I don't make any more horrible mistakes. I can only be careful, and carefully ask for help from those I trust." I looked around the circle. "And that, of course, means you all."

Works and Spark met my gaze, and they clearly understood—certainly better than I did—what kinds of changes were upon us. Hucklebark was studying the fire intently, as if to arrange the brands by looking at them, but I knew he was listening just as intently, trying to place all this in some kind of order. I looked over at Lyla, and her eyes were bottomless pools of feeling and concern. It seemed so strange that just a few moments ago we had been laughing and joking with Ev like carefree children.

Everett Longhaul had been so still and quiet I had almost forgotten he was there. His long limbs were ratcheted into as compact a form as could be managed. His eyes looked off into some other place entirely, and I wondered what depths he possessed that I had never suspected.

"Ev," I said softly. He started, and looked over to me as if returning from a long journey. "Where did you go?" I asked.

He shifted, uncomfortable at suddenly being the center of attention. I could see clearly the thoughts that passed through him. First, the impulse to make a joke and avoid answering altogether. Following that, the weighing of needs, looking for which component of his soul was strongest in the moment. And finally, the decision to answer plainly and directly.

"Mother Mountain," he said.

"Why there?"

"That's where we're headed, isn't it?"

"Yes it is," I answered. "What did you find there?"

"Darkness. Rain. Wind. And fire. But nothing is clear."

I felt a soft sigh escape me. "No, nothing at all is clear."

The silence fell heavy in the tent. The rain had begun again, still the light, nourishing patter of Mother Rain. The sound of it, and the whispering hiss of the fire, were comforting and hypnotic. We sat in silence, each working out our own thoughts, considering our destinies. Without explaining to anyone, I gently descended through the fir boughs and the ground into a river of the world's lifeblood flowing in a broad band beneath us. I placed my thanks before me and sat quietly as it whirled and eddied past and through me.

I needed Lupine here, and we would be complete. I asked, and offered, and twined the river about me. We traveled outward, seeking the life I called Lupine.

We ranged over the foothills, through the valleys, up over peaks. I gently guided us mainly to the south and east, not knowing exactly why. But in a place about ten miles to the south east of where I sat with the others in a warm, dry tent, I found her striding along a cold and sodden trail, the rain at that lower altitude much heavier. She was alone. I gently brushed against her mind.

Lupine.

Instantly I was buffeted by a blast of defensive energy, pushed back and fended off in an angry wave.

Lupine, it's me. You don't need to greet me like that.

Ray? Come closer. But not too close.

I approached again, still wrapped in the stream. I did not come as close this time.

All right, it is you. Forgive me; I've been beset by people who won't leave me be. What do you want?

I—we—need your help. Very soon I'll have to deal with the Destroyer. Will you come to us?

Of course. You seem to be able to find me, but I don't know where you are. And who is 'we'?

Works, Spark, Hucklebark, Ev, and Lyla. Works has been worried about you. We are in a small clearing on the lip of the Carbon Canyon, about a mile north of The Home.

Tell Works I will make my full apologies and tell my story in about three hours. After I get dried out a bit, that is. I am cold, soaked, and too hungry for small politenesses. Please leave me now—I need to concentrate on getting to you.

I withdrew, returned to the place where we all sat together, said my deep thanks to the river, and settled into my place at the fire. It was very hard to tell whether a minute or an hour had passed, but everyone sat exactly as before, quiet and contemplative. I caught Works' eye.

"Lupine will be here in about three hours. She apparently has something of interest to tell you." Turning to Ev, I said, "And it grieves me to say that she will be cold, wet, and furiously hungry."

Everett Longhaul frowned to himself in thought for a moment, then looked up with his more customary broad smile. "Yes, that'll do. Not a moment to be lost, though." Looking back to Works, he said, "You'll excuse me?"

Works, whose face had come back to life when I told him she would be here in hours, smiled widely. "From and for you, Everett, I will excuse most anything."

Ev was up and out of the tent before tossing back a "See you then!" We could hear the rattle of his pack as it leapt onto his back, and four or five of his great strides before the sound of his passage dwindled back into the lightly pattering rain.

I looked up to the circle with a question I had not thought to ask until then. "Where is Ev's tent?"

Hucklebark snorted. "I've always figured he sleeps in that pack of his, it's big enough you know."

Works gently waved the remark aside with a smile. "Everett is a very private young man, Ray. There is much we don't know about his life and habits, and our love for him is such we would never dream of prying."

I suspected Works knew a great deal more than that about Ev. But once more, Works had ever so gently and kindly asked me to mind my own business. All right, I said inwardly, maybe I'll learn how to do that some day.

Works said, "So in the two minutes of our silence, you traversed the landscape until you found Lupine, and then spoke with her. Do I have it right?"

"Well, um, yes," I stammered.

Works nodded. "Is there more you can tell us before she arrives?"

"No, not a thing. Except that she chased me off with the mental equivalent of a double bladed axe before I could identify myself."

He nodded again. "This is becoming as complicated as I feared it might." He sighed. "Lupine will undoubtedly bring us something important to consider. In the meantime, Ray, what is your intention?"

The next piece of unfinished business presented itself to me in no uncertain terms. "I have to at least try to meet with the People of The Home again. It's important—to me, at least—that they hear my apology for my behavior when I found that Lyla had disappeared."

Lyla had apparently heard the story from Works or Spark, for she simply nodded in agreement.

"When do you plan on this?"

"More or less immediately," I replied. "In a way it's a risk, but I would prefer to go there now."

"I agree on both counts," Works said. He turned to Spark. "What is your opinion?"

"I envision Ray returning to the place where I took him and sitting there quietly, without expectation or demand, in the hopes that The People will wish to speak with him." He gave me a significant look. "Is my vision correct?"

"In every detail," I said. "With the permission of you all, I'll get going."

Works looked tired and worn out again; knowing that Lupine would return soon had cheered him greatly, but now I was introducing another moment of heavy uncertainty directly on top of it. I regretted it intensely, and I wanted to find some way to tell him I was sorry to cause him such worry. But no good way to do that showed itself; I nodded to the company, and made my way through the tent flap.

I was back in the tent Ev had brought for me, searching to see if he had also brought me a jacket, or perhaps been able to salvage my old one. I found a jacket—not new, but in excellent condition, and perfect for the day's weather, and was slipping it on when I heard the tent flap rustle. It was Lyla.

"Ray, I want to come with you. I know it's something that only you must do, and I don't have any illusions about seeing them with you or anything, but I don't want to—"

I had moved over to the tent's entrance, and lightly placed a finger over her lips. She stopped, and I moved my hand away and kissed her.

"I don't want to be away from you for a minute. Come with me, then."

She was relieved and worried at the same time. "Are you sure it's all right?"

"I'm sure of *nothing* right now. But if The People can't see that if I go alone only half of my heart is with me, I don't know how I could explain it to them."

She smiled, hugged me fiercely, and then looked up and said, "I hope we have more than a day, or an hour, to get to know one another better."

I smiled too, though I wasn't sure that I felt like smiling. "So do I, lovely woman. So do I."

The rain had stopped and the sky had lifted a bit as we walked the mile along the canyon's edge towards The Home. I hadn't bothered to check the time of day, but even though the clouds still concealed the sun they couldn't hide the fact that it was heading downwards, getting ready to fall beyond the Mountain. We walked hand in hand, in silence, currents of feeling racing between us. Lyla's hands, after years of living on Tahoma, were much tougher than mine. And yet her skin was imbued with a vigor, a tender and ferocious love of life and all that lived around her, that shaped that toughness into something beautiful, wild, and fragile. I wondered how such a passionate, self-possessed woman could find in me someone she wanted to know better. I wondered how such an ac-complished, experienced and wise group of people could find in me someone who belonged with them, someone who had something important to offer.

But it all came down to trust, didn't it? In the midst of bewil-dering uncertainty, having no idea if tomorrow I might be alive, dead, or still human, Lyla trusted my heart, believed she was a part of it, and it a part of her. Works trusted me to do what needed doing, to learn what I needed to know, to become what the world appeared to intend me to become. Hucklebark trusted me to be nothing more than Ray Holdman, and trusted the world to make that possible. I would trust them all, for they deserved much more from me than trust. I would love them all, feeling like there was much more I should offer them. Lupine had taught me to examine all of my fear, and simply discard what wasn't necessary. I found now, in this moment, that very little of the fear I carried was necessary, and I neglected to carry it any further. It vanished as it hit the ground by the side of the rough trail we walked on, and I trusted the earth to deal with it appropriately.

We came to the small circle of level ground, beyond which the land sloped sharply downwards and then back up to the precipitous wall of The Home. I stood, uncertain.

"Spark had me lie down, with my head facing The Home, so that I was looking to the south. But this time that doesn't feel right. I feel like we should sit, facing towards The Home, but not staring at it."

Without hesitation Lyla said, "Then that's what we'll do." She sat down decisively, and with a brief grin I sat down beside her.

I took her hand again and we sat quietly, mostly looking at the ground in front of us. I made a point of expecting nothing, requiring nothing. I remembered all the unneeded fear that had seeped into the ground on the way to this place. I looked at what fear was left, and found there was nothing to do about it but wait and be alert to the world. And I remembered how I had learned to become still during the search for Lyla, and practiced that again now. I was prepared to sit through the night, though I confess I fervently hoped it wouldn't come to that.

I was deep in that stillness, allowing my thoughts to waft away like smoke, when I felt Lyla's hand squeeze mine, hard. Thinking to come back to the place and time where we sat, I discovered instead that it was dark; not the dark of nightfall, but the utter darkness that comes from being taken inside a mountain. For several minutes there was no sensation of any kind, neither warm nor cold, nothing to sense or perceive. Eventually I saw the faint glow growing slowly before me. Another few moments and I could see that I was again in the room of beautifully curved cedar planks, seated on the soft floor of fir and forest duff. In front of me lay the depression, with the small fire burning neatly within it.

Abruptly I discovered that Lyla's hand was still in mine. I turned to see her seated next to me, a look of deepest wonder across her face. I squeezed her hand to communicate my joy, and she returned it, all the while looking about her as I had done before. I breathed in the sweet smell of the cedar, and felt like I had already been forgiven.

A tiny gasp from Lyla made me look up. Tarn and Zephyr sat across the fire from us. As I faced him, all that Tarn had said to me at Mender's Camp came back in a rush, and I was suddenly not so sure of forgiveness. The fear began to return, despite its having been left behind on the trail. But it seemed to me that this time it was up to me to speak; I left the fear to fend for itself and spoke anyway.

"Thank you for allowing me this chance to make amends. And thank you for allowing Lyla to be with me. Once again, I have brought nothing to offer but my respect, my gratitude, and my apology for being so weak as to forget all that you tried so hard to teach me."

Zephyr smiled, and Tarn nodded. He looked towards Lyla. "Welcome, daughter."

Zephyr said, "Times change indeed. Now, not only do we greet one of the human people, but two."

Tarn cocked an eyebrow, first at her, then at us. "I think the first time we greeted a fragment of one, and now we greet something very much closer to the whole."

Zephyr laughed. "Well spoken." Turning to me she said, "Why do you return here, Ray Holdman?"

I stopped to collect my thoughts. I wanted to say what needed saying, and to say it well, for once. They waited patiently. Lyla had let go of my hand, as if to let me get on with it without distraction. She sat composed, every fiber of her being alert and attentive.

To Tarn I said, "When I realized that my fear and foolishness had made you regret reaching out to me, and made you feel that I had done violence to the Agreements you made with my people, I was devastated. By making that effort one more time—by coming to me with harsh but necessary words, you are the one who brought me back to who and what I must be, perhaps in the only way it could have been done. I already had more to thank you for than I could ever express, but now there is that much more again. I am here to offer my gratitude. I have no business hoping for forgiveness, but humans can't seem to help themselves, and I confess to hoping anyway."

Tarn spoke slowly, as if he too was collecting his thoughts and speaking carefully. "You will notice that neither Rill nor Riven, nor Fell nor Taiga are here. They found their first encounter with you to be important and necessary, but too difficult to wish to repeat. I will tell you that I also was reluctant to respond when we knew you were coming here again. Had it not been for Zephyr's opinion, I might have declined myself."

He turned to Zephyr, as if he had said as much as he wished to, and she should continue.

Zephyr turned to Lyla. "Daughter, we have observed your work for some time now, and we honor it. The trees love and respect you in ways they rarely if ever bear for your kind. Even when all peoples reverenced them and spoke to them, they maintained a strict reserve that they have willingly broken with you. Know that you carry our good wishes and good will."

Lyla sat stock still, gazing at Zephyr, her lips just slightly parted in complete astonishment. She suddenly flushed, and looked downward in confusion.

Zephyr turned to me. "I am by far the youngest of my clan, Ray Holdman. It is still just possible for me to have some inkling of how your people feel and act, and through recent ages I have watched them more than the rest of my family. You yourself have already wrought great change on the landscape, and yet that is minor compared to the changes being wrought within you. We are pleased with the courage you have demonstrated, and glad that you were able to act, so helping to preserve the daughter of the trees."

I was trying hard to hold on to every word Zephyr said, and it took a moment to realize she was talking about Lyla. I had already thought I knew that Lyla was a person of considerable depth and power. Was I being told now that what I knew barely scratched the surface? All I could do was to stammer, "Thank you."

Tarn began again, "We know that you remembered some of what we taught you. Do you also recall the Agreements?"

"I could never have found Lyla if I did not," I said quietly. "I now know all too well the consequences of forgetting them, and I will not lose them again."

Tarn nodded. "Your work is barely begun, Ray Holdman. Stay within your people, remember what you have been taught, and work well. That is all we ask, and all we expect. If you can do these things, we are willing to consider our Agreement with your people restored."

Stay within your people. How long ago, now—less than three weeks—was the time when I not only had no *people*, as far as I had known I had nothing whatever of any value? Now, there was nothing more in life that I needed beyond the necessities for keeping it going. And now too, there was everything to lose if I failed to keep well what was given. Did Lupine know how truly right she was to say, *remember?*

The smell of cedar and wood smoke began to fade, and the light dimmed. My hand sought Lyla's, and it was there, warm and reassuring. In the absolute darkness of our passage away from The People, I could neither feel nor sense anything at all except her hand pressed into mine.

Chapter 36

The darkness lightened, but not a great deal. It was enough to see the deeper blackness of the wall of The Home in front of us, and know that we were again sitting in the small, level circle at the end of the Carbon Canyon's east wall. The cloud cover still shut out the starlight and most of the moonlight, but I was glad to see that it had not started to rain again.

I got slowly to my feet, still holding Lyla's hand, and gently pulled her up too. She was silent, entirely absorbed, and I did not care to disturb her. We began walking slowly down towards our camp, side by side.

The darkness made the going difficult until I remembered that I'd been given another way to do this. Dropping my awareness a short distance into the ground, I found a river and lightly touched it. Once within, the way was clear without needing to see. Lyla stayed very close, still wrapped in her reverie. I could only imagine; not only had she not expected to be invited in—had been worried, in fact, that she might be considered an intruder—but they *knew* her. Knew her work, respected it, and considered her the *daughter of the trees*. I felt a surge of pride for her, followed closely by a stronger surge of affection. This in turn gave way to a stronger than ever sense of wonder that this woman was walking with me, her hand in mine. Despite the worry of whatever lay in store for me—for us all—I felt complete in that moment. And immediately saw that feeling as something equally important to remember.

When we reached our camp there was a faint glow emanating

from Spark and Works' tent, while all the others were completely dark. We stopped at the edge of the clearing, and I turned to Lyla, unwilling to break the silent spell we shared, but needing to.

"I have to tell Works about how this all went, and if Lupine's here I need to talk to her too. Do you want to come in, or do you need some time alone?"

"Thank you for asking, Ray," she said. "I need the time, I think. It's nice to be able to take a little while when someone turns your life inside out, whether or not it's a good thing. If nothing else, it takes a bit to figure out if it is a good thing."

I squeezed her hand lightly. "Will you tell me about it when you've got it better sorted out?"

"Of course I will. What are you going to tell Works about the People?"

"Everything about what they told me about me, and only that you were invited too. I'll leave your part of the story for when you want to tell it."

"Thanks," she said.

I leaned over, kissed her lightly on the cheek, and released her hand. She moved off slowly towards her tent, and I made my way to the front of the larger tent.

I stood in front of it for a minute, wondering what the protocol was with tents. It wasn't exactly possible to knock. Everett Longhaul had made a joke of requesting entrance with his theatrical throat clearing, but I wasn't in the mood for jokes, and I doubted Spark or Works were either.

In any event, the problem was solved for me when I heard Works' deep, mellow voice. "Come on in, Ray."

Spark, Works and Hucklebark were in the same places they had been when I had last been here. Ev was nowhere to be seen, off no doubt on one, several or many of his endless errands. Next to Spark sat Lupine, looking stiff and weary. Her clothing was clean and dry, meaning that as usual, Ev had performed the impossible and gotten back with supplies for her before she arrived. But her face and arms were a patchwork of scratches, and one arm had an ugly weal that had clearly been ministered to by Spark, and was just beginning to heal. I wondered if she had run afoul of a cougar, or something worse.

I sat next to Hucklebark with a smile of greeting. He grinned back, his expression cutting through the feeling of seriousness that lay like a heavy blanket on the gathering. He punched me lightly on the arm. "Hey, good to see you back in one piece."

I glanced over to Works, and was filled with alarm. He looked positively gray, and so tired that simply sitting upright was a challenging job. I felt a stab of remorse; maybe I was the cause of all this, maybe not, but it hurt to see him so drained. I resolved to get him alone, if only for a minute, at the first opportunity; perhaps I could work a little on his behalf as had happened with Lyla.

"Right on time, Ray," Works said with a smile that clearly required effort. "Lupine arrived less than an hour ago, and we thought we would wait for a bit to see if you returned tonight. We've filled her in, at least as much as can be done in a short time, on what's happened here. Before we get to her story, do you have anything to tell? And where is Lyla?"

"Lyla is taking time to absorb some things the People told her," I replied. Eyebrows lifted all around as the implications of that sank in. I described meeting Tarn and Zephyr, how we had been received and, in so many words, given their blessing.

"That's about it," I said. I turned and said, "Lupine, I'm more glad than I can say to see you here, and whole at least, if not in the best of shape."

As soon as I said it, I wanted to take it back. Lupine wasn't the sort of person to accept over-familiar remarks, and I knew that. But instead of a retort, or any other kind of answer, she studied me. I could feel her concentrating and focusing all the power she had accumulated through years, maybe centuries, of plumbing the deep places of the world, and bringing them to bear on her scrutiny of me. My first impulse was to escape. It required all of my willpower to sit calmly and allow her to study me. The second impulse was to resist, and I had to do the same with that. I used what Lupine herself had taught me, and asked once again what I was afraid of.

What did I think Lupine would find by searching me so deeply? I had to think it through step by step. She would find my work with the great world rivers, the way I had found and helped to restore Lyla, and my intense love for her. She would find remnants of the shame and regret that had paralyzed me after misusing what I'd been given, when I had so ludicrously tried to kill the Destroyer. She might even find the pieces of ideas in my mind, still waiting to be assembled into an actionable plan for how to proceed. Beyond all this, she might encounter those islands of history buried deep in my being, fragments from a lifetime of isolation, fear and pain.

And what of it? I had nothing to hide from Lupine. If she chose to judge me one way or another, there wasn't a thing I could do about it. And when I considered carefully, I knew that her judgment would change nothing. Although she was a formidable friend, a reserved, perhaps even an aloof one, Lupine was still a friend. So, then: I was carrying a great basket of unnecessary fear, which I promptly neglected to hold onto for another moment. It slipped away, and I waited patiently while she examined me, her whole body vibrating with the intensity of her gaze.

A small part of me registered the absolute quiet, the stillness of all the people around the little campfire. By far the greatest part of me was responding to Lupine, allowing her to see whatever she wished. Eventually, the tension she was holding began to subside; the energy she had brought to bear started to diffuse, and her gaze softened somewhat. When the questing electricity of her look had subsided to nearly normal—for her, that is—I spoke.

"Whatever you're looking for, if I can help you find it, I will," I said softly.

Her response was equally soft, a surprising thing from Lupine. "Spark is right, as he is always right. You are a deep mystery, Ray Holdman. A volcanic uprising, or an earthquake, they happen in an instant, a few moments. But it requires a long, long time of preparation to bring them to bear. What process has been working, and for how long, to bring you about?"

"I would tell you, if it was any less a mystery to me," I said.

Works spoke up at this point. "We have a number of mysteries to deal with at this point, and unfortunately, Ray's is the only one that doesn't pose an immediate threat to us. Lupine, are you ready to tell us where you've been, and what you've found?"

Lupine and I simultaneously broke the spell of communication we had woven together, and returned fully to the group seated before us.

"I didn't mean to be gone so long, as you know, Works," Lupine began. "I'm sorry to have worried you. But I needed to do some searching, some asking and some thinking on my own. This region has suddenly become a lot more unstable than any of us might have imagined. This Destroyer thing, in its movement and its attacks on people, has unbalanced some important places. If it isn't stopped, or made harmless, or whatever can be done, there will be some huge changes in the landscape. And I don't think we'll care for any of them."

Spark and Works seemed to understand immediately what she was saying. Hucklebark appeared to simply take it all in and store it. But I didn't know exactly what Lupine meant. "What kind of changes, I mean what kind of instability did you find, Lupine?"

She turned back to me. "You've traveled in some of these places way down deep, Ray. You must have seen and felt how delicately all those forces are balanced to hold them in equilibrium, so that movement, when it comes, is gradual, rather than a violent spasm. Many of these places are in imminent danger of losing that equilibrium, and we—and all the peoples in this region—can only stand so much violent change."

"I should have noticed that," I murmured to myself.

"How could you?" Lupine said. "You can't know something has changed when you've never been there before. I've been through those places any number of times, over a lot of years. If you'd done that too, you would have noticed."

At first I was disconcerted that she had heard me and chosen to respond. But then I realized that she was coming near to talking to me as an equal. That was as daunting as it was exhilarating, but I felt a glow of satisfaction, maybe accomplishment, to think that she might feel that way.

Works was regarding Lupine, concern and worry still written plain on his face. "Is there more you wish to tell, daughter?"

Lupine looked uncomfortable, then resolved. "My relations with a great many people—from many walks of life—have been disrupted. Many who I considered allies and friends have turned against me. It has become exceedingly dangerous, or outright impossible, for me to work with them. This thing is isolating us, Works. We have very little time in which to act, and there is no one else to help us. With every hour that passes, the urgency increases."

Spark had been silent so far. Now he turned to me and said, "Very well, then. Ray, if you have a plan, or even an idea, of how to move forward, now is a good time to discuss it."

I considered my reply carefully. "I have pieces of a plan. I need time tonight to try and fit them together. Whether or not I come up with it, it's clear we need to move tomorrow—the earlier the better."

Spark said, "And to where shall we move, early tomorrow?"

"It will be Mother Mountain. I think you all know from my story there is someone there who is instrumental in all this. I'm certain that's the place where I should do what I'm going to do."

No one spoke for a moment. Then Works said, "What exactly is it you plan to do, Ray?"

I smiled self-consciously. Despite Lupine's seeming new confidence, the feeling that I was totally inadequate to this task rose up, trying to smother my reason and courage. By looking around the circle at the friends who sat with me, I fought it to a standstill—for the moment. "That is where I have to beg your indulgence for one more night. If I don't feel clear about it in the morning, I'll say so."

Works looked thoughtfully down, and then back at me. He looked so exhausted I wondered how he could still be thinking and speaking. "All right, then. We'll let things rest where they are, until tomorrow."

Hucklebark and Lupine said muted good nights, and left for their own tents. I remained where I was. I wanted to ask Spark a favor, but a deep reluctance held me back for several moments. We sat quietly, no one saying anything at all.

As if he had heard my thoughts, or knew my need without any prompting, Spark rose to his feet, crouching so that his long frame fit under the tent's roof. "I believe I shall walk, and think for a bit before sleep." He glanced over in my direction. "Good night, Ray. I wish you a fruitful evening."

"Thank you, Spark, and good night."

He left the tent, and Works and I sat facing each other. I did not know how to begin, even though I knew exactly what was on my mind. I made several false starts, and lapsed back into silence each time.

Works smiled gently, through his exhaustion. "I don't see any way to make it easier for you, Ray. I would make it so if I could. Go on and say what you need to, and know that I don't bite—especially my own people."

To think that I was one of Works' 'own people' made my heart lurch with a stew of emotions that brought both pleasure and pain. In the wildest dreams I had spent a lifetime suppressing, I had never once considered the possibility that I could be noticed, let alone cared for, by someone like Works.

"I—I'm worried that you'll think me arrogant, Works. Or worse, still just an ignorant fool blundering into places of power and responsibility he has no business being involved with."

"Spark reminded you that at least in this part of the world, and maybe in all the world, there has been no Mender in living memory," Works said quietly. "Perhaps you haven't had time to consider the true meaning of this. First of all, it means there is no tradition from which you can draw inspiration and direction—none whatever. Secondly, it means that you have no choice but to travel and work in places most of us can never reach. For someone who didn't even know *we* exist until a very short time ago, that is a far greater leap than the world could safely ask of anyone. Thirdly," he said with another smile, "You would have to abuse what has been given you—without learning from your mistakes—more than once for me to consider you arrogant. Now, son, out with it."

I let out a deep breath in an explosive sigh. "I'm worried about you. I'm terrified of losing you; not just selfishly—though I won't deny that—but on behalf of all of us. I don't pretend to know anything more than how to get in trouble, but if there is anything in the world I can do to help you, I want to do it."

Works said gently, "Do you have any thoughts at all concerning what you might do to help?"

"I don't think I can take any credit for Lyla's recovery. I mean, it's as much a miracle to me as it is to anyone. But I can't help wondering why I shouldn't offer to try for the same sort of thing for you."

Works was quiet for long enough I thought he wasn't going to answer. Finally he said, "Whether or not you can take credit for that, you are responsible for it. But when you and I are finished here, Spark will come back, and he has some very specific things to work on with me. If we all get through the next few days, and there is time, come and ask me again. In the meantime, thank you for your concern. And thank you for bringing Lyla back to us, Ray. Her loss would have been a fearsome one we might not have recovered from."

"That at least I understand perfectly," I replied. "It's clear I need to leave you alone. May I ask just one more question?"

"Of course, Ray."

"Is everyone else all right? I mean, I haven't heard about anyone else since the gathering."

Works sighed, and seemed to grow heavier. "There have been a small number of attacks, with accompanying injury that ranges from moderate to severe. And there has been one other death."

I sat up suddenly. "Who?"

"I believe you met him at the gathering. His name was Douglas."

"But… he was in the same alpine fir I was, in Vernal Park," I sputtered. "He was never in the little cedar before the Destroyer struck it. What could have happened?"

"Douglas chose to ignore my repeated requests that he suspend his work until we could sort this out," Works replied wearily. "And as did our dear friend Henry, he paid for it with his life."

I sat silent, taking this in. I remembered Douglas saying, 'I fervently hope you don't need my help, but if you do…' Now it didn't matter if I did or not. Was he trying, like Henry had done, something or some way to resist the Destroyer? I'd likely never know. "I'm sorry. Truly sorry," I said.

"I know you are, Ray. But now I think you might need some time to work through what tomorrow will look like for us. And I'm quite ready for Spark's help."

I got to my feet abruptly. "It's high time for me to get going. Thank you, Works."

He regarded me with a twinkle in his eye that heartened me more than any assurances of his health could have. "You're welcome," was all he said.

Chapter 37

It had been dim in Works' tent, but the darkness outside it was far deeper. Without waiting for my eyes to adjust to it, I slipped softly into the ground, and let the river guide me over the few steps to my own tent.

Once inside, a few moments of careful scrabbling produced the candle lantern Ev had provided me with, and by its modest glow I put things in better order. I wanted everything to be perfectly ready for the dawn, though why it needed doing now I didn't know. With everything neatly stowed away I sat cross-legged, facing the tiny lantern now hanging from its loop in the tent's ceiling.

The night was a cool, heavy cloak that passed effortlessly through the thin walls of the tent and wrapped itself around me. The silence was profound; even the river canyon seemed to have decided to leave off dropping its stone and soil onto the glacier, for there was no rumbling, clacking rattle emanating from that direction. Nor was there the slightest sound from wind, trees, or any other form of life. Far from being oppressive, the silence felt like a welcoming place to be, and I gratefully began to settle into it.

I also settled back into the ground, with the same kind of heavy, gentle silence. I had thought I needed to spend this night thinking, hard and purposefully. Instead, I softly dropped into a life river and rested there, listening, sensing.

It felt right to be there. A part of my mind rebelled at quiescence; it insisted that I be planning, thinking through contingencies, figuring out what to say when I met the others in the morning.

That part of me was overruled by a certainty I had not realized was also there. This was what I should be doing—nothing. I should be here, immersed in this river, and I should wait, and listen, and neglect to hatch plots or even to think.

The less I *did*, the more deeply I entered into the river. The quieter I became, the further my senses reached without concerning themselves with reaching. I practiced allowing thought to pass through me and away. The river made itself known to me, and without thinking enough to be afraid, I allowed it to dissolve the last walls that kept me apart from the rest of the world.

I grew into the river, and the differences between it and myself became smaller and smaller. I was the river, and it was me. And yet there was still an *I* to experience and wonder at it all. The mystery of being truly submerged in another form of being while still thinking and sensing the world as myself was a deep one, and yet it was, for a change, a comfortable mystery.

I could sense everything that flowed within the river, touch everything it touched. The people I knew and loved were now not merely close by, they were *here*—here being everywhere—and I needed no movement at all to know their presence, though I chose to let them rest.

There were other rivers nearby. They ran as deep and strong as this one did. I admired them, watched them, too. They were on either side, and above and below. As I observed them, I began to think that perhaps they were moving towards me, very slowly. There was no disturbance anywhere; they simply edged closer to where I rested.

Ask, offer, join. They were coming, waiting only to be asked, waiting to receive my offer. I made the request, offered the pitiful scrap of life and consciousness that is me, and they accepted. The rivers began to merge, quietly and without fuss. They entered into me and I into them, for by now there was no barrier possible within me. It seemed like I could see and feel to the ends of the earth; all the rivers that had coursed through the palm of the old woman's hand were there to be sensed, including those where I was not permitted to go. The world was a map to me, a map through which I moved and lived.

I rested within a moving ocean of life and energy that was immense and irresistible. If I asked in the right way, perhaps it would move as I asked. If I were to wield this unimaginable force, perhaps it could help me to mend the great gash in the world's fabric, without creating havoc. Perhaps I could actually do what must be done.

But it was not complete. Something was still lacking, and I pondered this for some time, concerned and uneasy. What was still missing?

The People of The Home came to mind. Something Tarn had said lay just below the surface, something important. I had to force myself to be patient, to wait for it to slowly rise up to where I could see it. "I think the first time, we greeted a fragment of one, and now we greet something very much closer to the whole."

Lyla. Of course, Lyla was what was missing. I suddenly knew and accepted unconditionally the wisdom Tarn had expressed: apart, we were strong but incomplete; together, we approached a whole being.

There was no distance to traverse. She was simply there, part of a seemingly infinite multitude of life and lives. Lyla was asleep; I gently, carefully brushed against her mind.

I could feel her wake with a start, momentarily alarmed that someone was inside the tent with her. Wordlessly I greeted her, and felt a sharp instant of indignation that was immediately replaced by a quiet, serious questioning.

I answered by asking her to come with me into the rivers. Without hesitation, she accepted.

Communicating in this way with Hucklebark, and later with Lupine, had been difficult, almost laborious. With Lyla it was effortless, instantaneous. I drew her into the rivers and she came, wrapped in wonder and delight. We rested, weightless and substantial in the same moment, in the great stream. I let her alone, to get used to the experience, for quite a while.

I formed an intention and tried to grow it outwards. I wanted to encompass the rivers now running together with us in them; could I induce them to move with me?

I tried, but I could not wrap myself around them, as I had around the much smaller rivers when I had found Lyla. Whether it was spirit, experience, courage or intention, something was too small, or lacking in some other way. After another attempt that was thwarted like the others—as if I were reaching for something just beyond my grasp—I gave up and sat quietly, thinking and then trying not to think.

Eventually it was Lyla who broke the silence of thought. We were living at a level far below words and sounds. Her question was more like the echo of a sound long past that I understood and could respond to. I answered by allowing what understanding I possessed to flow towards her. Although it felt like something well beyond speaking and hearing, it also felt like something we were barely using, something we hardly understood. I hoped we would get better at it by tomorrow, for it seemed likely we'd need it.

Our minds, our senses and awareness lay side by side, deep, deep within the world. The stream around us continued to grow in strength and depth as more rivers altered their courses to coincide with ours. We rested in the midst of a mighty current, the kind of current that brings huge change to the world, and we almost had what was needed.

There was more to be done, but I did not know how to go about it. Lyla did, though.

It was as if she had simply been waiting for this opportunity, as if my coming and the things given to me were meant for her too. Perhaps it had to do with many years of deep communion with the trees, but Lyla knew what to do.

She entered me as she would enter a tree, which means she stood outside, and asked to come in. I was so startled it took a long moment for me to say without saying, *yes*. And then, though there were still two of us, there was also one of us. I explored the way that it felt, immersed in wonder at the place I had come to in the tiny fragment of time since Hucklebark had found me trying to talk to a willow.

My strengths, her strengths, were a single thing. Her understanding and mine combined, and the way each of us understood what was happening and what was to be done leaped upwards and outward. I had had to learn, laboriously and with short but hard practice, to leave off with my wall building, and to really let the trees, the glaciers, and the humans in. It was effortless with Lyla; she asked, I accepted, and we were thinking, feeling and working together as one.

I stretched our intention outward. We encircled the immense stream, enfolded it. We asked, and offered, and the offer was accepted. We joined with the streams that were joined, and plunged deeper still into the world and its life.

Gently, with the greatest of care we moved the great stream, a tiny movement that altered their flow almost imperceptibly. A little more pressure, still exerted gently, and it moved further. We moved with them, all of us moving in perfect synchrony. Slowly we began to divert the streams, moving them through the earth as delicately as we could; not so much for a particular purpose, not yet. But to understand how it felt to ask them to move, to nudge them, to feel them respond and then respond in kind. We practiced, and the great stream practiced with us.

An idea formed itself quietly in us, rising slowly to a place in our awareness where we could see it. Very nearby there was a dead, charcoal gray circle, where a great tree and all its attendant plants had lived. Would this strong, intense collective of life we were within be willing to help clear away the stain of that death, to restore that small area to a condition of hope?

We moved them, always asking, offering, responding. They moved. We could sense a roughly cylinder-shaped area of dead ground that extended far down into the earth, and we moved towards it. We came next to that place, and felt the stream resist moving any closer. We rested quietly, not demanding or pushing. We asked once more, offered to be a part of the work in whatever way we could. The stream moved up to the dead place, brushed against it. We felt the foulness, the piercing sense of pollution, as the great bundle of rivers pushed against it. Something seemed to crumble away from that place, and was carried off by the streams.

We moved them again, came up against that horrid place again, and something more broke away, taken by the rivers to a destination we could not guess.

We worked this way for what seemed a long time, moving, nudging, withstanding the foulness as it was abraded from that place and swept away. In time, the cylinder of dead earth shrank, became a pipe, then a tube, then a pencil pointing straight up and down in the ground, and with a final, swaying movement the rivers slowly broke over it and brushed aside the last of the pollution, breaking it into pieces and carrying it off as a river of water would break down an earthen dam. What was left was a place of emptiness; empty, but ready to begin again, to receive life and harbor it.

Lyla and I relaxed our hold, and the rivers relaxed theirs. We rested, radiating gratitude. The Destroyer had not come; had it not noticed the work? How was that possible? Perhaps we had worked in such stillness, with such quiet, that its attention had not been attracted. As grateful as I was that we'd been allowed to just work, I felt we must not depend on that going forward. I thought again of Henry and his incredible decoy, and had yet another reason for gratitude that would never diminish.

The idea came to us that it was time to leave here for now. It was time to go back, to get ready for the real work to come.

Lyla left me as she had entered, gracefully and without ceremony. We lay again within the rivers, side by side, watching and feeling as the rivers slowly unwound themselves from around each other, moving back into the courses they had left. When they had all moved away, and we were resting in the one river I had first entered, I brought Lyla out from it, left her as I had found her, and returned to a body, a tent, and a candle lantern.

Part Seven

The Mountain Spruce

Sometimes there is a tension inside that makes me want to scream, to run away, do whatever it takes to be distracted from it. Yet I gave up running from it years ago; there is no escaping it, and pretending otherwise always results in more pain and more danger when I try to flee.

Sometimes it feels like the only reason I'm still alive is that the trees have gifted me with something, imbued me with some quality that helps me to skirt the borders of human madness, and to instinctively avoid the worst trouble. But I have no idea what that something, that quality, might be, if it is even there. At other times it feels like the trees, the plants, even the stones in the ground are not just talking to me—they are shouting at me. The pressure they exert can be unbearable, and I want to yell back, What do you want from me?

For there is something they want, and they want it badly. I feel like pounding my temples to beat some understanding into myself, as if that would help. Why can I not understand them? Why must their language, their lives and their need be so far beyond me?

(Okanogan Wilderness, September 1997)

Chapter 38

I slowly rose to my feet outside of the little tent. In the course of two days I had become accustomed to it, and it felt as much like home as anything I could remember. I looked back at it with affection, a feeling of familiarity and gratitude that extended from the tent itself to Everett Longhaul, who had carried so many things on that strong, narrow back of his—including me.

The dawn was still at least an hour away, and the night still held the land wrapped in its cloud-covered darkness. The camp lay profoundly quiet. Yet I knew that everyone in it was awake, and all but Lyla and I were gathered in the larger tent that housed Works and Spark. At first I wondered how I could take that knowledge for granted, then realized that not only the feeling of intense connection with the world and its energy remained with me, but some of that connection itself remained also. The land was silent around us; not merely the hush that comes before a new day, but as if the landscape was holding its breath, ready to brace itself against some new or different thing just over the horizon.

I didn't need the soft rustling and the scritch of a tent flap zipper to tell me that Lyla had emerged from her tent. I could feel her presence like I could feel my own pulse. Perhaps it was not possible to completely separate after coming together to work in the way we had, not possible to go back to things just as they were before. I found I didn't mind that at all, if it were so.

Lyla's footsteps through the dew-laden grass were so soft I would have had difficulty hearing them. As it was, I felt her every movement as she came over to where I stood. She stopped only a couple of feet away from me, and then I could see as well as sense her.

Her expression was solemn, and yet it radiated a joy that made my heart leap with hers. We regarded each other wordlessly, as if seeing each other for the first time. It felt like finally encountering a long-lost, virtually forgotten part of myself, but the feeling was mixed with the fierce and tender delight of loving another, the joy of being both deeply inside myself and outside, too.

Lyla lifted her hand, and rested it lightly against my cheek. Her touch was warm and electric.

I said softly, "We did something important."

She smiled and said, "Several things." She removed her hand, letting it rest by her side. "But now we have to go to the others, and get ready to do some more important things."

We walked slowly over to the larger tent. The ground beneath me, and Lyla beside me, were alive and immediate. When we reached the tent flap, I lifted it and entered without preamble, Lyla directly behind me.

There were two spaces in the circle of people there, and we settled ourselves down in them, completing it. Works, Spark, Ev, Lupine and Hucklebark all wore serious expressions, as suited the occasion. No one spoke for a moment. There had been a swirling of energy as we entered and sat, that I was certain everyone could feel. We waited as it too settled, and became still again.

Spark looked at me closely, and spoke. "We see that you have been busy this past night."

"Yes, very," I replied. "I have to hope we've been busy enough."

"We are as prepared for what comes next as it is possible to be," Works said. I looked over to him, and saw that he looked better this morning. Whatever work Spark had done with him through the night had helped a great deal, though he still looked thoroughly worn and tired. Works looked around the circle once, then to me. "Do you have what you need to carry this through, Ray?"

"Nothing but the doing itself can answer that," I said. "But if I had asked for the most powerful, true and capable friends I could imagine, it would have fallen short of all of you here."

Lupine stirred, and spoke. "As usual, handsomely said, Ray. But can you finally end our suspense, and give us some idea of what you have in mind?"

I took a deep breath, and plunged. "Before anyone points this out to me, I'm well aware that this isn't really a *plan*. I have to meet the Destroyer, learn how to control it in whatever fashion I can find, and take it to a place where it can't do any more harm. I am certain all this will only be possible with the help of the spruce tree on Mother Mountain. What condition that tree is in, what will happen when the Destroyer comes for me, how I will deal with that—all those things and probably many others will have to reveal themselves in their own time.

"Lupine, I hope that you will be very near, ready and willing to help if I make mistakes, or do something that threatens the stability of the mountain or anything on it."

As I had feared, no one was at all satisfied with this. I lifted my hands in a gesture of helplessness, and let them drop into my lap again. "That is absolutely the best I can offer. I'm sorry if it disappoints."

"I'll speak for myself, only," Works said. "It isn't that it is disappointing, Ray; it's only that it could require a level of power and ingenuity from each of us that has never been tested before."

"You're quite right—it's true for every one of us," I said. "Who in our memory has ever had to attempt this kind of thing before? And for that matter, who has had to rely on someone as green and untried as me?"

Hucklebark made a low sound, deep in his throat. The rest of the circle turned to him in surprise.

"Green 'n untried, maybe," he said. "We all felt what you and Lyla did last night, Ray. I may not be all that smart, but I'm bettin' somethin' like that hasn't been done anywhere around here before, not in more time than anybody can count."

I gave him a look of thanks, and the circle fell silent again. I was beginning to feel restless. I knew I wouldn't be able to sit still much longer.

Lupine spoke then. "So what I take from this is that you need me to be some kind of cleanup crew, picking up the pieces of what you wreck while you're doing whatever?"

"I'm sorry you see it that way," I said softly. "'Green and untried' hardly begins to describe it, Lupine. I don't have any idea how much harm might get done. I want very badly to have someone with real experience there to help the idiot if he makes a mess of things."

"All right, I understand that, and it doesn't really matter if I like it or not," she replied. "What of the others here? How would you place us all?"

"I would trust each and every one of you with my life," I said. I looked to Spark, "As has already happened, more than once. I also trust each one of you to respond to whatever takes place, as needed." I looked around the circle, and I could not keep a note of pleading out of my voice. "Honestly, that's absolutely all I can say."

There was a short time of silence, while everyone sat with their own thoughts. The silence was broken from another surprising quarter—Ev Longhaul.

"Well, then," he said briskly, "I guess it's time to get a move on. Everyone, leave the tents with me, please, I have plenty of room for them."

"One moment, Everett," said Works, with a smile. He sobered immediately. "I have not heard from one among us. Lyla, you have been characteristically quiet; I must ask you to break that silence. How are you, daughter?"

She looked startled, and not entirely glad to have attention drawn to her. Lyla took her time in framing an answer.

"In most ways, I've never been better," she began slowly. "There is more to sort out than I am quite happy with, though. I guess I'm like the rest of us right now—I need more time to work it out than I'm likely to get."

"Yes, I'm certain that is so," Works replied gently. "If you can spare a few minutes this morning, come and find me, if it will help."

"Thank you, Works," she said.

His eyes twinkled at her. "You're welcome, daughter."

It was still dark when we went outside, but the dawn was not far away. Our thought was to walk quickly down the Wonderland/Moraine Park trail to the bottom of the Carbon River Canyon, cross the river and climb up to Mother Mountain following much the same route Lyla and I had taken to descend. I found that I did not relish the prospect, but when I examined my feelings I discarded all of them except the knowledge that getting up there would be very hard work. Hard work for me wasn't worthy of consideration, but I could not help worrying about Spark and Works, and the kind of toil that would be required of them.

The tents were down in a scant handful of minutes. Lyla was finished with hers well before I had gotten mine collapsed, and she silently helped me with it. I wanted to talk about a thousand things, but it was abundantly clear she needed no distractions, so I allowed the silence to remain, and merely worked on not allowing it to grow heavy.

Lyla and I left the little clearing first, walking rapidly down slope towards the Wonderland Trail. We turned down the trail when we reached it, hoping not to encounter any predawn hikers. Works in particular would need the gentlest route that could be found, though once we crossed the Carbon River there was no gentle route up the rocky sides of Mother Mountain.

Hucklebark and Lupine left soon after us. It would have been all right with me if they had walked with us, but it seemed they had their own things to talk about. Lyla's silence was beginning to worry me. For a short while after we reached the trail it was wide enough for us to walk side by side, and when I reached for her hand she took mine willingly. I was lightly touching the rivers that ran underneath us, and I let the energy and life that ran through me travel down to my hand and so to her. It seemed to help, for soon her arm relaxed a bit, and her walk took on its more customary fluid grace. I still did not dare to break the silence we shared, though it was a much less isolated sort of silence while I held her hand.

Eventually the trail grew rougher and ran downwards more steeply, and finally it became too awkward to walk side by side. By unspoken agreement, Lyla walked in front; she would be the one to know where we should leave the trail, to curve around the lower flank of the Echo Cliffs, and into the deep rift made by Cataract Creek that separated them from Mother Mountain. Letting go of her hand was hard to do; I took my comfort in feeling her presence through the river that ran up into the soles of my feet, and in the memory of what we had done and shared the night before.

We made our way quickly down the trail, with the lichen-studded Northern Crags rearing nearly straight up to our right—the trail was forcibly hacked from their lower slopes—and the Carbon River Canyon to our left. By then we had left the snout of the glacier behind us, and the first reach of the river bounded down the canyon in the glacier's place.

The boisterous rush of water was the only sound besides our own quiet footfalls. The land was still holding its breath, both above and below. We walked rapidly, silently, and it was as if there was no one else in the world.

I kept my touch on the river beneath me almost imperceptibly light, for I wanted to attract no attention at all until I was as ready as I could be. I was surprised when we walked all the way to the bottom of the canyon, never leaving the trail, and never encountering anybody else. The night was giving way to the twilight that announces another dawn, yet we turned abruptly onto the short path that leads to the suspension bridge that crosses the Carbon River, and made our way over it.

I had usually seen people cross this bridge one person at a time, for it swayed outrageously if two or more were on it and moving out of step. But Lyla stepped onto the decking of crosswise boards lashed to the suspension cables underneath them, and I followed immediately behind. I matched her footsteps, albeit with nowhere near the grace and sureness she possessed. The bridge swayed with a soft, slow rhythm as we crossed without incident.

We finally left the trail shortly before it forked on the other side of the river. The north fork led back along the river towards Ipsut Creek Campground, while the branch tending southwest—the Spray Park/Wonderland Trail—headed steeply uphill, hugging the west side of the Echo Cliffs. We crossed that trail quickly, and stayed in the bottom of the deep canyon formed by Cataract Creek as it flowed down to meet the Carbon. The Echo Cliffs loomed to our left, and Mother Mountain soared to our right, though in the creek bottom we could see neither because of the alder, vine maple and mountain dogwood that grew where the ground was always damp.

When we were well out of sight of the trail, we came to a large, flat glacial erratic that had been carried there long ago, and Lyla stopped decisively. Her voice, clear and soft as it was, startled me after our long silence.

"Ray, I need to wait here for Works. I won't ask you to do one thing or another, but I don't believe I can work the way we'll have to without some help from him."

"I can go ahead and stumble my way up Mother Mountain, or I can wait here with you," I said. "Whatever you wish."

Lyla smiled. "I wish you to not be away from me for a moment. After the work we did last night, I don't see any point at all in worrying about whether you should hear or be part of what I need from Works. Will you stay with me?"

I took her hand. Both our hands were cold with the chill of the diminishing night. "Of course I'll stay with you."

We sat down on the granite expanse that rose a few feet from the marshy ground, about thirty feet from the rushing creek. Our silence became more companionable again, and I watched with pleasure as the gray daylight stole into the world. The rivers that ran under the great slab of granite on which we sat were strong and numerous; each time I slipped lightly into one of them and found that the world was just as it had been the moment before, I felt better.

After what seemed like a half hour had passed, I turned to Lyla. "I would have thought Lupine and Hucklebark would have passed us by now. What do you think is up?"

She replied, "It doesn't surprise me at all that Lupine has chosen a route that will give her and Hucklebark as much time alone as they can manage. You've given her a formidable task, Ray, and she's going to need Hucklebark to help her in ways he may never have even thought about. I expect she's cramming as much skill and experience into him as he can hold."

I looked down at the rough intricacy of the granite between my legs, noting the veins of colored minerals running so intimately through the dark, dappled gray. "I wish I didn't have to ask anybody to do anything at all." I looked back up at Lyla. "But there isn't any use in wishing for what can't be, and I won't pretend to know what will be good and right in the future that looks hard and dangerous now."

She reached up and brushed aside a wisp of my hair that had fallen over my forehead, with a tenderness that took my breath away.

"You have learned so much since you came here, Ray. I have to believe you already knew most of it before."

I caught her hand and stroked it once, lightly. "And you, my friend, have awakened things in me that I could never have guessed were there, and that feel like they could either burn me to the ground, or make me live forever."

She laughed, giving my hand a pat before taking back her own. "Do refrain from spontaneously combusting, if you please. And let's be content with a beautiful morning."

She accepted my smile for an answer, and we lapsed back into a tightly twined quiet. We sat that way for a little while, and then heard muted footsteps crunching softly through the gravel and leaf litter towards us. Works and Spark emerged from a screen of willow and vine maple.

Works hobbled slowly over to the granite table on which we sat, and gratefully hoisted himself onto it. "It never fails to amaze me, but I can usually depend on the young people to find the best resting spots," as he settled down on the rock with a soft grunt of pain.

Spark remained standing nearby. "Unless you all feel strongly about my presence," he said, "I think I shall walk upstream a bit and consider the landscape."

I looked to Lyla, silently agreeing that the decision was hers. She looked up and said quietly, "Thank you, Spark." Their eyes met for only an instant, but in that time they spoke more to each other than a small mountain of words would have.

Spark answered her with a slight smile that contained more outward warmth than I had ever seen from him. He turned and silently walked past us, heading up the canyon.

To Lyla I said, "Spark loves you dearly."

Works looked up and smiled now. "We all do. How could we not? Now, daughter Lyla, since Ray is with us, I conclude you choose it to be so. Let us begin then; how can I help you to move forward?"

Lyla began by telling all that happened when we had visited the People of The Home together. Works listened attentively, a grave expression on his face. He made no comment or interruption until she was done.

"That would deeply change anyone's way of feeling, daughter," he said. "How has it changed yours?"

"It has blown apart the boundaries that surrounded my work, and the way I walk in the world, is how it's changed me," she said. "But if that was all that had changed, I expect I could deal with it, even though it means assuming a responsibility I can barely imagine."

She launched into her own telling of the work we had done the night before: how I had come to her, brought her into the rivers, how she had sensed my failure to enfold them all. And then how she had suddenly known what was required, and had entered me as if I were a tree. And further how we had, together, wielded a great knot of power to dismantle a seemingly unassailable mass of corruption, inducing the rivers to break it apart and carry it away.

Lyla turned to me. "I would never try to be dismissive of what's been given to you and what it means, Ray. But when I try to think about it from your perspective, from where you have come from, it seems like it might be easier to accept somehow. I have worked this way for a long time, and it's very hard to have to rethink it all."

I answered slowly. "That makes sense to me, I think. I mean, you were really happy already, you had your work, and it was strong and beautiful work. Why would you want to change? I confess I hadn't thought of that at all, and it worries me a lot."

"That's it exactly," she replied. "I *was* happy, and I saw no need for more of anything. Knowing you, and what we've done together, has been wonderful and exciting, and powerful and rewarding. But I'm afraid of what I might have to give up, I'm afraid of losing myself. And I'm afraid of losing the work I've only just begun, after all." She turned to Works. "I'm afraid of handling this kind of power, and the harm it could do if we make mistakes. I've never felt this much fear in all my life, and I don't know what to do with it."

"Even if you used the technique Lupine has taught Ray, and examined all of these in minute detail—much of which you have already done—you would not be able to discard any of this fear, for it is all meaningful and real," Works responded gently. "Which simply says that another way must be found. Perhaps we need to turn to Ray for a moment," doing exactly that as he spoke.

My eyes widened as he turned to face me. What could I possibly offer Lyla, except my feelings and devotion? As far as I was concerned, I was at the bottom of the pile when it came to wisdom and experience. What was Works getting at here?

"In your telling of your first visit to the People of The Home, Ray, you mentioned that there was a point where you did exactly what I have described: you examined, identified, and named all of the fear you were feeling, and discovered that almost none of it could be discarded. And yet you did not stop doing things, nor did you appear to make any grievous mistakes. How was that possible?"

"I—I need a minute here to remember, and get things sorted out, Works," I stammered. "I'm sorry—can I just think for a bit?"

"Of course," Works said with an encouraging smile. "I am vastly in favor of thinking, over any of the alternative ways to respond. Take as much time as you need." He sat, composed and upright even though it was clear he was in considerable pain. Lyla sat quietly, determinedly not focusing her attention on me.

I sent my memory back to the dim, cedar-scented room deep within the Mountain. There had, in fact, been more than one moment when all the fear I felt—which at the time threatened to overwhelm me—was quite valid. How *had* I gotten through that?

One of the People had said to me, 'Remember what your brothers and sisters have taught you, and act anyway.' Who had said that? It came quickly: the voice had belonged to Taiga, who had taken pity on me when I had reached the absolute limits of my endurance and understanding. And where had her advice led me?

Once again, I started slowly, thinking very hard as I spoke. "It was Taiga who told me to remember everything that you all have taught me, and to *act anyway*, in spite of all my fear. In a way, each one of the People gave me that message. And every time I was in danger of being paralyzed, something that Lupine, or Lyla, or Henry, or one of you had said to me came to mind. And then, when that would happen, I would realize that for me it always came down to trust."

"What kind of trust, Ray?" Works prodded.

"Well, as I've said several times, I trust all of you implicitly. And I trust the People of The Home to mean us well. Beyond that, I've had to learn to trust—very carefully, mind you—the rivers themselves, to take me where I needed to go, and to help me do what needed to be done. As if that weren't enough, I have to learn to trust the world in which all of this—us—exists, to believe that there is room for all of this, that it all has a place in the world, and that it all has meaning."

Works nodded with approval, and turned to Lyla. "Change is the only thing we can always depend on, daughter. And true human change only happens when the spirit moves beyond its own self imposed boundaries, to come closer to its intended depth and breadth. It is never easy, and it is always essential."

Lyla, who had been listening to us in turn with an almost quivering intensity, sat back suddenly with an indrawn breath that caught somewhere in the middle and turned into a drawn out sigh. "What is the 'intended depth and breadth' of a spirit, Works? How would I try to reach it?"

"There you will find one of Lupine's mysteries to get comfortable with," Works replied with a grin.

I didn't mean to break in, but I couldn't stop myself saying, "But sometimes people, I mean people like me, really need to know where the boundaries lie, Works. How can we live without knowing that?"

"Some boundaries are good and necessary, Ray," he said. "And others are no more than impediments to a deeper understanding and acceptance. It takes courage to learn the distinction, and more courage to make it. You in particular have already had to do this many times. I have said before I am not at all happy about young people being pushed so hard to achieve so much. But there is no help for it, and all any of us can do now is find the right way to 'act anyway'."

We sat very still for some time, Lyla and I trying to absorb what Works was teaching us, Works himself simply being still. Suddenly Lyla scooted forward on the rock and wrapped her arms gently around Works. She buried her face in his shoulder, and though she was quiet I knew she was crying. Works laid a hand on her arm, and let her be that way for a few moments. Then he gently disengaged her, and brought her facing him. "Why do you weep, daughter?"

"Because I love you so much, Works, and I'm so grateful for you. And because I'm so afraid of losing you. And because—because change is so hard, and it's harder still to think about it always happening this way."

Works laid a hand on the side of her face, held it there softly. "Children should never be required to carry this kind of burden. And yet," he went on reflectively, "I must remember that you are not children. You only seem so because I am so ridiculously old. I hope you will always remember that I trust you absolutely to become who and what you are intended to become. And remember too that it will not always be this way; fortunately for us, most change is much more gradual.

"Now," he went on gently, "We must get ready to move forward. The day won't wait for us, and we have a long climb ahead."

I uncrossed my stiffened legs, and slowly made my way off the granite table. Lyla jumped down easily, and held a hand out to Works, who accepted it and lowered himself gingerly back onto the ground.

A noisy rustling just behind the screen of willow and maple through which Works and Spark had come made me jump.

Immediately after, Everett Longhaul came striding towards us.

He was carrying what looked like a canvas-wrapped house on his back. A closer look showed it to be his ever present pack, over which must have been lashed countless things: tents, probably, and who knew what all else. The whole was covered with a dun colored tarp. If it hadn't been so impressive it would have been comical.

His timing was such that I figured he must have been behind the trees for some time, waiting for us to finish our talk. For once, good judgment prevailed, and I did not mention my suspicion. What did it matter? I trusted Ev just as I trusted the others.

He slipped out of the huge pack—which at the moment appeared to be about as big as Lyla—like an otter would slide into the water, and leaned it against the rock. Without ceremony he whipped off the canvas and began rooting around in an upper compartment, after rapidly unhooking several tents and tossing them aside.

"Let me guess, Ev," I said. "You've just spent the last ninety minutes running down to Northern California and back to fetch some things that are harder than usual to come by here."

"Greetings, greetings, my fine and credulous friend," he looked up at me with his wicked grin. "Even you should know I can only make it to Portland and back in an hour and a half." He extracted three waterproof bags from his pack, and tossed them at me in quick succession. I managed to catch the first, while the second and third bounced off my chest. "There is heavy weather coming our way, my dears—very heavy weather indeed. These will help."

I opened the first bag while he tossed three more to Lyla—a good deal more gently, I noticed—and then solemnly handed three more to Works. Inside the bag I found a pair of the lightest, warmest feeling longjohns I had ever seen. Another bag contained an undershirt of similar material, and the third an incredibly light, tough set of rain pants and jacket with hood.

"I didn't expect to find Lupine or Hucklebark here," Ev said to no one in particular, "But where is Spark? After all, even the toughest old coot on the Mountain needs a little protection when it gets rough outside."

Works allowed his hearty laugh to ring from one side of the clearing to the other. "Everett Longhaul, I imagine Spark might render you into a pile of dust at any moment, but that he's never done it yet. Not without provocation, I'll have you know."

Ev pulled on an innocent, astonished expression that made both Lyla and me burst into laughter before he even spoke. "Works, I am amazed. Me, into a pile of mere dust? Provocation? I am but a humble, minimally amusing Stuff Bringer, after all. And who but myself would hotfoot it to Portland, or Northern California (assuming I had an extra hour), I ask?"

Works, still chuckling, said, "All right, all right, Everett. I am certain Spark will rejoin us any moment. Now what's this about heavy weather?"

Ev instantly switched back to brisk and businesslike. "The clouds are roiling at the summit, and the wind is picking up the snow on the heights. I'd say we have an hour, maybe two at the outside, before it cuts loose." Turning to Lyla and me, he said, "I recommend getting into those underthings right away, and waiting for the real rain to put on the outer gear. No sense wicking off any more sweat than you have to."

Lyla retired to a secluded patch of willow. I was free to stay where I was to shuck off jeans and shirt, and put the new clothing on. I instantly felt their warmth, and was amazed to realize it did not feel like I was wearing anything extra. I started to ask Ev where he had acquired such wonderful stuff, and bit the question off. Works had told me more than once, in his kindly way, to mind my own business, and I was going to do just that even if curiosity drove me crazy.

Spark came in from one direction just as Lyla returned from the other. Despite his earlier wisecracking, Ev handed three waterproof bags to Spark in a respectful silence, and Spark responded with a nod of thanks. He simply placed them inside his own pack, and then turned to us.

"We must make the best time we can up Mother Mountain," he said. "Everett is quite right in predicting difficult weather, and soon. Lyla, I suggest that you and Ray choose your own route and get up the mountain as quickly as you can. I expect that Lupine and Hucklebark will be waiting for you." Turning to Ev, he said, "Would you consider accompanying Works and me on the ascent?"

Ev bowed, not in his exaggerated, comic way, but gently and with respect. "I would be honored, sir."

"Very well, then," Works said. "Ray, if you and Lyla need to commence your work before we arrive, I suggest you do so. Hopefully, Spark and Everett and I will join you soon."

He came to stand in front of me, placing his hands on my shoulders, and it felt like a river running through me, warm and bracing. Works looked earnestly into my face.

"Whether you know it or not, Ray, you have everything that is needed. Whatever may happen today, you must keep moving forward, working with what has been given to you. Will you promise me this?"

I looked searchingly into his eyes. His words filled me with dread; was he saying goodbye? After all that had happened, did I still not understand what we were undertaking?

I started to ransack my mind for the response that would match the depth, the understanding and compassion of his words, and then stopped it abruptly. I was beginning to learn that any truly important things I could say would come from a place that wasn't accessible that way. I waited, without trying to force the words, and they came of their own accord.

"On my life, Works, I promise you."

He graced me with his broad, warm smile, and I knew that he understood exactly what I had just felt and done, and approved. He gave my shoulders a light squeeze, and moved to stand before Lyla.

Her eyes were shining with tears. Works took her hands in his, held them lightly.

"Daughter, you are one of the most cherished people in my life," he said quietly. "And now you know that others love you as dearly as I. Take those gifts, accept them, carry them well. Whenever events become frightening and uncertain, remember that that love has been given, now and forever, and it cannot be destroyed or taken away by anyone or any thing."

Lyla struggled for words as she looked up into his face. The tears that had threatened to flow again began to run lightly down her cheeks.

"Oh, Works…"

She moved forward, rested her head against his chest, and cried silently for a moment. In a muffled voice she said, "You mustn't leave us now. You *mustn't.*"

Works gently took a step back, still holding her hands so she wouldn't fall, and looked into her face again.

"I have no intention of leaving you, daughter, if it can be avoided. But we both know what today might bring, and there are some things that must be said in the hope they will be proven unnecessary." He smiled again, and lightly brushed a tear from her cheek. "In any event, they will never need to be unsaid."

He let her hands go, and turned to face us. "We must all be moving now. "

Lyla and I wordlessly hoisted our packs, turned and left the little clearing.

Chapter 39

We began making our way up the canyon, following busy, rocky Cataract Creek for a short way. We came to a place where crossing the creek was relatively easy, and Lyla led us over to the north side of it. Soon the main tributary of the creek veered off towards the west side of the Echo Cliffs, and we continued on up the canyon, following a side stream.

This smaller fork of Cataract took us steeply uphill, and after a while I could tell we were hugging the northern wall of the canyon, hard against the flank of Mother Mountain. The trees grew smaller and sparser, and the undergrowth thinned out rapidly as we rose. We walked in silence, wrapped in our thoughts. Moving through our dread of what lay ahead was as much like physical work as climbing the steep canyon, and I barely noticed the beauty of the land we were passing through.

I kept a part of myself immersed in the small life river below the ground while we walked along the little unnamed branch of the Cataract watershed. There was no suggestion of unrest in the earth, and I could not tell if the continuing feel of suspense I thought I detected was real, or my imagination. Through the river I could sense Lyla just ahead of me, in a way that was far more direct and deep than simply being able to see her striding up the slope. Piercing through everything else I was feeling, her presence was an endless happiness that none of it could abate.

I remembered almost nothing from the last time I had been here, when she had half carried me down the slope and found a safe resting place for me next to the Carbon River. When we stopped for a moment to catch our breath I said so. She smiled, and then became thoughtful again.

"I wouldn't think you'd remember much of that hike, Ray. You were only slightly better off than the spruce at the time. But do you feel too," she mused, "that all of that is already a lifetime in the past, that so much has happened since then it might almost have been someone else's experience?"

"Speaking strictly for myself, it did happen to someone else," I replied. "Or at the least, it happened to a Ray Holdman who was so far away from this Ray you see now, he was as good as someone else."

She leaned over and kissed me briefly. "I don't believe I've said this yet, but I think I already loved that Ray Holdman. And I love this Ray that I see now very, very much. If there is no other chance, I want to be sure that it gets said now."

I looked down at the ground and tried to contain my joy. Not because I wanted to, but because there was something vital we needed to discuss before anything else happened to us. I stored that joy carefully away in the deepest, safest part of me I could find, and hoped with all my heart there would be time for it later.

Looking back up I said, "I hadn't really thought about how frightening and hard it might be to twine with me, as well as with the rivers. I will never ask you to do something you don't want to, Lyla. But it's very clear that I can't do it alone, and I don't know what to say now."

She smiled again. "Dear Ray, you and Works already gave me what I needed to go forward with this. I would have said yes even if I thought I would lose everything in the doing of it. But now I think that may not be so, and I'm prepared to trust, from the energy of the world on down, that what needs to happen, will."

I smiled back. "I've been thinking some about what Zephyr said to you, and about what happened when the old tree took you inside itself. And as I see it, there are two things to remember. One, the trees are immensely more powerful than any of us thought possible, and two, they love you passionately enough to sacrifice one of their elders to save you. Knowing that, I don't imagine they'll let you go; I expect you will be with them for a long time to come."

"Assuming we make it to tomorrow, I suppose—and hope—you're right," she said. "Sometimes I like the way you use logic, Ray."

The rain began, softly for a moment, but almost immediately it started to come down in a more businesslike fashion. Lyla opened an outer pocket in her pack and extracted the raingear Ev had given us. "I don't know about you, but I'd rather be a little sweaty than soaked through."

I agreed, and we clambered into our rain pants and jackets. Unlike most of the raingear I'd ever had—which was not much—these were easy to move around in. We stood, adjusted our packs, and began upward again.

The trees thinned out, and then disappeared. The salal and Oregon grape remained, bravely covering their little patches of ground, until Lyla turned away from the creek and headed us more sharply uphill, to where only broken rock lived. The rain continued in a steady fall. Rivulets of water sprouted from the ground, running past us down towards the canyon, the Cataract, and the Carbon River. The clouds were still hanging above the highest ridges of Mother Mountain, for which I was grateful; I didn't like the idea of making our way up there if they came down to meet the ground. I was also profoundly grateful for the lack of wind, so welcome on a hot, sunny day, and so shockingly cold at other times.

Once turned away from the creek, we began to climb in earnest, moving diagonally along the mountain's flank. We came to a slope that required us to climb with hands as well as feet, and I asked Lyla if we had come down this way.

"No, we took a slightly easier route that was longer. We're in much better shape today, so I think we should take the quickest way we can manage."

"All right by me," I huffed, "As long as you don't leave me in the dust."

She turned to answer over her shoulder, still moving slowly upward. "Not much dust today, I think. And no, I won't leave you behind."

I could either use breath to climb or to talk, so I climbed. We zigzagged, doubled over, up a slope too steep for upright walking. As the slope lessened it opened into a canyon about fifty feet across, wrinkled with small ridges that ran crosswise from either side of it, making a maze-like path leading upwards.

I wondered if we should worry about flash floods, and then decided it had not been raining long enough. I hoped we were nearing the top so I wouldn't have to think about it any more. Then it occurred to me that moving a little deeper into the river under my feet might tell me something.

I could feel water moving everywhere. The thirsty gravel swallowed a great deal of it, and what was left was in a hurry to travel down the mountainside. It flowed in a thin, flat sheet just under the surface of the ground. The sheet of water grew thinner with every few feet of movement down slope, as the innumerable crevices and the coarse sand and gravel invited it in, leaving some of what could not soak into the ground to rise again and make the rivulets that flowed past and over our feet. But nowhere was there the threat of a large mass of water rushing down to meet us, and I was finally satisfied.

The rain fell harder as we moved upward. As we approached the top of the wrinkled canyon it was pelting down. The feel of the earth underneath us had told me we were almost to the top of this part of Mother Mountain's crest, and would soon be heading downwards again.

It was still somehow a surprise to reach the top, and stand on a relatively flat space no more than six feet wide looking down towards the canyon carved by Ipsut Creek, with the spire of Gove Peak beyond it. It was even more surprising to see that even up on the ridge the wind was not blowing hard. I mentioned it to Lyla.

"Don't get your hopes up, Ray. The wind usually kicks in a while after a good, soaking rain like this one has started. We need to be ready for it."

"What should we be doing to get ready for it?"

"Nothing practical that I can think of," she said. "I just meant we need to accept the fact that it's going to blow really hard, and not get upset when it happens."

"Maybe Ev will pull something out of his magic pack for us," I said hopefully.

She gave a tight smile, and said, "I won't bet on it, but when it comes to hoping so, I'm right with you. Look, the next hundred feet or so is difficult, especially in the rain. Watch your feet carefully, take your time, and remember it's only a hundred feet. After that it will be easier."

I looked down and blanched. It wouldn't quite be like jumping off a hundred foot cliff, but I would have preferred it to be far different from what it was. The slope, so steep I didn't think I could possibly stand on it, was completely bare, obviously because nothing larger than a pebble could stay on it. Lyla hiked her pack a little higher on her back, bent deeply at the knees, and started down. I waited for her to move several steps and change direction to a sharp diagonal, hoping that if I made a mistake I wouldn't trip her up in the process, and then followed behind.

I leaned back as far as I could and dug my heels into the gravel with each step. The rain was coming down hard enough now that it was difficult to see my feet clearly, and Lyla was a dark blur ten feet ahead of me. Once when I dug in a heel, I hit a pebble that sent a shock up through my leg, and I thought about the river just underneath me. Perhaps it would help, perhaps not.

It helped a lot. As soon as I moved farther into it, I felt like there was something holding me on to the side of the mountain by sheer force. I could feel where each step should go, and once again there was no distance between Lyla and me. I thought about trying to catch up and offering to bring her into the river too, then realized she was moving faster than I was, and without its assistance. Moving clumsily, but with myself firmly entrenched in the energy running below us, I made my way down.

Lyla was waiting for me when I reached the place where it leveled off and I could walk normally. "That wasn't so bad, was it?"

We had to speak loudly to be heard over the rushing percussion of the rainfall. "Well, yes it was," I said. "But I had help. I would have offered it to you, but it was clear you didn't need it."

"Thank you anyway. The hard part is done now, Ray. We're

about ten minutes from the place where you and I stopped after leaving the spruce. Are you ready to go on?"

"As ready as I'll ever be."

She was, as always when it concerned the landscape, perfectly correct. The rest of the way was quite straightforward by comparison, the rain notwithstanding. It felt comforting to keep myself partly in the river, since with its help I didn't need to depend on eyesight alone, so I stayed with it, listening all the while for unwelcome attention from the Destroyer. There had been no hint of it yet, and for the moment that suited me perfectly.

But in that short walk I felt something changing. There were other rivers running below, very close to the one in which I had still only lightly entered, and more were coming into my awareness. That alone would have been no more than a mild surprise. What I was totally unprepared for was that they were taking hold of me.

They were entering *me*. Unlike Speakers, or Change Bringers, they did not stand outside and request permission; they simply came in, whether I willed it or not. I stopped in my tracks, and felt a stab of absolute panic. Whatever was happening was instantly beyond anything I had felt until now, and nothing I had heard or learned to this point told me how to respond, or what to do. The rivers were coming together of their own accord and moving into me like a massive ocean tide. I stood immobile, surrounded by immense, roiling, slow moving waves of power and energy.

Lyla had turned to be sure I was directly behind her, and found that I was not. She came loping back up to me, concern written large on her face. "Ray, what's happening? Are you all right?"

I was expanding, growing outwards in ways that blew past my understanding like a herd of wild horses streaming around a bewildered boy. I couldn't speak; I was more intensely aware of my surroundings than ever before, but I was far beyond them at the same time. I could hear the rain pounding down on us, but I did not feel it. I concentrated on moving my hand, lifting it before my eyes, and heard a gasp from Lyla. Light sprayed out from my fingertips, as had happened on the ridge overlooking Vernal Park, but much brighter. It shot out from me and splashed against the slope above us and off to the right, making weird patterns on the broken rock, turning the intervening drops of rain into flashing, multi-colored globs of light.

The rivers were still assembling themselves below, and still spilling into me. The feeling was like being stuffed into a live light socket, and it was becoming unbearable. Frantically I ransacked my mind for something I could hold on to, anything that would help me find my bearings. At first there seemed to be nothing but a random jumble of words, ideas, hopes and fears. But searching was enough to hold off the blind panic that threatened to overwhelm me, and I thought of Lupine. I looked closely at what was happening, what I was feeling, even though I wanted to look anywhere else at the moment.

These rivers, this incredible locus of the planet's power and energy—how could I possibly live within this, and still be me? From somewhere in the maelstrom of thought and feeling, a familiar, nasal twang rose into my consciousness.

C'mon, bub, pull yourself together and get a move on.

Henry/Holdman? What are you doing here? What are you?

No time for trivialities. In case you haven't noticed, you're very busy right now.

What do you expect me to do? I'm about to be obliterated, and you want me to pull myself together?

You're not being obliterated. You're being pushed a little harder than your lazy butt is used to. Can you think about Lyla, or the others right now? How do you feel about them?

It was easy to think about Lyla, effortless to remember how I felt about her. There in my mind were Lupine, and Hucklebark, Everett Longhaul, Works and Spark. I was suddenly certain that an obliterated nonentity would not be able to think about beloved friends this way.

All right, then, I'm still here, and likely to remain here, wherever 'here' may be. What's going on?

Ask what's being given to you, and be quick about it. You can dither around, deciding which tea cups and cakes to bring to the party, but even a mountain spruce doesn't have all day to wait.

Okay, I'll work on seeing it that way. Any other pithy tidbits of advice from whatever realm of something or other you're in now?

Like the old man said, Get to work, child.

I could tell, though I didn't know how, that if I asked any more questions I would not get an answer. Whoever or whatever this Henry/Holdman thing was, it was gone again.

What was being given to me? I focused on the panic I was feeling, looked carefully, and saw that Ray Holdman was not dissolving, or being eaten alive, or anything else. Ray Holdman was being *joined*, and the rivers were still coming. The awareness of what was around me continued growing; I could already sense everything over a huge swath of territory, and it was expanding as I considered it. I looked at the panic again, named it, and it began to slip away. Clearly a few minutes would be needed here to learn how to live in this sea of energy, to move with it and within the world.

I looked outward, and Lyla was standing in front of me, her eyes wide with terror. Without knowing how—only knowing I wanted to—I shifted my perception slightly, and saw myself through her eyes. No wonder she was terrified. I looked like a cross between human and ball lightning; light was leaking out of me as if I'd swallowed the sun, the rain was turning to steam as it landed on me, and I seemed to be wavering. This won't do, I thought, I'm not willing to scare my partner to death.

I tried to say something out loud to her, and couldn't manage it. With an inward start I realized how much easier it would be to speak to her more directly. She was simply *there*, and all I had to do was carefully brush against her mind.

Lyla—wait, dear one, just wait a few moments. I think it will be all right.

Ray? What's happening to you? You're frightening me!

I'm sorry. It was frightening me, too. I need a little time to learn how to be with this, and then I'll be okay. Please—just wait a bit.

I started to gently withdraw from her mind.

Stop, Ray! Don't go. I need to know where you are. Stay with me!

All right, I can stay. But let me work for a minute.

No effort was needed to stay with her; it was as if I simply kept a hand resting gently on her mind. And at the moment I had thousands of hands to work with.

More rivers were bending from their accustomed paths, and joining with the ones that had already joined with me. I began to feel like I couldn't hold all the energy, the roiling force that was crowding inside me. It felt like I might burst apart. What would Henry/Holdman have to say about that?

Grow into it, bub. If the shoe's too small, make it bigger.

It figures he would say something like that. He had a point, though. It occurred to me that Works had said something important along this line, to Lyla, just a short time ago. "True human change only happens when the spirit moves beyond its own self-imposed boundaries, to come closer to its intended depth and breadth." Very well, then, Lyla had told him that her own boundaries had been blown apart by the People of The Home, and by the work she had done with me. It seemed only fair that mine should get exploded too—again. But how to deal with it? How to *grow* your own spirit?

Relax, bub. Quit holdin' back, and you'll be all right.

Was I willing to grow outward this way? I wondered if I'd spent as much energy building walls to keep myself in as I had spent building them to keep everything else out. The glacier had taught me about neglecting to maintain walls, and it was fitting that an echo of Henry's spirit, or whatever it was, should point me in the right direction.

Works had specifically called them *self-imposed* boundaries. However and whenever they had come about, I was going to have to un-impose them, and very quickly, before the massive power that was flowing in took me apart. I ransacked my mind for assumptions, for the most deeply held beliefs I could find.

I am small. And stupid. And useless.

At this point these were interesting and quaint, but I set them aside as almost superficial. Where were the ones that really defined how I made my way through the world?

I am separate—utterly alone in a world that will never include me.

Now I was getting somewhere. In this moment, when I was bursting with the flow of unnumbered rivers of the world's life blood, and was resting gently against Lyla's mind, it was never more obvious that my idea of being separate, of being *alone* in the world, was pathetically mistaken. It would not do to simply try to jettison such a deep-seated belief, but again Lyla came to my rescue. She had said, "I'd say that unlearning something means to replace it with something that works better." There was no need to search for what to replace it with—I was living it that instant.

I pretended that my belief in being separate from the world, my belief in the impenetrable barrier between the world and me, was a living creature. When I looked closely, I saw it to be a goldfinch—I had no idea why, and I simply allowed it to be what it seemed to be. I held it in my hands, watched it quiver there, its heart pounding so much faster than my own. I lifted my hands and gently thrust it into the air, and in the same motion I allowed everything I was experiencing in that moment to take its place. The bird vanished as soon as it left my hands, and in that moment I felt the pressure inside me lessen. There was more room for everything; my body hadn't changed a bit, but there was room in my mind and my heart for what was happening, more room in my very being for the enormous, rolling swell of power that had come barging in.

Was there anything else I could do to make space for all of this? I looked into my heart, my innermost being—not without trepidation. I saw that for most of my life, that place where my heart lived had been a dark, airless, featureless room, more like a prison cell than the home of a human soul. I could see that it was an artificial construct, and that I'd built it that way myself some time long ago, for some reason that was irrelevant now.

I didn't need a broom closet here. What I needed was a palace, a mansion. On second thought I discarded both of those. What I needed was a forest. *That* was where I wished the heart of me to live. I wanted a place like the woods that Lyla had taken me to near The Home, a place of ancient and sacred beauty. I considered the broom closet, its walls and the single, small door, and I neglected to support them. They disappeared like smoke being carried off by the wind that sweeps down from the mountain top, and instead there was a forest. It had always been there, and I had no idea how big it was. Nor did it matter. *This* was where I lived, the deepest part of me, the part so well hidden I had not known it existed, and there was room in it for more than I could imagine. It felt like I had shrugged a great block of stone from my shoulders. The pressure from the rivers receded further; they began to calm, to fill the space that had been made for them.

There was nothing whatever between myself and the world, and I had discovered a huge, open, spacious place in me where I could live. I calmed down along with the rivers, and we were simply flowing together, though I was still tingling with the immense hum of power that flowed around and through me. I looked at my hand again, and the light that had so fiercely sprayed from my fingertips was no more than a warm glow. I looked up at Lyla.

She had been waiting all this time, tense and expectant. I found that I could speak again. "I think I'm going to be okay now. Are you all right?"

"Yes, I'm fine, Ray. What just happened?"

"I had to grow a new pair of shoes," I said. Her expression was as baffled as it had every right to be. "I'll explain it better later. Do you want me to stay with you, I mean inside mind-wise? Or shall I just go back to my own head?"

The question surprised her so much she laughed, and then looked thoughtful. "You are still there, in my mind, and yet you're talking to me too." She considered for a moment, then said with decision, "For now, stay with me in whatever way, shape or form we have to work with, Ray. At least until all this is done."

I had hoped she would say that, and a burst of affection found its way from my mind to hers.

She took my hand and said, "Can we get started again? It's almost dark."

"Yes, let's go. Will you allow me to bring you a little ways into the rivers? We won't need any light to keep our footing that way."

She nodded, and I carefully brought her into one of the rivers coursing through me. We started again towards the place where she had taken me that morning—the morning that now felt so long ago, when I did not know her name.

We walked surely, efficiently in the heavy rain and gathering dusk, each of us knowing where we were going, knowing exactly where to place our feet. Lyla rested lightly in one of the rivers; all of them rested in me, massive and quiescent now that I had made room for them. Lyla had not entered me yet, nor did it seem necessary at the moment. She was closer than if we had been touching side by side. Talking was unnecessary now, and we shared thoughts and feelings effortlessly.

When we reached the somewhat sheltered place where we had stopped on our way down from this mountain, we paused at the rim, looking down into the shallow bowl. Just upslope from the bottom, on the side away from us a lean-to was just visible in the last glimmer of twilight. It was set up with its lower side facing the Mountain, its higher side about four feet off the ground. We knew without seeing that Lupine and Hucklebark were sheltering there, waiting for us.

The rain continued to pour down on us, hard and purposeful. If it kept up like this for a few more hours, there would definitely be flooding to think about, at least in the low and sheltered parts of the landscape. On Tahoma, as in all the high elevations in this part of the world, the rain is never warm; even if there is no wind it is quite capable of pulling every ounce of warmth from an unprotected body. And for what seemed like the thousandth—and I hoped not the last—time, I thanked Everett Longhaul from the bottom of my heart as I felt the rain bounce off my jacket with its tight fitting hood, never getting the chance to move inside to my skin. Now too I felt the wind beginning to blow down from the top of Tahoma. It was a burly, chilling wind that so far was merely strong, but carried within its push the threat of a vastly greater force.

We walked down and across the sodden meadow, with the rain drops kicking up countless little splashes, to the lean-to on the other side. Lupine and Hucklebark sat near the back of it. They had not lit any kind of light, and the darkness deepened as we moved inside, pushed back our hoods, and seated ourselves facing them.

It was too dark to see faces clearly, but it was easy enough to feel Lupine's tension and Hucklebark's quiet, almost feral stillness.

When Lupine spoke, it was with the same kind of softness that had surprised me in Works' tent. "Ray, what is going on?"

"The rivers are entering me this time, Lupine, and there are more of them than I can count. There wasn't room in me for them, and I had to find a way to create a place for them to be, or else be taken apart by their force."

I sensed rather than saw her nod slightly. "You're carrying more power right now than any human should ever be asked to carry," she said. "Do you believe you can work with this, you can do what needs doing?"

"What choice do I have?" I replied. "This is completely out of my hands, Lupine. I'm just going to have to deal with it. And with Lyla's help, I do think there's a chance."

Since no one but Works had heard the details of Lyla's and my work the night before, I briefly recounted it.

Lupine sat quietly, thinking. Hucklebark stirred, and I could tell he was looking my way. "You're lookin' a bit larger than before, Ray," he said. "You havin' a growth spurt or somethin'?"

I laughed in spite of all the tension and dread surrounding us, and blessed him in my mind. "Well, yes, I suppose you might have to call it that, Hucklebark. As Henry said, 'when the shoe's too small, make it bigger'."

"When did he say that?" Hucklebark asked.

I stopped in confusion. *Did* he say that? Did I, or did *we*? "I don't know, exactly. Maybe I should just say that's how he might have put it."

I could tell Hucklebark wasn't satisfied; he knew in some way there was much more to it than that, but his silence made it clear he was willing to wait for some other time to hear the real story. I felt a flow of gratitude and affection for him. "Thank you, Hucklebark."

"Huh? What for, Ray?"

"For being Hucklebark."

He snorted, then chuckled. "Not much to that, I reckon. I don't seem to be able to help bein' Hucklebark."

"Don't change a thing, then. I treasure you as you are."

He lapsed back into a now embarrassed silence. The restlessness was coming over me again, and there was no more time for anything but getting to work. I didn't need to communicate my feelings to Lyla; she had already felt them, and when I posed my question to her in our minds, she answered without hesitation: *Let's go, then.*

"Lyla and I have to get to the mountain spruce as soon as possible. Would you consider waiting here for Works, Spark and Ev? That reminds me: Ev has some raingear for the two of you, and I can heartily recommend it tonight."

Lupine said, "Do you have any ideas for how they should find us, or are you suggesting we wander around looking for them?"

"Good point," I replied. "Hold on a second."

The rivers were running so strong inside me it took nothing more than a short flick of attention to find them. In an instant I took in their position, which was not at all what I expected. Ev had lashed Works' pack to the already bulging back of his own; he had Spark's pack hung backwards, over his chest. He looked more like a huge, long legged pillbug than a man as he toiled up the rocky slope, about a mile from where we were. Spark was bent over almost double, carrying Works on his back; Works' arms were weakly wrapped around his neck, and Spark's hands were hooked under his legs, holding him up by main force. Without going anywhere near Spark's mind, I could tell it was in a grim place.

When I brushed against Ev's mind, he responded immediately and without surprise. He was living and thinking in the most businesslike mode I could imagine.

Hey, Ray. What do you need?

Nothing, Ev. I want to show you where Lupine and Hucklebark are.

I pictured the depression, the lean-to, and the surrounding landscape.

Lyla and I have to go on to the tree immediately. Can you care for Works, set something up for him there, where Lupine is?

Sure. I have it. I'll join you as soon as I can.

I let him go, intensely aware of how hard he was working and wanting to distract him as little as possible, and turned my attention back to Lupine.

"Ev knows how to find you here. Works is very, very weak." Lyla had seen them with me, and she was filled with shock and alarm. I thought about the fact that we might have to do anything we could to help him before much else happened, and felt her vehement agreement.

To Lupine and Hucklebark I said, "We need to go now. Will you join us when you can?"

Lupine said softly, "Will we be able to join you in time, if you go now?"

"There is a lot of work to be done—this instant—in several places. I think, and I hope with all my heart, that we'll have the chance to do some of it before we're overtaken. At any rate, I don't know any other way."

Lupine sat very still for a long moment, then said, "All right, Ray. Hucklebark and I will be with you in some way when you need us." In the darkness, I sensed that she had stretched her hand to me.

I hesitated, and then grasped it firmly. I heard a stifled gasp from Lupine, and felt the highway of energy that her touch created, and the incredible flow it prompted. Nothing was gained or lost in either direction; we were simply conduits that an astonishing range of the world's energy chose to pass through.

Lupine let go of my hand, and turned to Hucklebark. "I'm sorry to say it, Hucklebark, but I can't recommend shaking hands with Ray right now." Turning to me she said, "Be extremely careful who you touch when you're in this state, Ray. Just a warning for the future."

I said, "Thank you for everything. I'm putting all my hopes on there being a future for me—for all of us."

As one, Lyla and I rose and made our way out from the lean-to.

Chapter 40

The darkness was complete now, but it meant nothing to us, and the pounding rain meant little more. The wind was another matter. It blew straight down from the summit of the Mountain, and it was increasing with every moment. We held hands tightly, moving up over the lip of the bowl and directly into the wind's teeth. It was a force to be treated seriously, like a great hand shoved against our chests, pushing hard to prevent us from going forward. I thought about bringing Lyla a little farther into the river, and she agreed. We rooted ourselves in energy, and concentrated on moving ahead. I feared for all the trees tonight; some or even many of them would be destroyed before morning if the wind grew fiercer, and I feared much for one tree in particular.

From a good ways away I could feel its roots thrust deep into the rough, rocky soil, and sense its branches already whipping back and forth in response to the wind's increasingly violent caprices. When we were a hundred feet or so from it, I stopped us, telling Lyla that she would need to come much farther into the rivers, and that now was a good time to enter me. She hesitated for only a second, and then she was completely, entirely a part of me. I brought her as far as I dared into the rivers, and as before left her alone for a bit to find her bearings. I saw with a burst of pride that she had no need to expand her spirit to make room for all that was pouring into her. While our bodies stood, hands clasped, leaning hard into the wind, all the rest of us was immersed in the world, gathering energy and—hopefully—understanding for what must come next.

We walked slowly, leaning far forward, until we were about four feet from the mountain spruce. I had thought that I would examine it closely for signs of damage or healing, but it was too dark to do that with eyes. Lyla and I sat down side by side, on the lee side of the tree, and waited.

Its invitation came immediately; it seemed that the tree had had enough waiting itself. We entered it from below, through the smallest, finest tips of its furthest roots. They were deep enough below the surface that the rain had not penetrated there yet, but as we moved upwards into larger roots, we passed places where the water muscled its way into every available tiny space that the gravel and sand created. The roots were doing what they were supposed to—pulling the water in as fast as they could. Still, it was a slow and stately process, and the vast part of the water flowing under the tree would pass it by.

Moving up from the roots into the short, slender but incredibly strong trunk, we found an understanding that neither Lyla nor I had had before. This tree had its own vast, sprawling forest of spirit within, a place that was entirely capable of carrying all the rivers that were flowing through me. We entered that place, filled with admiration and astonishment. Without waiting for an invitation, the rivers came rushing into that place too, and if I had thought them capable of human feeling I would have said they were glad and gleeful. There were moments of bustling, jostling movement, and we were all humming with the power of what was being joined.

I held a short, silent council with Lyla. When the rivers had begun to settle into a semblance of quiet, we wrapped our intention around a great bundle of them, and gently nudged them into a twining, sinuous flow around the mountain spruce, both inside and out. We spread into every cell of the tree, touching, sensing, considering what we found.

We found a great deal of damage that had been partially healed. My first encounter with this tree had indeed very nearly killed it, and the work it had done since then to repair itself and simply survive was heroic in scale. In this great interior forest there were wide swaths that had been knocked down, as if trampled by a herd of panicked giants. It was humbling as well as humiliating to know that the destructive herd had been me.

Asking the rivers, offering, becoming ever more a part of them, we wound ourselves around and through the tree's internal landscape, and the work became a wordless song. This time the rivers played Lyla and me together, and we played them as one. Little by little, we saw the ravaged places in the landscape mend themselves, the broken forest raising itself back to its proper height and vivid life. We worked, and played, sang, and were sung.

In whatever way I tried to think about it, this tree was probably the strongest living being I had ever encountered. While we worked within it, within the rivers, I asked Lyla if she had known this tree before she found me beside it. She had not, and her wonder at the immensity of its spirit and the ferocity of its will to live was even greater than mine. We continued working it, seeking out every place we could find in the tree that had been harmed by me, or simply needed mending or reinforcement.

The rivers were still coming, bending their courses from farther and farther away to join, as if we were magnets, and they simple streams of iron filings. I began to wonder if there was any living thing that could hold them all if they kept coming. And when that thought began to make me feel afraid I set it down—something maybe useful later but not helpful at the moment—and turned my attention elsewhere.

Lyla was moving the rivers herself, nudging, coaxing, and sometimes, in a gentle but matter of fact way pushing them outright, steering them to the places within the mountain spruce that needed strength and repair. I took a moment to turn my awareness back to the depression and Hucklebark's and Lupine's lean-to.

It was empty. I hoped that meant that they were on their way to join us, but I was immediately distracted by a tent that had miraculously appeared nearby, on a piece of ground about halfway up from the bottom of the bowl, in a place that was almost level.

I could not imagine how Ev had possibly erected the large, circular tent that housed Works and Spark in this madhouse of darkness, rain and wind that was happening. But not even the tearing, muscular wind had prevented him from getting it done. The tent was held to the ground by six crossed lashings of heavy mountaineering rope over its top, looped firmly to stakes driven deep into the earth. I could sense the windward side of the tent bowing inward from the pressure, but aside from that it stood as if nothing less than the end of the world could harm it.

Ev was not there, but Spark and Works were both inside. Spark sat cross legged next to Works, who was prone, and laboring. I left them alone for a moment, rushing my attention back to the mountain spruce and Lyla.

Lyla was still moving the rivers through the tree, persistently seeking out the weak and damaged places, washing ours and the rivers' song over and through them. I showed her Works, and posed a question.

You need to go to him now, Ray. I can work all right here for a short time. But remember that even if your attention is elsewhere, I'm not doing this alone. Don't leave me for long.

Our attention, and all of our awareness, was suddenly snapped to a place some distance away, in the southwest. We knew in an instant that the Destroyer had found us, and was careening towards us at a fearsome rate of speed.

Lyla had felt its loathsome, predatory presence before, but it didn't make it any easier. Her distress tore through me; without stopping to explain, I picked a shard of memory and flung it, with the strength of the rivers behind me, to the southeast. It went crashing across the landscape, making such a disturbance that I thought immediately of what Lupine had said about the perilous state of the land's equilibrium, and feared that I might after all wreak havoc in the attempt to mend it.

The Destroyer continued heading straight towards us for a long, heart-stopping moment. It suddenly veered sharply towards my decoy, which was moving faster each second; it would have to catch up with it before it could strike.

Lyla was in wonder. *What did you just do, Ray?*

This is Henry's gift to us, love, that made it possible for me to find you. I can do it again, if need be. If you sense it coming back before I do,

let me know in no uncertain terms, all right? I have to go to Works now.
I will. But hurry, Ray!

If we had been living a little more in our bodies at the moment, I would have kissed her. As it was, I had to be satisfied with brushing her mind in a quick caress. I gathered up the largest bundle of the jostling rivers I felt I could work with, and made my petition to them. I offered the life of Works—an extraordinary, crucial life. I felt sure they would accept, but still a flood of relief ran through me when they did, and I sank far down into them. We moved quickly out from the mountain spruce, towards a newly-sprung up tent not far away.

Works was weakening rapidly. I could sense Spark sitting next to him, his head bowed down, with one hand resting lightly over Works' chest. I brought the rivers up with me and twined them around Works, getting them to work their way into him. By necessity, I had to go where they went, but I did so with great trepidation. It felt like I was violating Works' privacy, the very definition of his boundaries and his being, in a way that I had known without thinking would not have been important to Lyla when I had entwined the rivers with her. Nor had it been a problem when she and I had started this work on the mountain spruce, which was still going on; the tree had clearly had no concerns about what we were doing.

But here with Works it was different, and I could not decide if the reasons for that were real or my own immature fancy. Works was truly ancient—there was no living, mortal being anywhere here that even approached his age. He was humanly responsible for many people, and for all I knew responsible for any number of other beings. He possessed a deep, substantial authority—and a very definite privacy—that I was loath to intrude upon. Yet to pull back now, perhaps to even hesitate, might result in his death. I had to decide to trust him to forgive me if I was doing wrong, and to trust myself to work well with what was given to me. I decided what I had to, and the rivers and I entwined him.

The first thing I discovered was how close he was to dying. The thread that held him with us was perhaps a little stronger than Lyla's had been at its lowest ebb, but not by much. I encouraged the rivers, nudged them into the deep places that were Works, and concentrated on playing the rivers, and responding to their playing of me.

Lyla, back with the mountain spruce, and I both felt the Destroyer turn back towards us at the same time. I stormed through the upper reaches of my mind and grabbed the first thing I found, which was a piece of what I felt for Lyla. If I should lose this, I would lose something as dear to me as life itself. But there was no time to find a substitute; I halted the rivers' questing into Works, and with them inside me I threw my offering with all the force I could summon. This time I aimed it to the northeast, and the Destroyer spun around, screaming after it.

I needed to be thinking, feeling and sensing in several places at once, and even with the immense power rippling through me, it was a daunting task. I tried to keep parts of me not only watching for the Destroyer, but working with Lyla too, while the rivers and I turned back to Works.

The next thing I learned about Works was that he was connected to the world in ways far deeper and more profound than I had ever imagined. To say that his roots ran deep would have been a ridiculous understatement. Pathways opened up to my awareness; pathways leading from Works into every part of the world, leading upwards into the sky, downwards farther than I could see, and outwards in every direction. Seeing Works as I had, and simply thinking of him as being pretty much what I had seen, was like looking at the outside of a great library and deciding I knew what all the books inside it were like.

The pathways that radiated out from him were not simple connections to other places and things. They carried his spirit, his energy, and all his life out into the world. And when the world was well, they carried much back to him in the way of strength, understanding, vigor and compassion. But the world was not well, and seeing him in this way made horrifyingly clear how unwell it was.

Most of the paths that led to and from Works were polluted, fouled by the same poisons that had rendered the charcoal gray dead places in Vernal Park and at the Carbon River Canyon. I saw that every piece of damage, every poisoning of the ground that the

Destroyer had brought about had hurt Works directly and person-ally. Being connected to the earth in such an intense and intimate fashion cut both ways, and those cuts were killing him now.

There was not enough time to care for all of the places that were sickened, to ask the rivers to carry away all of this poison. I was faced with a desperate quandary, and Works' survival depended on its correct solution: what must I do in this instant to keep Works alive until Lyla and I could come to him together, to do for him and all he was a part of what we had been able to do for the circle at the canyon?

I could not tell; I didn't have the experience or the wisdom to know what, in this instant, would help him and what would not sustain him. The only thing I could think of was the rivers themselves. I placed my ignorance and desperation before them and asked *them* to move *me*. I had a flashing vision, there and gone so quickly I almost missed it, of the old man who had said to me, 'Get to work, child.' He had smiled at me, as if in approval, but there was no time to ponder or savor. The rivers were not as tentative as I. They took hold of me, moved me forcefully with them, and we attacked one of the pathways leading from Works that was cruelly fouled. With me at their center, they wrapped themselves around it, pressing in fiercely. Touching the poisoned path was like pressing up against a wall saturated with acid; I screamed at its vile touch, in my head if not with my lungs and throat. The rivers would not back away from it; they pressed harder, and the pain was enough that for a moment I lost all sense of where I was and what I was doing. I swam through a red haze of agony, and even in the midst of it managed to wonder at how something besides a body could feel such pain.

A chunk of the poison I was pushed up against broke away and was instantly carried off by one of the rivers. The pain lessened at once, and I took the hint. I battered my own life against the foulness, flinging my intention against it, and was absurdly excited when another piece of it broke loose and was swept away.

Now that I had a way to work, the pain lessened more quickly, and I threw myself at the masses of poison, as the rivers were doing in their own way. If this was a song, it carried a very different sort of power from the gentle ones I had sung with the rivers to Lyla, and that we were even now singing to the mountain spruce.

A great mass of foulness fell away from Works, was broken up by the rivers and carried off. The pathway we had been involved with was nearly clear, but before it was done the rivers brusquely picked me up, and we moved to another one that was just as bad.

They were all hard and painful, but the first one was by far the worst. As the rivers and I learned about this new way of working together, it went faster, and I took less of a beating in the process. We wrapped ourselves around more of the polluted pathways that were Works, and learned to batter, break apart and fling away the poison that had been killing him.

The Destroyer was coming again. Almost without thought I picked something from myself, without bothering to hope it was something I could live without. I flung it, again to the northeast, and the rivers helped me send it shooting through the land. After an instant to sense that Lyla was still working and was all right, the rivers and I turned once more to Works.

The thread that held him to life had grown in size and strength. I asked the rivers to slow down for a moment, to give me a chance to think and to sense. I brought myself to a place where I could see him; Works was breathing normally again, and his skin had resumed its normal dark, olive coloring. Spark was still sitting next to him, a look of deep wonder on his face. I was almost as reluctant to touch Spark as I had been Works, but time would not permit me to do otherwise. I touched his mind carefully, diffidently.

Spark, I can't tell—is Works going to be all right, at least for a little while?

I don't know exactly what you have been doing, Ray Holdman, but it has brought him farther back into life than I would have thought possible. He will be able to sustain himself with some help from me for a while, now.

I know you'll stay with him, and keep him safe. Thank you, Spark.

Very well, Ray Holdman. And I thank you also.

I turned myself and the rivers, preparing to return to the

mountain spruce and Lyla. But my awareness snapped to attention as I felt a great current of distress sweep into me from her.

Ray, it's still coming!

Perhaps it had learned, or perhaps I had thrown my last decoy too hard, too far. Whatever the reason, I could sense the corrosive wave of hatred and malice streaking towards us. In my mind it felt like I was sniffing the wind, and catching the first whiff of the real encounter with the enemy. And in my mind, I snarled in return.

Chapter 41

It was still a long ways away, but coming to us as fast as it ever had before. I wrapped myself around the rivers that had shown me how to help Works, and we raced back to the tree and Lyla. During the tiny span of time it took to return, images flashed past me, brief as if illuminated by a flash of lightning. I saw Lupine and Hucklebark, still in the depression that also held Works' tent; they were part way up one side of the bowl. Lupine had spread herself flat on the slanted ground, and was looking for something. Hucklebark was on his knees, bent forward, arms locked with hands planted on the earth in front of Lupine, shielding her from the wind, which was howling now. I was sure that Lupine was searching for the right entry place into the earth from which she could work, but the image of them was gone even as I thought it.

I saw Lyla's and my bodies, sitting in the lee of the mountain spruce, in spite of that being battered by the wind and the rain. Our heads were bent down nearly to our knees, hands tucked under our legs. In that instant I was puzzled to see that someone—it must have been Ev—had wrapped several turns of wide canvas pack strapping around our torsos, and run the straps around the slender tree trunk.

The last thing I saw before plunging with the rivers back into the mountain spruce was Everett Longhaul. I could not tell what he meant to do, but he had more of the canvas straps, and was winding them around the tree's trunk too.

The Destroyer was getting close now. I was fully present in the mountain spruce, and it was clear that the tree was strong, vigorous, and ready to meet what was coming. The work we had begun, and Lyla had continued, had wrought its changes quickly.

Ray, there's no time. How are we going to respond to this?

There's no more point in waiting. We might as well let it begin now—work with me, dear one.

In the last moments I was astonished to see that there were still rivers making their way into us and the tree, bending their courses from who knew where to join us. The tree was still making room for them, and it was crackling with energy and power. Lyla and I wrapped our intention around them all, stretching ourselves and our spirits near to the breaking point. We pushed them farther into that great, spacious place the tree had made for them, until we and the mountain spruce were so embedded in them it was not possible to tell where we left off and they began. The last thing I did was to make certain that the ground around the tree—which still held our own bodies and Everett Longhaul—was also deeply embedded in the rivers.

The wind was screaming, the rain lashing almost horizontally when The Destroyer struck us head on. It was moving at an enormous rate of speed, and we were standing still. The ground beneath us, the air around us, we ourselves crackled, shivered, and shook with the force of that blow. But we did not break.

The tree, aided by the immense body of energy within it, had fended off a great volume of the malignant strength that was flung at us. There were intense flashes of piercing blue light that tore into our senses, and all of us reeled at the shock of the blow. the Destroyer veered off, deflected by the mass of power brought to bear against it.

It turned with remarkable speed, and was upon us again almost immediately. I had not had time to do anything but feel what was happening when it struck again. The ground trembled, and for a moment it felt like we were falling.

But again the tree had deflected much of the force. I could feel that each blow weakened it a little; even with the help of a great body of world's energy, it was too much to believe that this ferocious little spruce tree could withstand an instant of that killing assault. I made my plan to Lyla; we asked the rivers to help us, offered what little we had, and joined them as best we could, willing our minds and spirits to stretch just a bit more to take them all in. They accepted.

The Destroyer returned for a third blow, but this time we rose up as one to meet it. In helping Works the rivers had shown me that there were times for gentleness, and other times that called for abrupt, forceful work. Instead of standing still and expecting the mountain spruce to be our defense, we thrust ourselves and the rivers forward to confront the coming strike.

The two immense, coursing streams met head on, and it was as if two great tidal waves had collided. Energy, both toxic and clean, was flung in every direction; the rocks beneath us shivered and cracked. There was a roar that cut through us as if we were tissue paper, and went on and on. For a bare instant I could see the ground around us: Lyla's and my bodies were flung backwards so that we lay flat on our backs, hoods blown back and eyes shut tight against the whipping of the rain. The webs of canvas wound around us were all that kept us from being blown away. Everett Longhaul, on the other hand, had wound innumerable loops of the canvas strap around the trunk of the mountain spruce, and tethered them to himself. It seemed impossible, but the wind was blowing harder; as if the tree didn't have enough to contend with, there seemed no way it could stand against what felt like a hurricane.

Ev had other ideas, though. He was still on his feet, bent almost double and facing directly into the wind, his hair streaming out straight behind him. He had wound the straps around the trunk to even the strain on it from top to bottom, and like a lanky draft horse was pulling against the wind with all his formidable strength. He looked to be rimmed with scarlet St. Elmo's fire that danced around his body, sizzling and popping even over the howling of the wind. It was much more than electricity, of course: Ev was standing very near the edge of the space that was embedded in the rivers, and he was exposed to much of what happens when two huge, opposing forces meet violently.

A sudden, percussive snap ran through us. It was followed by a surge of pain that peaked quickly and began to subside just as quickly. We knew that one of the tree's branches had broken off in the wind. I could only hope that not too many more would give way, and that with Ev's help the tree would stand.

The Destroyer broke away from us, veering off in what we sensed was a wide, circling movement. It was roiling viciously with malignant energy, leaving a poisonous trail in its wake. It moved away, then turned and came screaming back towards us.

To Lyla, I thought, *We must not let go of it this time.*

How can we hold this thing?

We won't find out until we do it, love. Help me to hang on to it; there's no other way.

We had thought we were doing everything possible to hold this incredible, unmanageable collection of rivers. But it was clear now that something more was required, and there was no time to search for it. I could sense Lyla's internal landscape, and knew from being so close to her that it had been generous and substantial for a long time. Now I could feel her desperately trying to make it larger still, to grow it in an instant in order to better accommodate the streams that were crammed inside us, to hold them more firmly.

She was right, and I needed to do the same. Within me was a great forest, whose limits I was not even aware of. Right now it was teeming with rivers of the world's lifeblood. Despite what was to me an amazing expansiveness, it was filled to bursting with them, and there were only seconds with which to do something about it.

I was certain that straining against the borders of my spirit would bring no help whatever. The alternative was to find a way to relax them. How in the world could I relax anything at a time like this? Since I could think of nothing else to do, I tried again what I'd done before and placed the limits of *me* into a small bird that I lifted up and gently thrust into the air. It disappeared, and I replaced it with a belief that I hoped and prayed was larger. I felt the forest waver, and shift, and from one instant to the next there seemed to be more room inside. The rivers shifted too, and in that moment it appeared that perhaps I could hold a few more, a little more firmly.

I had no idea what exactly I had just done, but there was no chance to consider it. The next collision with the Destroyer was upon us, and it would be worse than any of the ones before. Another percussive snap went through us, followed almost immediately by a third. The pain was worse, but the mountain spruce discarded it with a tree's equivalent of an impatient shrug.

We held ourselves around all of the rivers we could reach. They strained and stretched, barely under any kind of control, ours or theirs. We flung it all—including us—at the Destroyer, wrapped ourselves around it, and felt a searing, terrifying jolt of horror and revulsion rip through us at the contact.

The rivers were coursing madly over its surface, into and through the Destroyer. The first awful moment of really touching it diminished as the rivers hurled themselves against it, trying to tear it apart as they had broken the great clots of pollution that had sickened Works. The Destroyer itself was another thing altogether, of course, and no simple battering against it would suffice. It jerked, heaved, and thrashed in our embrace, but it could not shake us loose. Neither could we seem to even weaken it, for all the indescribable energy we marshaled against it.

The two great streams remained locked in a lethal embrace. Though the Destroyer continued to buck and writhe, we were not moving through the earth, or above it. Even though so much was in motion, for a moment it seemed as if we were all standing still.

In that moment it came to me as it had before, the hideous, skeletal figure with its lank, filthy hair, red flashing eyes, and mouth contorted in a grimace of hatred. It pushed its face directly into my awareness, as if my own face were only an inch away. Its breath was hot, and foul beyond bearing. Without knowing how or why, I thought of Works, and of how he had taught me to consider the horror of this, and I responded without speaking aloud.

Whether or not I had a hand in making *you, I'll have a hand in* unmaking *you.*

I held my ground, my awareness staring into its mad eyes, watching its mouth twisting and leering, opening and closing spasmodically, nostrils flaring, willing myself not to flinch. Lyla was with me, and she was like the lioness I'd imagined at the gathering, waiting for the moment to spring, her ferocity goaded to a pitch that would send any sane being howling in the opposite direction.

We stared into its foul visage, refusing to budge. Time seemed to stretch out behind us, and there seemed to be none of it before us. For the briefest instant I turned my attention towards Everett Longhaul. He was still strapped to the tree, still pulling with all his might against the unrelenting wind. If I had not understood what I was sensing, I would have thought he was completely engulfed in flame. But he was simply caught in the awful confluence of the two massive streams. I had no idea how he was surviving it, but there was no doubt he was still working as only he could do.

Lyla saw him with me, since there was no barrier between us to stop any kind of thought or understanding. Even as the Destroyer loomed in the very midst of our being, we saw Ev with a brilliant clarity. We saw his open defiance of forces that any conventional reasoning would assume must crush him like a bug, and the incredible, steadfast devotion to doing his work as he found it, whatever it took, in whatever way it must be done.

We saw the mountain spruce that had brought us into itself, had made room to hold a world's worth of energy. We saw them both, and were filled with wonder. And suddenly we were filled with pride, and admiration, and love, and rage. And we knew what to do.

The lioness redoubled her ferocity, and it was a fearful thing to behold for anything in this world. Lyla reared her spirit up higher, and still higher, until she seemed to fill the earth and sky together, and her rage was from another realm. And a simple, lost man whom the world had somehow decided should be a Mender reared himself up, filled to bursting with all that had been given, and gathered it, lioness, innumerable rivers and all, in an unbreakable grip. I hurled us into the face of the Destroyer with the force of Mother Mountain beneath and behind me.

The horrible face wavered, crumpled grotesquely, and began to dissolve. The earth trembled and shook far below us, and we could feel a great crack forming deep beneath the surface. It was as if the ground had decided it would not tolerate such treatment, and was determined to swallow this mountain and everything in and on it. The Destroyer's horrid features vanished, but it remained, locked in our embrace, still thrashing and writhing.

Lupine had known how strong was my fear of doing great damage while trying to mend the Destroyer's killing harm, and now it looked like I had been right to fear it. Even as we fought to prevent its escape, we could feel the earth getting ready to give way in what would surely be a catastrophic failure, that nothing anywhere near this mountain would survive.

Even as I thought of Lupine, we found her. She and Hucklebark were deep down in the ground, though we could still sense their bodies on the slope of the depression nearby. Beneath the surface Lupine was rapidly wending her way downwards, stopping for an instant from place to place to deliver a shove in one direction, a sharp tug in another. Hucklebark was holding on to her somehow, as if to help her find her way while she spent all of her energy and awareness on the immense slabs and sections of earth that had come unhinged. He was an anchor that kept her oriented without slowing her down.

Lupine worked feverishly, racing from crisis to crisis, plowing through the earth in a desperate effort to prevent disaster. Hucklebark moved next to her with massive grace and speed, with an unerring guidance that made their motions look like a flashing, ethereal dance. They continued downwards into the earth, their spirits dwindling into the distance, and I wanted to follow, to stand somewhere near them, watch them in the beauty and power of their work.

But we were still clinched with the Destroyer. For the few instants that we had regarded Lupine and Hucklebark it had been quiet, as if trying to decide what to do. Now it resumed writhing and thrashing, with more violence than before. The rivers bucked and shoved against it, and we had to use all of our will and concentration to hold them together. Even if Lupine managed to prevent the earth from collapsing out from under us, it was obvious we could not remain in this vicious stalemate for much longer.

We needed to move the Destroyer, not just away from here, but somewhere that it would not be able to cause harm. Lyla agreed wholeheartedly, but made it clear she had no idea where we must go or how it could be done. I did have an idea; when I gave it to her, I could feel the fear warring with her ferocity and rage. But in the absence of anything else to do, when *something* has to be done, what choice is there?

The rivers had been moving around the Destroyer, but also within it and through it, trying it seemed to take the Destroyer apart piece by piece, until the confluence of energies felt like a muddled chaos, and it was hard to separate friend from foe. We called out to the rivers, asked urgently that they come back together and allow us to help move them. We offered the chance to move this revolting invader away, to muscle it out of our world, and they accepted.

They flowed back to us, never entirely letting go of the Destroyer, until we once again had our combined will and intention wrapped firmly around them, and they in turn wrapped tightly around the Destroyer. It continued writhing, grappling with us, but now it felt like it was trying simply to get away. With ourselves so deep inside the rivers, and our minds occupying exactly the same place in the world, Lyla and I began by nudging the rivers, then gently shoving, and within a moment pulling with all the spirit we could muster to get the whole mass moving.

We felt a shift, and very slowly we began to pull the Destroyer along with us. For a moment we thought we would be able to control this motion, and that my plan would succeed. But whether the Destroyer had been quietly deciding how to respond, or marshaling its immense power, it suddenly shot into violent motion that nearly tore it from our grasp, and screamed forward at an immense rate of speed with us in tow. I had a last, flashing glimpse of Everett Longhaul faithfully pulling against the wind, and of the enveloping scarlet fire that had surrounded him being sucked away in our wake.

We held desperately to the rivers as the Destroyer dragged us screaming across the landscape. I had just turned my awareness away from Ev to learn where we were headed, when a bolt of horror tore through me; we were headed directly towards Works' tent, within which he still lay, partly conscious, Spark still kneeling beside him. If we collided with it, Works and Spark would be blown out of the world just as Henry had been.

We wrenched with everything we had, trying to turn the malignant juggernaut we were riding, and at first it seemed like nothing could change its course an inch. Something huge and shadowy reared up before us; it was massive, and menacing, and it seemed that the Destroyer—and we with it—would be crushed to oblivion if we collided with it. Another second of speeding towards it, and I could see that it was coming from Spark, or perhaps it somehow *was* him; I couldn't know which.

What mattered was that whatever Spark had expressed or produced, it was enough to convince the Destroyer to change direction, just a little. The instant we felt it start to veer, we pulled the rivers as hard as we could in the same direction. The result was that the whole screaming train of Destroyer, rivers and us lurched wildly away from Spark, and Works behind him, into a great circling arc. There was no time for relief, though, for as soon as we saw that our direction had changed, we found ourselves headed straight towards the place where the bodies of Lupine and Hucklebark crouched, bodies waiting in silence and stillness while their spirits worked feverishly deep beneath the surface of the earth.

It was no surprise to learn that the Destroyer would always orient itself towards something to destroy. I recalled—a tiny fragment of memory—that working in anger had nearly killed me, and almost lost me the help of the People of The Home, but anger welled up high in me then, threatening to overrule all else I was thinking and feeling. It was Lupine herself—who now lay directly in our deadly path—who had said that more often than not anger grew directly from the fetid ground of fear. I was afraid for her, now, and there was only time to try, as best as I could, to dispassionately direct my rising anger into the right action.

I gave another thought to Lyla, and she responded instantly. With all the force of my anger and her still coursing ferocity, we shoved downwards on the rivers, and the Destroyer.

Abruptly we plunged deep into the ground, spiraling downwards at a pace that would have rendered my body paralyzed from dizziness and fear had it been with me. It was impossible to tell in which direction we were going, only that we were moving too fast for conscious thought.

Let go of where and how we are being taken, I thought to us. *There is nothing to do now, but to trust them.*

I placed the thought of a fearsome, forbidding place to which I had been taken once before, in front of the rivers. I asked and offered; there was no more joining to be done, for we were already so enmeshed in them there was nowhere else to strive to.

Though we were careening through the planet at a pace beyond understanding, we could feel something change. The rivers now had something to aim for, and though we were thoroughly disoriented, we could tell that all was being carried in a particular direction. The Destroyer never let up its bucking and thrashing for an instant, but now the rivers seemed to anticipate its every move, responding to those changes in a way that reinforced the direction I had asked for.

We roared through the world, going so fast that our awareness could not catch and hold the least detail of our passing. It seemed at that rate we could travel around the planet in an instant, yet we went on and on. Perhaps we had outstripped our own sense of time; nothing made any sense then, and there was nothing to do but hold on.

We sensed it looming in the distance, while it was still very far away. I felt Lyla's shooting sense of terror as it made its presence known. Though I shared that terror with her, I had been here once before, and I understood what we faced. I brought up the memory, and though the fear diminished a little it was still running deep and strong in us, and rightfully so.

The mountain of not-life was buried so deeply in the earth it was beyond the reach of all but the most persistent rivers. Yet Riven and Rill had brought me here before. I had accepted their solution, and the entire mass of uncountable rivers, our own spirits, and the Destroyer held captive within us plunged towards that immense mass of Opposition. It grew larger more quickly than I would have thought possible, and then it was imminently near.

I placed my final thought before Lyla and the rivers, and they understood. We waited for another instant, but that was all the time there was. With a last, desperate wrenching motion that sucked up the final scraps of our will, we flung the Destroyer away from us, towards the looming mass.

The Destroyer struck it with a roaring, booming percussion that buffeted us mercilessly in a backwash of force. It seemed to disintegrate as it struck, and pieces of the Destroyer seemed to fall into the inverted mountain as they broke away from the whole. Perhaps it only took an instant, but it seemed a long time that we watched in fascinated horror as the Destroyer was blasted apart and the pieces of it swallowed whole by the mass of not-life before us.

Whether or not we had needed to wait that long before releasing the Destroyer, it had been too long for us. There was no way to stop, or even change the direction we were plunging in. The rivers, Lyla and I struck the mountain too.

The violence of that impact was beyond anything we could have imagined. Although there was nothing physical of us to break or wreck, the pain of it was overwhelming. The rivers themselves splashed off the surface of the under-earth mountain as if they were streams of water, bouncing off it, breaking into millions of pieces and then immediately coalescing back into themselves. Lyla and I, still unbreakably together, were flung away from them. There was a rolling, grinding thunder that felt as if it would shake our spirits apart. We had no idea where we were being thrown; only an idea of endless noise, and chaos, and pain. Our will was spent, our awareness overwhelmed, and in the next moment, there was nothing.

Chapter 42

It was quiet. That is not quite right: it was silent in a way that is impossible when there are ears to hear, and air to vibrate, no matter how small the sound.

And it was dark. Not simply the darkness that expresses the absence of light, but a darkness that signals the absence of everything; a darkness that not even nightmares can produce.

An instant of dire panic arose, and then subsided as quickly, for I could feel that Lyla was still with me. Her mind lay quietly next to mine. It was there, but she would not or could not communicate. For a moment I was frightened by her silence; yet I could feel that we were still connected as one being, and I knew that she was resting somewhere in the midst of a deep, deep stillness. It was easy to understand the need to rest, immobile and impassive, after what we had endured. When I had brought her into the rivers I had let her alone for a time, to work out her own way of being there. I would do the same now, and return to her soon; it was enough to know that I was not alone.

The last moments of our struggle with the Destroyer began to reassemble themselves in my mind, and it required a strong effort of will to consider what had happened without actually reliving it—something I was entirely unprepared to do. But if we were to understand where we had come to, we would have to consider what had happened, and what it might mean.

It was clear that we had been thrown out of the rivers by the force of our collision with the Opposition, the inverted mountain of not-life buried so deeply within the earth. And also clear that the rivers, which were all that could take us back to our bodies and our lives, were nowhere to be found. We floated in nothing. I thought it likely that we had been thrown downwards by the impact, but here—if nothing could even be called *here*—there was no direction, no up or down. Even if we could learn how to move in a place such as this, which way should we go?

For that matter, I wondered how it was that we could live at all in this place. An absence of everything meant, naturally enough, an absence of any life, a lack of the energy required to sustain it, even in the form of simple awareness. Perhaps Lyla and I survived at all because there were two of us, and at least for a time we would sustain each other, until our own gifts of life dwindled and then faded away.

We would have to find a way to move—that was all there was to it. The problem of *where* would not be a problem at all, until we solved the *how*.

The silence, the darkness, and the absolute lack of anything to feel or sense was eerie and uncomfortable. But when I considered it, I found to my deep surprise that I was not afraid. Not long ago I would have been paralyzed, unable to even think, if this had happened; now, I rested calmly in the midst of the negation of all life and pondered how to deal with it.

Perhaps it was Lyla's heart and mind—nestled within my own— that made it possible to be this way. Maybe too the part of my being responsible for the manufacture of terror and uncertainty was exhausted, tapped dry by all that had happened in what, after all, was a short period of time. Perhaps we weren't alive at all, and there was nothing left for us to know or fear. This was not a mystery I was inclined to get comfortable with, but until I could think of something to do about it, it would remain just as it was.

I felt Lyla's awareness stirring, emerging slowly. There was nothing but me to be aware of here, and our gladness at being together was enough, for the moment, to overcome anything that threatened to interfere with it.

We did it, she thought to me. *The Destroyer is gone.*

Yes it is, love. But I'm beginning to think that we are gone too.
Have you been in this place before?
Never. I have no idea where we are, or how to move away from here.

She put many questions to me as we tried together to understand what needed to be done, but I could answer none of them. After some time of fruitless thinking, we sat quietly, waiting and hoping for inspiration, or at least a useful thought.

Ray, it's changing. I think something is coming.

She was right, though what or who it could be was unknowable. Bit by bit, the absolute darkness in which we were entombed was being diluted by the faintest possible light. It was so diffuse we could not tell where it came from, but it grew slowly, gently, like the door into a darkened room being opened with infinite care—except there was no room, no door, and who was there to take care?

We waited, having no alternative, as the light gradually filled our minds with its warmth. We were both far beyond fear by now, but even if there had been any left in us, it would have been hard to fear the light that was coming in. It felt right, right and proper, as if it were a splendid gift we had not dared to hope for.

One moment there was nothing but the growing illumination. The next there were two people in front of our minds. They sat on nothingness, composed and alert, looking at us. There was the old woman, who had shown me the rivers of the world in the palm of her hand. Next to her sat the old man, who had shown me how to find the People of The Home, and had recalled to me the power and generosity of a mountain spruce. Lyla saw them with me, and was filled to overflowing with wonder and awe. Her feelings, already a part of me, amplified what I felt, and we were silent.

The old woman bore a soft expression that may or may not have been a slight smile. She gazed at us intently, and we fell into the bottomless depths of her eyes. They held all of the living world, and all that lay beyond it, and within that world we saw where we were. Far below the tip of the inverted mountain of not-life was where we lay; we had been flung so deep into the earth there was nothing anywhere near to us. We saw the multitudes of life upon the world's surface, and that life which lived within the thin skin of it, both just above and just below the ground. We saw the rivers coursing through it all, and we knew that until a short time ago, many of those rivers had been coursing through us. They were all so far away, now. If there was a pathway between the rest of life and us, we could not see it.

We emerged from the old woman's vision, retreating back to where we faced them both. The old man was smiling broadly now, though I had to think Lyla and I had little to smile about. But he continued beaming at us as he spoke in his creaky, grandfatherly voice, which we heard without hearing.

"Well done, children. You're almost finished, now. If you want to get home, you'll need to reach for it."

The old woman lifted a hand towards us and gave it a turning motion. We felt ourselves—our awareness—being turned with it, until we were faced away from them, looking out onto a nothingness illuminated by only the barest scrap of light from the old people, that shone faintly past us. We felt what would have been hands on our backs, if we had had backs, and there was a gentle but firm shove. It sent us pitching forward, and in that instant we realized which way 'up' was, and that we had been pushed that way.

We moved slowly, dreamily, making our way upwards and out from that place of nothing. There didn't seem to be anything we could do to help ourselves along, for there was nothing to hold on to, nothing to push against; only the motion that had been given to us, and the light that was almost gone again.

It seemed such a long time that we went that way, going on and on, all because of a single shove from behind. We began to think about the possibility of actually returning, about the incredible chance that we might get to come back to our own place in the world. But there was nothing to be seen ahead or above us. I tried extending my senses, straining to find the merest hint of a river, or any kind of world's energy, and nothing came back to me. As time went on with no change in anything, we began to worry that perhaps we were slowing down, that we would be stopped before we could reach a place where we could move ourselves.

We began to think of some of the people we knew and loved. We thought of Works, and Spark, Lupine and Hucklebark, and of course, Everett Longhaul. We thought of the People of The Home; not with the same kind of intensely human love, but with a reverence and respect that is also a treasure to hold. They were all a part of us.

A memory bubbled up, and I showed it to Lyla. When Riven and Rill had brought me to the mountain of not-life, there had been a very bad moment when I had felt utterly alone in the world. But I had finally understood that it was not possible to be truly alone, and I had known that if I reached out to those that mattered to me, they would respond whenever it was humanly possible. Lyla understood immediately, and we placed the thought of all of those people before us, and reached out to them.

Were we moving a little faster again? There was no way of knowing, but doing something—anything—was better than doing nothing. We kept our dear ones ahead of us, stretching our spirits to get to them, and if we only thought we were moving, that was all right.

This journey back to ourselves, our lives, went on, extending backwards into irrelevance and forwards into an ever-diminishing end. We were so very, very tired, we had been through so much, and now it began to feel to me like everything we strove to return to was so far over the horizon we would never return to it. My reach towards life and the people who made it real for us began to shorten, and I started to consider giving it all up, and letting myself simply fade away into the nothingness through which we strove.

Be still, Ray. Remember who it is that gave us that push back to life, and have a little faith.

Lyla had felt the discouragement rising in me, and gone directly to the spot in my heart that was faltering. In all the life that had brought me to this place, I had never trusted any kind of faith. What had there ever been that was worthy of trust? What had there ever been to show me that faith could be repaid?

And yet: the only reason we were here, struggling to make it back to a life we loved so passionately, was that I had discovered trust, and stillness, and—the thought shook me to my depths—faith.

In order to do what had had to be done, I had placed more trust in the rivers than I had ever known existed anywhere, let alone in my own being. I had found Lyla, hidden away from the world so thoroughly that no one knew how to find her, by learning to be still. And I had been compelled, through some deep alchemy of the spirit, to turn that trust into faith, as I had played and sung those rivers, and unconditionally allowed them to play and sing me.

Move back into your heart, dear Ray. I am already here; come back into this beautiful forest, and work with me.

How could I have possibly forgotten this place? Perhaps it was too new; in any event, I would never forget its presence again. I did not have to go there—remembering it was enough. I came back to her, and back to myself. All the people I loved, and the Mountain that had become a part of me, were before us. We reached for them, not knowing how or if our reaching would take us there. Time returned, and I entered into it with Lyla, and we worked within a sphere of stillness, trusting that whatever would happen was how it was intended.

We were still reaching, striving through nothingness, having no idea if we actually moved or deceived ourselves with hope, when I sensed something far ahead of us. It was so far away that I could not be certain it was there at all. I wanted it to be there, wanted it with all my heart, whatever it might turn out to be. For a moment I was afraid to believe that it was there. But Lyla sensed it through me.

Go on and believe it, love. What would be the point in denial?

And so I did believe it. Time continued to pass, and I tried to still my racing hopes, to give whatever might or might not lie ahead of us the chance to become more than hope, to become real.

From one moment to the next it changed. In one small bite of time it was no more than a hopeful dream, something so insubstantial I was afraid of accidentally blowing it away from us like a dandelion seed. In the bite of time that followed, it was something real—there were no bodies, no life, no flesh and blood where we were, and yet it seemed to be a hand, reaching out to us.

In the next moments, it became two hands, and we strove to reach them, straining our exhausted spirits and wills, urging them on as if asking a spent team of horses to burn that last particle of strength. The hands grew closer, larger. We had but one, small burst of effort left in us, a burst whose very presence was an enduring surprise, and if it failed, we knew there would be absolutely nothing left to save us. We spent it, and if our bodies had been doing the reaching, our bones would have cracked with the effort of it. The hands grew close, closer, and they grasped us in a grip that was warm, and firm. They pulled, and we went with them, and I could sense ahead of us places of life and energy.

They were the hands of Riven and Rill; I could feel them, even though they themselves were far from us. They pulled us upwards, and soon there were more hands extended towards us, high above. The People of The Home did not speak to us, didn't enter into us in any way. But they drew us onwards, towards the others who were waiting.

As we rose through the lifeless places I could feel rivers of the world's lifeblood above, following their courses, carrying those who waited for us. Though there was no energy left in us, we felt a surge of joy run through the forest of my heart, where we lay drained and hoping, dreaming of the return to life.

The first river we were drawn into felt like the first, convulsive breath of air that comes leaping in when the water overhead still seems infinite, and yet we have finally broken through to the surface. We clung to it, drew it into us, inhaled it, and lived. The hands of Riven and Rill slowly released their hold of us, but now the river held us gently in its grip, and moved us towards the hands beyond. They grew nearer, and soon those hands grasped us. We had thought that the joy leaping through us was as much as life had to offer, and were well content with that; but there was more, and it surged higher still to feel the touch of Works and Spark as they held us firm and safe, drawing us ever closer back to the world.

We moved faster now, and faster still, until our passage was a blur of movement and energy. We let them carry us, passive and inert, too spent to do any more than know that we would return after all, and to feel an exhausted delight.

The movement began to slow, gradually at first and then

more and more definitely, until upwards and ahead of us lay two bodies, flat on the ground, next to a small mountain spruce. We approached them with wonder, with an astonished happiness, and slipped gently into them.

It was a revelation, a stunning discovery, to feel air on our skin, to know that there were muscles that could be moved, eyes that would see. But they would have to wait: right now, sleep seemed like the benediction of the world, and it would not be denied. Before our eyes had opened, we entered back into ourselves, and slept.

Chapter 43

"What are you thinking about, love?"

Lyla's voice drew me sharply back into time and place, from some dreaming land. Her hand rested gently on my arm; where were we?

I was lying on my back, looking upwards into the ceiling of the tent that Ev Longhaul had brought up the Mountain for me. Sunlight pushed its way through the tan colored skin of the tent, and a light breeze played about its edges outside.

There were rivers running through me. I felt certain that they would always be there, that I would never again be away from them. The thought made me supremely happy. Within that happiness, I tried to work my way back to where I had been, trying to answer Lyla's question.

"I was thinking about Henry."

She leaned over me, brushed her lips lightly across my forehead and then kissed me, settling into it, graceful and strong, as I wrapped my arms around her.

Some time later she lifted herself to look at me more clearly.

"What were you thinking about him?"

"I know what happened. I understand now how he tricked the Destroyer so completely into thinking he was me. And I also know who that Henry-type voice inside me is."

She sat up alertly. "All right, don't keep me in suspense. Out with it."

"Henry knew how to reach in and take out a little piece of me, and leave a piece of himself in its place. He must have done it some time when I was sleeping, when we were at Moraine Park before the gathering, or maybe the first night we were there."

Lyla's eyes unfocused as she considered the implications of that, and a small sigh escaped her.

"You believe he was that powerful."

"Yes, I do," I replied.

"It strikes me as horribly dangerous knowledge," Lyla said. "And for all the awful price something like that could extract from a person, I don't think it ever made him happy to be that powerful, or to keep it such a profound secret."

I considered Lyla's way of thinking and understanding, and realized with a start that she was not within me, not in the way we had been when we had worked to mend this part of the world. But perhaps it wasn't right to want that all the time; besides, there was a whole world of delight and discovery to be gained just by being people again. Having thoroughly distracted myself, I had to take some time to reapply my mind to the problem Lyla had set before me. She waited, patient and attentive.

"I don't think Henry was at all concerned with happiness. I expect he had set that aside, in the same way that Lupine taught me to set aside unnecessary fear. Not that I'm in any kind of agreement with that way of being," I said, as I reached up and drew her to me again.

There was a sudden restlessness in her, and after a moment I honored it, and let go. She sat up again, regarding me with what looked like a mixture of love, curiosity and anticipation. I wondered what she was thinking, and nearly laughed aloud to think that this person, whose spirit had been so deeply enmeshed in mine there had been nothing whatever between us, should now pose me a mystery.

I started to ask her where Works was, and then realized there was no need. The rivers took me to him instantly. He was walking along the top of Mother Mountain, and Spark was at his side. Works was by no means completely healed, but the sickness that had been killing him had been arrested. I was certain that if he allowed us to bring the rivers into him again he would recover, to live for a good while longer. Perhaps—I thought, having learned much about who and what he really was—as long as he chose to.

Lupine and Hucklebark were nearby, clear in my awareness. Hucklebark was studying the ground intently, as if retracing the tortuous path he and Lupine had taken through the earth. Lupine herself simply sat, quietly taking in the sky, the sunlight, the air, the sand, gravel and stones beneath her. I had not been able to think about it before now, but she had done it. The fact that we were still alive, and still on Mother Mountain, meant that she had done the impossible, and the genius of her power and skill had shoved the ground beneath us back into a balance that had averted disaster.

Everett Longhaul was nowhere to be seen. For a short moment I was torn with worry that he had not survived his work. But the rivers found him for me; he was only a couple of miles away, off on another of his mysterious errands, and there was no reason to bother him now.

And finally I sent my mind out to a little mountain spruce, which I found still standing just a short way from where I lay. It was tattered, still disheveled from the storm that had tried in all its fury to kill it, but the tree stood as steadfastly crooked, wind-blown but upright as it always had. The innumerable loops of pack strapping had been removed, and it stood unencumbered and open. I gave it my greetings, blended with a gratitude that was far too great for words. It extended its invitation, and I promised that sometime soon, when we could, we would return to it.

Whether Lyla's restlessness had wormed its way into me, or I had produced an abundance of my own, it was time to be moving about again. Lyla sensed it in me, and we got up in the same motion, and went out into the sunshine.

The sky was the brilliant, cobalt blue that blesses the mountain places after a particularly ferocious storm has passed. It was punctuated by small, intensely white clouds that were moving across the dome of blue much faster than the breeze lower down was pushing against us. The air was warm, but under the warmth I could feel the first edge of autumn, such a short season up here. That slight edge would sharpen from one day to the next, until in much less time than seemed right, the biting cold of winter would be upon us. I turned to Lyla.

"So…" I suddenly felt self-conscious, and then realized how ridiculous it was to be self-conscious with this woman. "So where do you stay for the winter?"

She smiled radiantly, and gently pulled my face close to hers. "I've been wondering when you were going to ask me that," she said softly. "Shall I show it to you soon?"

My heart leapt upwards, and a ripple of happiness swept from one end of its great forest to the other. I could barely breathe, and my voice was as soft as hers.

"Yes, please. Is it a fine and private place?"

She laughed, and—for the moment—the most intense part of the spell was broken, though all of the happiness remained. "Yes, it is indeed a fine and private place. I recall telling you in some past age that this really is a lovely home." Looking thoughtful, she went on, "Though it is a bit small for two. We'll have to ask Ev for help in acquiring some materials for making it a little bigger."

"How much would you care to bet that's what he's up to this very moment?" I said.

Her eyes widened at the thought. "Are we that transparent, or is he simply that presumptuous?"

I laughed. "Yes. And we shall take him most severely to task for such presumptuousness, while we're gratefully accepting whatever he has brought us."

A movement nearby caught my attention, and I turned to see that Lupine had risen to her feet and was walking slowly towards us. Hucklebark had looked up from his study of the stones and the gravel, and seemed to be deciding whether or not to come too.

Lupine reached us, turned to Lyla, and hugged her with a tender ferocity that expressed Lupine perfectly. As long as I live, that's how I want to remember her.

"Welcome back, Lyla," she said, and kissed her on the forehead. Lyla blushed, looked deep into Lupine's eyes, and said simply, "Thank you."

Lupine turned to me then. She stood on her toes, placed her hands on my shoulders, and said, "Welcome back, Mender." She stood back down, and bowed her head just slightly. I carefully raised it, bent down and placed my forehead lightly against hers. The rivers flowed from me to her, and back again, but gently this time. I moved back again, and took my turn gazing into her fathomless eyes that were filled with fire, and stone, and still brimming with humanity.

"You did it," I said softly. "Thank you for saving all our lives."

Smiling, she said, "We all did things we didn't know were possible, Ray." She turned around to face Hucklebark, who had quietly come up behind her. "Especially this particular friend of ours."

I looked over Lupine's shoulder at him, looming over her like a great human cliff. He took this as his cue to sidle carefully around Lupine with a diffidence that would have been comical, except for the fact that without him Lupine would never have been able to rebalance a mountain; that was how I would choose to think of him from now on.

Once he was before me, he grabbed me in a bear hug that squeezed the air out of my lungs in a long whoosh. I returned it as best as I could, even though it wasn't possible to get my arms all the way around him.

He eventually set me back on the ground and eyed me, beaming. "For a while there, I didn't reckon I'd ever see you again, Ray. But here you are: and now, of all things, you're a real Mender." He chuckled. "I'm a pretty lucky guy, I suppose—not too many folks get to see something like that happen."

He turned to Lyla, and wrapped her in a great hug that was as enthusiastic, though not quite so strong, as the one he had bestowed on me. "And you too, you know. What would we have done without our Lyla?" He looked down at her tenderly. "Girl, I am so *happy* for you!"

She looked confused for a moment, then glanced at me, blushed the deepest pink again, and then burst out laughing. "Hucklebark, the world is a richer place for you being in it," she said when her breath returned. "And I hope it stays that way for a long, long time."

It was Hucklebark's turn for confusion, and he looked at the ground, muttering something none of us could make out. He was rescued when Lupine looked up towards the lip of the rocky bowl. I had known he was coming, and when I looked up too, Works was just appearing over the top, Spark beside him. Works was grinning broadly, and though he was not fully healed, his stride held no hint of the sickness that had come so close to killing him.

They came up to our little group, Spark standing a bit off to one side. Works took my hand in both of his, and simply said, "Ray."

The skin of his hands was warm, and firm, despite the wrinkles of great age. The rivers bounded through me and into him, and I could feel how far he reached into the earth, and up into the air, and to touch him was to be cradled by the planet. I basked in that feeling for a moment. His eyes led directly into the most spacious, expansive heart I would ever know, and in that moment I felt so much love for him, and at the same time so much awe of him, that I didn't know what to do.

My eyes filled with tears, and I could not speak. Works seemed to know exactly what was happening, even though I didn't. He said gently, "There will be time to talk, and listen, and learn. You are a part of us, now, and we are a part of you, and there is nowhere else you need to go, unless you wish it so."

The tears made their own, tiny life rivers as they ran silently down my cheeks, and I realized with amazement that for the second time in my life, I was crying for joy. Works gently let my hand go, and I stood uncertainly before him, wiping my face with a sleeve.

"I've come home," I said, and then stopped in wonder at the words.

"Yes, you have indeed come home," Works said.

"'Bout time too, is all I can say," Hucklebark put in.

I looked around me. Everyone was smiling, not trying to avoid my feelings, not trying to make anything of them. They were simply there, and we were simply together.

My glance rested on Spark, who was still standing quietly just off to one side. "Thank you, Spark. Thank you for everything. And

I really, really promise to try not to get killed any more."

He nodded slightly, and his face relaxed into what was just barely a smile. "I shall hold you to that, and help you to it also, in whatever way I can. You have earned as much of my gratitude as I can offer also, Ray Holdman, our Mender."

I nodded back silently, taking in what he had said—*Ray Holdman, our Mender.* I remembered to send a stream of gratitude towards The Home, in hopes that the People would receive it, and know that I knew what I owed them, now and forever.

I took a deep breath, and let it out in a gusty sigh. "I just wish Ev was here right now. It's not like I'm leaving or anything, but it doesn't feel right that he isn't here."

"Doesn't feel right? Doesn't *feel* right?" rang a high, nasal twang from the rim of the rocky depression. Everett Longhaul came striding down its side, taking in as much territory with one long-limbed pace as I would with three. "Well, I *am* sorry, ladies and gentlemen, but that simply won't do. *Some*thing will have to be done about it." He grinned as he reached us, sweeping his gaze to encompass everyone. "Any suggestions?"

I moved over to him and grasped his hand, laughing as I did so. "Everett Longhaul, Lyla's right—and I swear that whatever theatre you ran away from must have been filled with crazy people to let you go like that."

Still holding my hand, he drew himself up to his full height which, though it seemed to change from moment to moment, was always formidable. "My dear Holdman," he began in his most pretentious voice, "There is no glittering proscenium in the world that can hold me, for, as you already know, I am much larger than life." He dropped his character suddenly, and winked broadly. "And that's only seven-eighths hogwash, you know."

Still laughing and looking upwards at him, I shook my head. "I'm not convinced it's hogwash at all, Ev. But how are you? How did you survive that mayhem, while you were saving the mountain spruce's life? And if I may be so bold, what kind of mysterious errand have you been galloping to now? Oh, and one more thing— did you bring any coffee?"

He dropped my hand as if it had turned red hot, raising both his own in mock horror. "Please, *please*. Do not pepper the sensitive *artiste* with such questions! Well, anyway," he said, shucking off his ever present, enormous pack, "That last one is pretty easy. Hucklebark, would you consider doing the honors?"

"Sure thing, Ev," Hucklebark said, chuckling. "Whatever the great man says." He turned and headed towards his pack, a bag of coffee beans in his massive hand.

"So tell us, Ray," Ev said, turning back to me. "What's next for you? Are you heading off to new and exotic realms, to chart the unchartable, plumb the unplumbable?"

"Of course not, Ev," I said, smiling. "I'm staying right here, as long as that's possible." I took Lyla's hand in mine. "There isn't anywhere else of interest."

Ev directed his most benign, chivalrous gaze at Lyla, swept up her other hand, and kissed it dramatically.

"By all means, my dear ones, by all means. Let me know your needs when the time is right; I am at your disposal." He smiled wickedly. "And if I dare say so myself, I can be of some assistance in the architectural department."

I turned to Lyla. "You see? Didn't I tell you? How can we deal with such a man?"

She laughed, and turned back to Ev. She stood on her toes, as high as she could get, and he bent down as she tenderly kissed his cheek.

"Dear Ev, thank you for everything, now, past, and future. We love you with all our hearts."

He stood straight again, gazed to the sky like a moonstruck calf, and sighed melodramatically.

"Ah, yes. Paid in full already. What now is there to look forward to?"

Chapter 44

When dusk was turning to the soft dark of a late summer night, we sat on the rim of the depression in the top of Mother Mountain, above the living place of a small mountain spruce, and watched the stars and a waning crescent moon pour their silver onto Tahoma. We had been silent for some time, letting its beauty wash over us, when Lyla turned to me.

"It isn't really gone, is it, Ray?"

I didn't have to reflect at all on her meaning.

"No, not at all. The Opposition, or Destroyer, or whatever we'll call it when we know it better, is as much a part of the world as we are, I think. It will be back, sometime."

"What will you do?" she asked.

"I'll keep watch, and if we're lucky, I'll catch it before it has the time to gain strength." I turned to look at Tahoma. "I don't know what it really means for the world to be in balance. If I ever do learn that, maybe I'll have a better idea of how to take some part in keeping it that way."

She smiled, and rested her face on my shoulder. "That sounds like it could take a good, long time."

"I don't doubt it for a moment," I said, stroking her hair where it flowed down her back. "I don't want to be greedy, but I can't help hoping the rivers will help me to age as gracefully as you, and the others."

I thought, because of how I'd said it, that she might respond lightly. But she surprised me, and looked deeply thoughtful.

"I don't believe the world would ever consider giving such a gift to a human without helping them to use it properly. And that will definitely need time."

"Is this a comfortable mystery," I mused, "or a prickly one?"

Lyla dug an elbow into my ribs. "Comfortably prickly, wise man."

She sobered again almost immediately.

"Ray, I can't help feeling there is some kind of unfinished business that's on your mind. What actually is next?"

I thought, letting one of the last warm evening breezes of the year move over us, and then turned to face her.

"You are next, love. And after that, you. And when we've worked that through and through, I hope that you will be next."

She laughed quietly, gave my arm a gentle shove. "You've been listening to Ev again. Come on, tell me."

"It's not a lot, really," I said. "I need to go down into the glacier and visit Henry, just once. And there is also the matter of a very dead circle of ground in Vernal Park that needs attention. And, of course, we need to finish what was begun for Works. Will you work with me?"

"Of course I will," she said, kissing my cheek. "And after that?"

"I'm hoping that you will show me a fine and private place, and that we will work together, be alive together, and remain happy for a very long time to come."

"Then we are in complete agreement," she said, smiling.

I turned and looked at her, sitting next to me in the moonlight, while I thought of what to say. Then, with the satisfaction of remembering a lesson so recently learned, I stopped thinking.

"Thank you, Lyla," I said.

She crooked her arm through mine.

"You're welcome."

END
OF
BOOK TWO

Acknowledgements

Though many of the places (particularly on Tahoma) that are described in *The Fireweed Entrance* and *A Mountain Spruce* are physically, intimately familiar and dear to me, others are places I have only visited in wishful imagination and by way of excellent topographic maps. I am indebted to the U.S. Geological Service and the National Parks Service for maps and information that allowed me to envision places that I don't get to just hike to. For his descriptions of some of these places and many of their remarkable details, I have Floyd Schmoe to thank. Mr. Schmoe first arrived at The Mountain in the winter of 1919, as caretaker of the lodge at Paradise, and stayed as a Park employee off and on for many years, eventually becoming the first Park Naturalist. His eloquent and observant book *A Year in Paradise* has been a treasure trove of information and inspiration.

I also owe a great debt of thanks to several people still with us: Joe Schonbok, for careful readings and crucial feedback; Larry DuBois and Gates Johnson, the other two thirds of the world's nearly-smallest writers' group; Jim Burke and Mary Shackelford, for an irreplaceable friendship and some important hikes.

My deep friend Rex Morris passed away in November of 2019, but he had the chance to read the manuscripts of both volumes. His advice and encouragement, as well as some of his own writings that he allowed me to read, were invaluable.

My daughters, Clara, Elena, and Ramona, have taught me far more than they may suspect. They have also given me, at times when I needed them the most, all of the truly primal reasons for living. And finally, my deepest love and gratitude to Nancy Olszewski, without whose support, wisdom, and firm but gentle nudges this work would not have been possible.

Richard Jones
Salish Sea, Washington, April 2020

Richard Jones has spent decades hiking in the wilderness areas that are the setting for Speakers of the Earth, and many years imagining and creating the work he has set there. He lives on an island in Western Washington with his wife, where they share the land with an elderly pygmy goat and an alpaca.

www.ingramcontent.com/pod-product-compliance
Lightning Source LLC
Chambersburg PA
CBHW050251110726
47898CB00007B/2368